CREAM OF PLANKTON SOUP

CREAM OF PLANKTON SOUP

GRANT SUTTON
Artwork by Ayesha Drew.

Matador
9 Priory Business Park,
Wistow Road, Kibworth Beauchamp,
Leicestershire. LE8 0RX
Tel: 0116 279 2299
Email: books@troubador.co.uk
Web: www.troubador.co.uk/matador
Twitter: @matadorbooks

ISBN 978 1788032 759

British Library Cataloguing in Publication Data.
A catalogue record for this book is available from the British Library.

Printed and bound by CPI Group (UK) Ltd, Croydon, CR0 4YY
Typeset in 11pt Gill Sans by Troubador Publishing Ltd, Leicester, UK

Matador is an imprint of Troubador Publishing Ltd

INTRODUCTION

The lunatics have taken over the asylum. More precisely, the reader has taken over the story. All writing in italics after each story represents the readers' thoughts in a 'Blog'. You are encouraged to join in the blogs via www.planktonsoup. co.uk or the Facebook page, Plankton Soup.

All comments are welcome; the more pedantic, scientific, disgruntled, crazy they are, the better!

- *I like Sutton's 'Can Do' attitude. Is he American?*
- *Alas! Judging by the size of his penis, I would say he is Welsh.*

Please consider this an interactive book, where the readers are not only invited to run their eyes across and down each page, physically turning each leaf, mentally digesting the content and translating their thoughts into suitable emotional responses, but in one story they are encouraged to roll the dice to decide the ending! Amazing!

CRITICAL ACCLAIM

"They say that there's a fine line between genius and madness. Sutton comfortably inhabits both sides of the divide, like buttocks in a G-string."
JOHANN SEBASTIAN BACH

"Destined to become a modern classic!"
NOSTRADAMUS

"I didn't know what to make of this book!"
ORIGAMI EXPERT

"A bit rough around the edges but that's the way I like it."
TREE HUGGER.

"I'm Sutton's biggest fan!"
ROBERT WADLOW (8'11")

WARNING!

The following stories contain flashing images, contentious scientific theories, poor grammar, a variety of foodstuffs and lashings of tea. Some stories may be unsuitable for human consumption. Ensure soup is piping hot before serving. Do not exceed recommended dosage. Store in a cool, dry place. May contain a sprinkling of nuts.

INGREDIENTS

The Gabrielle Courvoisier Trilogy

The Emergency Meringue Base

The Plot That Thickened

The Prog Rock Trance Affair

The Colourless Odourless Man

Mull Doon's Lives

The Jive Talkin' Turkey

A Friesian Cow In Repose And Associated Questions

Buddy Guards

The Cat Sat On The Mat

The Day Our Underpants Saved The World

The Show Must Go On

Paradise Tossed

Watching Paint Dry

And He Kept It In An Oily Rag

An Interview With The Deity Formerly Known As God

Me And The Captain

Problems With A Mechanical Flange, Lemon Soap And An Unwatched Kettle

In Which I Do Battle With A Silver Blue Demonic Gnu With Iridescent Lime Green Eyes In A Cupboard Under The Stairs

The Secret Society

Window To The World

The Ballad Of Purity Calou

Frank Gladtiding: Tug Boat Owner, Part-Time Detective And Fathers' Rights Activist, With Mild Tourette's, Oh And He Was Allergic To Floral Print Curtains Too!

Short Straw

MEET AND TWO VEG

"You were made pregnant by a vegetable?" My voice is abnormally high-pitched due to the shock. I am both disappointed and concerned for my friend Pippa. I am... (I'm searching for a good word)...aghast!

"What kind of vegetable?"

Pippa is evasive with the answer but stresses that it shouldn't really matter; the main thing is that she's happy.

I try to calculate the gestation period for a vegetable-human hybrid. I decide that by adding the initial germination process of a tuber to the flowering process of a vine, and then to four and a half months (half a human) I will arrive at an approximation of the birth date. I must remember to buy a card and present.

Six weeks later I see Pippa in the park by the river. She is pushing a heavily laden shopping trolley. This is not allowed. There are strict rules governing the misappropriation of supermarket trolleys. You should certainly not take them further than the car park.

I say "Hi" to Pippa and she smiles. She indicates two pumpkins in the trolley and tells me their names are Pierre and Melone. They are twins, she adds needlessly.

3

They look very fresh.

I ask was it a difficult, erm… (birth or harvest?)… I say birth.

She laughs and says, "No, a couple of weeks ago they were only the size of tomatoes."

She offers me the chance to hold one, but to be honest I find other people's babies repulsive and so I politely decline, telling her that due to my restless legs syndrome I don't think it would be a good idea.

One of the pumpkins, I think it is Melone, starts to cry and this disturbs the other, who perhaps is Pierre and who also starts to cry.

Pippa unhooks a wooden stepladder from the trolley and then takes off her rucksack, but now I can see it is not a rucksack, it's actually a piano accordion. Noticing my quizzical expression, she explains that the only way to soothe the crying pumpkins is by sitting on top of the stepladder and playing a constant, haphazard noise with the accordion… for about an hour.

I ask how she had discovered this method and she tells me 'by trial and error'. This makes me wonder what else she had tried previously in order to arrive at this solution.

I suggest that maybe a concertina would be more convenient. She answers that although it is easier to operate and certainly not as heavy, the concertina does not have the range of power and tone of the piano accordion. Also, concertinas remind her of barrel organ monkeys and clowns, neither of which would she allow to have contact with the pumpkin children as they may induce nightmares.

For some reason I suddenly take on the mantle of child psychologist and begin to lecture Pippa, although my intention is only to put her mind at rest. I look up at

4

her sitting on the stepladder, squeezing and expanding the bellows of the instrument.

"Pippa", I say, "children are born without fear. It is our own fears that we instil in them. They are innocent… until um… proven guilty. It is the classic 'nature-nurture' principle. In nature, there are no clowns, no barrel organs and no fez-wearing monkeys. It is the parent that teaches the child what is good or evil, safe or scary. In nature, the pumpkin has no reason to fear the concertina. They have no natural enemies… except perhaps the stag beetle… oh and greenfly."

I have to raise my voice above the sound of the accordion.

"Nurture them Pippa!" I urge. "Encourage them to embrace all musical instruments, no matter how menacing they may seem. The lyre, the lute, the hurdy-gurdy and the glockenspiel are all out there, waiting to be discovered by smiling, happy children, or pumpkins or… whatever."

Pippa suddenly stops playing.

"I think Pierre has shit himself," she says.

I am about to correct her with the word 'shat', but see the look on her face as she climbs down from the stepladder and I realise she is in no mood for pedantry.

She looks slightly jaded. Of course she must be. Bringing up two pumpkins alone cannot be easy.

Alone?

"Is the father helping at all?" I ask.

Pippa launches into a foul-mouthed tirade which I do not intend to share with the reader, but needless to say the word 'arsehole' appears more than once.

She finishes with, "Men! They're all the same!"

But I know that she knows that I know that we both know… the father was a vegetable. And not all vegetables are the same. Some are long and pointy, some are round and knobbly. Some make good fathers, some don't.

READERS' BLOG:

- *Sutton has made a prick of himself again! A pumpkin is not a vegetable. It is in fact a fruit, or to be more exact, a pepo.*
- *The author is a cabbage!*
- *Scientists should keep their noses out of food classification. I would serve pumpkin as a side dish with spicy chicken, but never, I repeat, never with custard. Therefore it is a vegetable.*
- *Yeah, and Jaffa Cakes are biscuits!*
- *All men are bastards and (apparently) so are male vegetables!*
- *Some people leave pumpkins in a basket at the end of their garden so that passers-by can help themselves. They are encouraging theft. It's a national disgrace!*
- *Wait a minute, wait a minute! Pippa had sex with a pumpkin? How the…?*
- *Pumpkins? Bleuch!*
- *If you want to see something that induces nightmares, what about Halloween 'jack-o'-lanterns'? They are made from pumpkins. Poor Pierre and Melone. Their lives will be short and their deaths will be hideous!*

SEND YOUR COMMENTS TO
www.planktonsoup.co.uk

CHEESE ON TOAST

A dark, nightmarish cloud gathers on the distant horizon. The sky is in transition and the failing sunlight glints in the eye of an eagle that has taken flight as if suddenly disturbed by the spirits of cold winds that are now extending their tentacles into every contour of the mighty cliff face, worn ragged by countless aeons of glacial friction, sandstorms and confused woodpeckers.

Atop this monolithic natural fortress, at the pinnacle of the croppiest of outcrops stands a lone figure, resplendent in the scarlet robe of a nobleman who is at peace with his sexuality. His handsome, regal jaw is set in defiance against the threat of the oncoming storm but, although his stance is heroic and god-like, somewhere deep in his psyche there is a cold fear, an emotion previously unknown to this King of men.

He clenches his fist tighter around the staff of his trident, the favoured weapon of his once proud army, and forces the unwelcome doubt from his mind. He frowns at his mental weakness and glances back at the small fire he has built for some kind of reassurance. He knows he is running out of time.

Far below, a black shape climbs up slowly and inexorably towards the start of the jagged rock face. It is the shape of a man, but no ordinary man. A man with superhuman powers of endurance and resilience. A man of almost supernatural skill. The greatest assassin that ever lived. This night, a legend walks the earth.

The assassin stops at the base of the cliff and looks up fearlessly towards the apex, calculating the best route for stealth and speed. He has travelled many hard miles across the wilderness to reach this point. His beloved stallion died of exhaustion five days before and since then he has made the journey on foot, carrying the heavy load necessary for the success of the mission strapped to his powerful back.

Having satisfied himself that the climb is indeed humanly possible, at least for one such as he, the legendary killer briefly turns to look back across the vast plain of the Mascarene Plateau where he had said his final farewell to his steed, where even now the storm is venting its anger onto a cowering landscape. He must begin the climb now. He must climb through the night and reach the summit before the storm crosses the plain and blows him off the sheer rock face. He knows he is running out of time.

At the cliff edge, the King, unaware of the assassin's approach, stares into the fire and his mind wanders into an unwelcome memory. It is the memory of the lost one hundred.

He'd known each one by name and had loved them like brothers. Brave warriors. Men of steel. Men of girded loins. Muscular men in leather underpants, chain mail vests and face paint. A tear forms in the corner of the King's eye and, brushing it away irritably, he mentally blames it on the smoke from the fire.

One by one the warriors had given their lives in their quest to fulfil the King's demands. One by one they had failed and died. Each day the sad news was delivered to the King and each day he had felt his soul get heavier and heavier with the guilt of their deaths. He could have ended this slaughter with a single command but somehow he felt compelled to persist until he finally tasted victory… at any cost.

Now he has one chance left. He has almost given up hope. The storm is coming and the fire is burning low. Night has fallen during his trance. He knows he is running out of time.

The assassin's body convulses in spasms of agony. He has fallen quite some way back down the cliff, pulling out fingernails and gouging flesh from his legs and face. He grits his teeth against the pain and curses his gods. His gods are the kind that you can curse without fear of retribution. He curses them regularly and extensively. Somehow it helps with the pain.

Now, with his warm, sticky blood oozing from gaping wounds, he allows himself a smile. He smiles at the challenge before him that his gods and his leader have set. He will not fail, has never failed, and the taste of victory will be ever sweeter.

He is near the top. He can smell the wood smoke from a fire. He feels the weight of the load on his shoulders and visualises the face of the person on top of the cliff and its expression when they finally meet on this fateful day.

The King is not just a King, he is a warrior and his instincts have roused him from the shallow sleep. He can hear the crackle of the fire and the moans and wails of various wind spirits. But there is something else. He strains his senses and picks out the sound of leather sandals scraping against rock. He can smell fresh blood.

He jumps to his feet and reaches for his trident. The sounds are coming from the cliff edge. Suddenly, in the weak grey light of dawn, a head appears over the edge. A bloodied head, followed by a battered and torn body of immense musculature.

"Back so soon?" says the King, amazed. "I didn't expect you before the storm."

"Sire!" gasps the assassin. "I have brought you a gift."

He takes the near indestructible 'bag for life' off his mighty shoulders.

"Chocolate biscuits your Majesty, and just as you ordered, bread, tea bags and butter."

The King eagerly impales a slice of bread on his trident and thrusts it close the fire.

"Great! I'll get the toast ready. Have you got the…?"

He stops and catches the look in the eyes of his last and greatest warrior.

The assassin's face pales and he almost falls to his knees in despair.

The cheese!

"Oh, for fuck's sake!" cries the King.

And as the assassin wearily begins to climb back down the cliff, the King spins round, raises his face to the heavens and his furious roar trembles the ground beneath his feet. Shaking his fists at the unseen gods, he screams out every terrible obscenity his educated royal brain can concoct.

In spinning, his robe has caught fire and, as the King is engulfed in flames, the roar of the fire drowns out the cry of agony… and in turn is superseded by the crash of thunder as the first hammers of rain smash into the King's upturned melting face. He knows the quest for cheese on toast has evaded him forever.

READERS' BLOG:

- This makes grim reading. So much death and suffering, and for what? Cheese on bleedin' toast! The madness of war and kings!
- Any leader of men worth his weight in scarlet velvet should have arranged a strategic logistics re-supply protocol before embarking on an expedition into the wilderness. The wanker.
- He is a king. If he wants cheese then somebody better find some quickly or heads will roll. Honestly, you just can't get the staff nowadays.
- Serves the assassin right. If he hadn't been such a kiss-ass, buying needless chocolate biscuits as a treat, he may have remembered the all-important cheese.
- I'm surprised that the cloak burnt so easily. The velvet must have been of inferior quality, perhaps a polyester mix?
- The King is his own worst enemy. If only he had shared a biscuit or two with the assassin before sending him back for the cheese they might both still be alive today. Perhaps we'll never know.

SEND YOUR COMMENTS TO
www.planktonsoup.co.uk

A PICTURE PAINTS A
THOUSAND WORDS

I am looking at a beautiful painting in the gallery. The painting I am looking at in the gallery is beautiful. I am in the gallery. I am looking at a painting. It is beautiful.

I'm sorry, but those words don't even begin to do it justice. When I first saw the picture, some hours ago, I was so stunned by its beauty that I had to sit down and stare at it with my mouth open in awe!

How can somebody create on canvas the feel, the sensation, the reality of silk, and yet next to it using the same substances create the texture of velvet, of skin, of steel and pearl? What kind of brush or knife can apply paint so softly as to create the illusion of glass, mist, candlelight or deep, still water?

It is incredible to visualise the original bare canvas, stretched across a frame as it awaited the first dab of oil, or would the artist begin with a wash of colour to create the background? Nevertheless, however humble its origins, that same blank canvas now lies underneath a masterpiece.

Who did this? The signature is illegible, almost as if there has been an attempt to paint over it as an afterthought. The information about it is sketchy (which would be a good joke if it were a pencil drawing and not an oil painting!). I can only try to understand the artist through this work.

The painting is so lifelike, I feel I am able to climb inside the picture and actually watch the artist as he works, as if I have somehow travelled back in time. I wonder, when he had finished, did he stand and stare at it as I am now? I start nodding at thoughts of an imaginary connection with the artist. I create in my own mind a portrait of the artist as a young man.

I try to 'remember' the artist as a student. Was art in his blood from a young age or did he come to it later on in life? Was he a poor student at school, producing clumsy renderings of stick men, giant flowers and a smiling sun… or did he stand out as a protégé; a budding genius? Were there any women in his art class?

Had the artist actually witnessed the scene he has painted or has he constructed it through imagination? How many times did he begin a canvas and then discard it in hot-tempered frustration? Did he simply paint over the failed work and start again?

How did he arrange his palette? Did he work feverishly or did he apply time management to the project with regular breaks and a strictly defined relaxation period at the end of each working day?

He was probably feverish. That's how I imagine him. He did his best work that way, driving himself into a frenzy, falling over items of furniture, shouting obscenities, rending his blouson in twain with his multicoloured fingers.

Was the artist irritated when his wife or mother called him down for his tea? Yes he was! A genius hates to be distracted whilst inspiration is in full flow. The only thing more hated than disturbed inspiration is not having any inspiration at all.

A blank canvas! A blank canvas can drive an artist crazy. It is said that if you stare long enough into the blank canvas, very soon the blank canvas will stare back into you.

"How can pork medallions ('Come and get them whilst they're hot!' shouts Mother) be more important than overcoming the mental challenge of a blank canvas?" the artist cries to himself. "No matter how good the sauce!"

Although the artist loved his mother, she didn't seem to value his work. He would sometimes ask her opinion and she would glance at the painting, shrug and say, "It's OK, but it needs to show more light."

But what could a woman know about art?

His wife was even less enthusiastic, sometimes even refusing to come to the attic studio at all. Once, when she actually did venture upstairs, she irritated him by quoting from a brochure that introduced the work of his archenemy at a gallery in Florence.

"The artist affirms the objectivity of the imagination, not as sentimental fantasy, but as a function of the mind that leads to a harmony with both the self and others – a necessity for life. His use of materials is heterogeneous, utilising raw linen, milk paint, verdigris, silver pigment, mica, oil sticks and lithographic ink, which are combined in different permutations. They create a variety of painterly surfaces, which mirror his notion of the self as a fragmentary experience where the only constant is 'the continuity of discontinuity.'"

His wife put down the brochure, looked out of the window and sighed dreamily.

He noticed that whilst listening to her he had crushed the pastel chalks he was holding and his palette had dried out.

15

"I was thinking of experimenting with impasto," he said defiantly, "and maybe a little chiaroscuro."

She didn't turn but continued to stare from the window, a wan smile struggled to her lips and the beginnings of a tear formed in the corner of her eye. She knew what she would have to do.

For the next few weeks she crept into the studio whilst the artist slept and slowly corrected his work. She added depth and light, using a mixture of techniques and mediums to create a feeling of life in the picture. She worked so delicately and with such infinite patience that the artist did not notice the minute increments of improvement. Not until the end.

With a final, violent flourish of blue across the canvas, he gasped for air and staggered back from his easel, grabbing the curtains for support. "Voila!" he cried triumphantly. His chest heaved with artistic exhaustion and drained emotion. Through bleary eyes that ached from the months of concentration, he regarded his work as if for the first time.

Yes. Over a century ago he stared at the painting in awe, just as I do now. Then slowly and with increasing wonderment he came to the same conclusion as I have.

"Only a woman could have painted this!"

READERS' BLOG:

- *This story reminds me of the fairytale by Andersen (or was it the Grimms?) about the old shoemaker who had help from the elves (or were they goblins?) to make beautiful shoes (or were they slippers?).*
- *Why don't we hear of any female classic artists?*

- Ask the Pope… the Catholic Church has been guilty of the subjugation of women for centuries!
- The previous reader should calm down; this is not the appropriate forum for bitter, socio-political or religious protest, no matter how valid.
- There is plenty of evidence to suggest that history has been doctored to hide the achievements of women and pass them off as achievements of men. Needless to say it is usually a man who writes the history books too!
- I think Sutton is saying that women should come out and paint, not skulk around in the attic like Frankenstein's monster. That was written by a woman by the way. Shelley. Not sure what her second name was though.
- Women need to be careful. Look what happened to Thatcher. Also see Joan of Arc, Queen Boudicca, Enid Blyton, Princess Di and the poor woman that Prime Minister Gordon Brown slagged off. None of them have been seen or heard of since.
- Yeah and what about old Ada Lovelace? She helped develop the first computer! Ada would give that nerd Bill Gates a run for his money, and kick his puny ass up and down Silicon Valley.
- I have heard it said that if women ruled the world it would be a better place. But who would do my laundry?
- Yes I'd like to see more women in art… and not just the nude ones on canvas.
- Bill Gates? Weird! Last week whilst out tomcatting, I met a geeky-looking guy at the back gates of an office car park. After three failed attempts at 'booting up', he apologised about his 'Microsoft' penis but paid the bill anyway. I didn't ask his name.

SEND YOUR COMMENTS TO
www.planktonsoup.co.uk

NIGEL FORGETS THE PEAS

Lucy was upset. Nigel had forgotten the peas.

"I specifically underlined the importance of *not* forgetting the peas!" she said, stretching out her arms and letting them fall, slapping her thighs in exasperation.

"These things happen," shrugged Nigel, taking a large slurp of red wine and looking in the fridge for no particular reason.

"One thing that will not happen is the shepherd's pie I was planning for this evening," threatened Lucy. She considered abandoning the peeling of an onion. What was the point now without peas?

Nigel was oblivious to the series of circumstances he had set in motion and continued in the wrong direction by saying, "We could be adventurous and try it without peas. After all, it's not as if they add much flavour."

He made a joke about them not bringing much to the table.

Lucy remained miffed. She pointed out that Nigel also did not bring much to the table, including peas.

"At least they add colour and texture," she said, quoting something Delia had said in a book.

"Why don't you dice a few carrots?" he suggested helpfully.

"We don't have any carrots. That's why I sent you to buy peas."

"I don't see the logic in that."

"Of course not. You can't understand simple logic, you're a man."

And then, unable to help herself, she huffed at that description, as all women seek to ridicule a man's manliness during an argument, whatever the relevance.

Nigel's ire was of course promptly irked.

"Oh, I see. I forgot the peas and it's all because of my low sex drive is it? Did it ever occur to your tiny mind that my lack of interest is due to you having such a fat arse?"

"What's that got to do with peas?"

"Nothing, it's all the chocolates you eat!"

"Maybe I'm eating chocolate to compensate for the lack of something else."

"Right, that's it! You want peas? I'll show you fucking peas!"

Nigel stormed out.

Four hours later a rather handsome policeman knocked on the door.

"Good evening madam. I'm sorry to tell you that your husband has been arrested for drink driving. The car has been impounded. However, it did contain forty-three bags of frozen peas. I wonder if you could shed any light on the matter?"

Lucy growled silently with contempt for her husband. Frozen peas! What fucking use were they? What was she going to do with her cooking now? She would simply have to change the menu.

"Come in officer. Do you like hotpot?"

"Yes, I'm very partial to that particular dish."

"I'm afraid there aren't any peas in it."

"I'm allergic to peas as luck would have it."

Keeping her legs straight, Lucy bent at the waist to open the oven and then looked up at the policeman with her innocent brown eyes.

"Would you like a big portion?" she pouted.

He caused his own eyes to shimmer with a glint of harmless mischief, hoping to convey forbidden thoughts with subtle movements of his lids and brows.

"Would you?" he answered.

READERS' BLOG:

- That Nigel sounds like a complete tosser!
- Frozen peas? They are good for soothing bumps and bruises. The policeman should donate them to the local A&E unit.
- I think he will be giving a large donation to Lucy very soon!
- I've got a feeling that Sutton has confused the ingredients for both dishes. When my grandmother used to make shepherd's pie she put onions in it. Hotpot is best served with beetroot. Sutton should not be allowed anywhere near a kitchen.
- Or a typewriter!

SEND YOUR COMMENTS TO
www.planktonsoup.co.uk

"CAN WE COHERE THE RANDOM FLUX?"

IMHO

Good morning class, and also a warm welcome to those of you joining us from the virtual world by reading this book. Thanks to the wonders of modern science you are able to be with us today, no matter how far into the future you may exist!

Yes, science and matter. These will be our topics today and I shall begin with a statement about that impostor that has been given the name 'gravity'. Let me make this perfectly clear. There is no such thing as gravity! There, I've finally said it. It's been bugging me for years and I just had to get it off my chest. There is simply no such thing as gravity.

I know some of you will be shocked at this. I'm sorry to disappoint you; sorry to come right out and say it as bluntly as I did. Perhaps I should have let you down gently… unlike gravity which would have caused you to slam into the pavement. (Not that it exists of course.)

So now you're probably wondering what it is that stops you floating out of bed. Well to be honest I don't really want to go into too much detail right now. And I'm sure you readers in the virtual world have got plenty of other things you'd rather be doing than listening to me droning on about quantum physics.

What's that? You're free for the next hour or so? No work today? You got the sack? Why? You were caught photocopying genitals! But not yours, the bosses… during the board meeting!

The mind boggles!

Anyway let's get back down to earth and to gravity. I'll just skim over it quickly and then move on to the next subject as we've got a lot to talk about before the end of this lesson.

So, what attracts objects to each other if not gravity? Well I'll tell you. Nuclear attraction. There! Easy! Nothing more. Nothing less. Nuclear attraction! Check it out! Google it!

Once we have accepted that fact then we can move on to the idea that it is the polarity of electrons that causes the nuclear attraction. And it is only a small step further to realise that if you can reverse this polarity, you can fly! Q.E.D.

Let's talk about time travel. "Impossible!" I hear you cry. Misguided fools! It simply hasn't been invented yet. When it is, we will then be able to travel *back* in time. Only then will we be able to travel *forward* in time, but only up to the dates since time travel was invented. The future does not exist for us but it will for those that are already dead… if you get my drift? Well I'm glad that's all cleared up.

Next topic: the great 'vacuum' of outer space. People, people, people… there is no such thing as a vacuum in space. If we agree that light consists of super-fast particles travelling through space then we have to agree that space is very busy indeed and is certainly not empty. It's chock-a-block with dark matter for a start and that's not all. Space may be 'filled' with a very thin gas called ether, or as I like to say, aether (you can spell it either way). Did you notice how I pronounced 'either' as 'aether'? Just a little joke there to 'lighten' the mood, and ho ho, there's another one. OK, everyone settle down.

There may be one molecule of ether per one million square miles of space, but it could be enough to conduct the power of light and radiation. That could be why light travels so fast through space. It jumps from one molecule of ether to the next, and because this jump is sometimes one million miles, well, work it out, speed equals distance divided by time. When light hits a more solid object like our atmosphere, it begins to slow down as there are more molecules to jump through… and when it hits a mountain, it may never get through at all. Too many molecules, you see?

There is a new theory that suggests certain particles can exist in more than one place at the same time. So maybe light is *not* travelling, it just appears instantaneously from its point of origin. And if it *is* travelling, then we could argue that there is no such thing as 'the dark'. Dark is just light that hasn't reached us yet.

The Big Bang? Hogwash! This theory is based solely on the supposed 'fact' that the universe is expanding. Expanding? Says who? Oh, you're telling me about the red shift? Well I say "red shift-shmed shmift", and that's not an easy thing to say, but I think it indicates the strength of my feeling.

Some starlight is blue, which indicates the star is moving towards us, or we are moving towards it. All that can be deduced is that objects are moving around in space in relation to one another. Nothing more.

The starlight we see from the so-called expanding universe was sent to us millions of years ago. Those same stars are probably already on their way back towards us as they have swung around on their colossal orbits. The Big Bang is a baloney sandwich and I for one am not hungry.

I won't go into detail about perpetual motion. I've said it all before and you're probably sick of hearing me go on about it. All I will say is… the spinning of the earth, magnetic poles, cohesion of the universal random flux, coiled wire and gyroscopes. Make of it what you will.

Aliens are everybody's favourite science 'fiction' topic, but I'm here to tell you that aliens really exist. They have been with us for thousands of years, sharing our planet, our oceans, our skies, our breakfast cereal.

Think about insects and bacteria. You believe they are of this earth? Think again. Now think again, again!

Does the Bible say that Noah welcomed onto the Ark things that buzzeth in the ear? Things that are so small that a billion can do star jumps in a Petri dish? No it doesn't. These things came from outer space on an asteroid! They are aliens!

I once read a scientific report (actually I read it more than once) that claimed if aliens came to Earth, the most amazing thing they would find is… the sausage. Where does that leave us in the grand scheme of things?

Now a quick word about evolution. We are merely the leftovers… the failed models… the detritus of creation.

We have been left behind like all the other unwanted, unsuccessful species. The best have gone on to better things… natural selection… supernatural selection. They are with us now but living in a superior dimension, flitting

26

around us as we amble along in our ignorance. Sometimes they revert back to their physical selves, where they live on the inside of the Moon's crust, like the Clangers did in the seventies.

Now I'd like to quickly mention my current favourite topic: The case for wearing spacesuits *now*. Why should we wait until the future? For me it is already the future. When I was a child I fully expected to be living on Mars by the year 2000 and walking around in a silver spacesuit. What's the hold-up? What are we waiting for?

Here are some of the things that an all-encompassing, computer-controlled bio-suit could do: protect our lungs from air pollution; protect our skin from cancerous solar radiation; protect us from cuts and bruises and perhaps even broken bones; regulate our body temperature; protect against airborne diseases; protect against electromagnetic disruption of the brain, act as a monitor for medical conditions; assist weak muscles and joints; and because it will be made from a hybrid of spider silk, Gore-Tex, silver and Kevlar, ironing is a thing of the past!* It would come in a variety of colours, including see-through for those of you who like that sort of thing! (* Pat. Pending).

- *If I were a Warren Buffett or a Bill Gates I would pour money into that project!*

Finally, the big one. As is customary, I've saved the best until last. Ladies and gentlemen (can I have a drum roll please?), I have an announcement to make. Shush! Silence! Thank you. Pause.

There is no need for any of us to die.

"What's that?" you ask. "What did he just say?" "Please repeat!"

With pleasure! There is no need for any of us to die!

(The experienced orator pauses to allow this information to sink in before continuing.)

We are made of atoms. Atoms do not 'end'. Therefore we should not 'end'. There's simply no reason for it. Theoretically we could live forever. All we have to do is find a practical solution.

Oh and by the way… just a quick one, food for thought… E does *not* equal MC^2. Think about it! Work it out for yourselves.

Well, thank you for joining me during this brief explanation of our universe. I hope things are a lot clearer for you now.

And please don't forget your homework. All assignments must be in by the end of the week. Don't discuss your findings with anyone outside this room. Don't put the title on the outside page. Remember, it's top secret! For my eyes only!

What's that Tompkins? You weren't here last week and don't know what the title is? There's always one, Tompkins, and it's always you. The title is…

'CAN WE USE VOODOO TO TURN LEAD INTO GOLD?'

READERS' BLOG:

- *Can we really cohere the random flux?*
- *I can!*

- *The only way to live forever is to find a way to increase the Hayflick limit from 50,000 to infinity.*
- *Where did Sutton get his science degree, Albanian goat-herders' summer camp?*
- *I don't know which is more ridiculous, Sutton's writing or the tanga briefs he wears when mowing the lawn! Not that I've been watching him of course.*
- *That's just reminded me of a funny story I once heard. Apparently, Archbishop Desmond Tutu visited Tanzania last year and when he asked how many hours it takes to drive from the airport to the coastal town of Tanga, the taxi driver replied, "It takes two to Tanga." And that's a true story by the way.*
- *Imagine if the taxi's call sign was 'Two-Two-Tango'. The newspaper headlines could say, 'Two-Two-Tango takes Tutu to Tanga'.*
- *Better to say, 'Tutu takes Two-Two-Tango to Tanga'.*
- *No. What about, 'To get to Tanga, it takes Tutu two in Two-Two-Tango'?*
- *Bah! You've ruined the joke now.*
- *Dear oh dear! Sutton does like to harp on about gravity. If it didn't exist we'd all be flying off at tangents, just like he does with his stories!*
- *I hate ironing! I'm ready for spacesuits!*
- *Archbishop? Weird! I met a defrocked priest under the railway arches last week, and guess what? His name was Desmond and he certainly wasn't defrocked... he was wearing a ballerina's leotard under his mackintosh! Crotchless, naturally.*

A MAN OF FEW WORDS

The meeting was drawing to a long overdue conclusion. The man was suddenly aware that his mind had… what was that modern expression? Ah yes, 'zoned out', his mind had zoned out, having lost track of what was being said quite some time ago.

He had spent the last few minutes contemplating some cigarette ash on the knee of his suit trousers, which was odd as he hadn't smoked today. It was somebody else's cigarette ash and that disgusted him. He brushed off most of the ash but succeeded only to create a fine dust that embedded itself further and deeper into the knit of the fabric, leaving a grey patch on the otherwise immaculate blue twill.

He noticed that the Director had closed the meeting with the usual solemn tones and people were beginning to leave the room. He tried to stand up but suddenly found the Director's hand on his shoulder, pushing him back into the seat.

"Not you," said the Director sternly. "You stay here. We need a serious talk – alone!"

The Director then launched into a frank and vicious

criticism of the man's work; banging the table with his fists and throwing his arms wide in the direction of the boardroom window and the great city beyond to indicate the extent of his emotions.

"Not only has the company lost a valued client," said the Director, between clenched teeth, "but the damage limitation analysis predicts a shortfall of new contracts for the first time in thirty years!"

He leaned across the boardroom table and fixed the other man with a steely glare. "You have been here less than a month and almost destroyed the company! What have you got to say for yourself?"

The other man returned the glare, steel upon steel, his eyebrows narrowing slowly into the sort of condescending frown a professor gives to a student who simply does not grasp the basics. He breathed in deeply and held the air in his lungs for what seemed an impossible amount of time. He then formed his right hand into the meditative 'Palm of Buddha' position and slowly moved it forward from his chest in a controlled manner whilst exhaling forcefully, releasing the breath rather more noisily than was necessary, but he felt that under the circumstances it would underline the irritation he felt with the Director's tirade.

He took a silver cigarette case from his jacket pocket and looked at it for a while as if considering taking out a cigarette, and then coming to a decision, put the case back into a different pocket. He smiled to himself then shook his head and looked up at the ceiling.

He seemed lost in thought for some moments then suddenly, pushing his chair back from the table, he stood up, thrust one hand into his trouser pocket and walked to the far end of the boardroom where he then spun around on the Cuban heel of his expensive boot to face the Director.

As he walked back towards the Director, he wagged an index finger in mock admonishment and pointed it from the Director to the folder of documents on the table, so bringing the Director's attention to its contents. He shook his head again and laughed noiselessly.

He walked casually, almost arrogantly to the door, took his hat and coat from a wall-mounted hook and put them on. Then pausing with one hand on the doorknob, he gave a cheeky salute with the other and left the office.

He was smiling as he walked across the floor of the reception lobby. It seemed that he hadn't a care in the world. He felt that a weight had been lifted from his shoulders; a stark contrast with his first day at the job when he had anxiously expected to be weighed down with the weight of expectation.

The only furniture in the large reception area was a maple wood desk with a beautiful vase of flowers on top. The secretary was just in the process of putting down the phone.

"Excuse me, sir, but the Director would like a word with you before you leave," she informed him sternly. He dismissed her with a sardonic wave and strode towards the exit.

"Sir? Sir!" cried the secretary.

Failing to get a response, she motioned to the security guard to stop the man.

Seeing that the security guard had taken up an intimidating stance blocking the exit, the man returned to the reception desk and looked with an amused smile from the secretary to the guard as if to make sure they were both paying attention.

The man then took ten dollars out of his wallet and held it dramatically in the air. With his other hand he slowly slid the large vase of flowers towards the edge of the reception desk.

The secretary and guard both looked on as if in a trance. They watched spellbound as the vase teetered over the edge and fell catastrophically onto the marble floor.

"That cost one hundred and fifty dollars from Bloomingdale's!" cried the secretary, as the man gave her the ten-dollar note.

"Bloomin' 'eck!" swore the security guard. "The most I ever paid for a vase was six dollars and ninety-nine cents!" (He pronounced it 'varse' not 'vayse'.)

The guard shook himself from this thought and dived at the man, knocking him to the floor.

"Six-ninety-nine, but my wife loves it! If you ever come around my house and start knocking vases over, why I oughta…"

Meanwhile, back upstairs in the boardroom, a fly that had previously been eating some wayward sugar grains from the complimentary drinks tray, landed on the open folder that the man had left on the table for the Director to read. The top page was almost blank except for one line of scrawled handwriting.

'Me no speaky Ingrish!'

READERS' BLOG:

- *I don't get it. How did he pass the interview if he can't speak English?*

- *Don't be so naïve. Many people lie on their C.V. to get a job.*
- *I like this guy's attitude. Don't take shit from anybody. There's a job waiting if he wants it. Go Marines!*
- *I knew a man once. But he didn't know me.*
- *Why is the guard shouting "blooming heck" (a very British turn of phrase), yet the story is apparently set in America? Sutton should take more care with continuity of plot if he wishes to become a successful author.*
- *I object to the author's apparent invitation that we read the man's scribbled message over the shoulder of the fly, which I consider to be an inferior species. If I want to read something I shall jolly well swat the pesky fly to kingdom come!*
- *The above reader is bang out of order. We are all God's creatures. The fly has just as much right to eat sugar, read books and spread disease as we do.*
- *The Fly? That was a crap movie. You can't change something's molecular structure and expect it to come back perfect. It's like reconstituted milk, i.e. it ain't milk.*
- *Yeah, I've used that powdered stuff. There's something missing. Like that other shit movie… Lost in Transmutation… or whatever. No substance to it.*
- *Apparently if you pronounce 'vase' as 'vayse' you are a pretentious twat… or so my stockbroker told me over a glass of Pimm's at the yacht club the other day.*
- *By what right can the guard prevent the man leaving the office? Until the moment he broke the vase he was a free citizen and legally entitled to go about his daily business unhindered. This is typical of modern-day fascist America.*

- *I wonder what kind of flowers were in the vase? Perhaps we'll never know.*

SEND YOUR COMMENTS TO
www.planktonsoup.co.uk

THIS IS NO ORDINARY DAY

PROPER CHARLIE

There is nothing unusual about this day. Just as every other day in his miserable life over the last few years, he has been to work and drifted aimlessly through the hours. For him there is no feeling of achievement and he is unable to remember what he has done with his time.

His drive home has been the usual slow crawl through the grey streets. The avenue where he lives looks the same as it always has. His front door is the same colour it was yesterday and still opens inwards as opposed to outwards, which is perfectly normal.

He throws the contents of his coat pockets into the empty fruit bowl on the hall table and hooks his coat onto a wall peg. He walks to the kitchen and switches the kettle on, then stares out of the window into the back garden.

But there is something odd about the garden. It appears to be an inverted image of its normal state, and what used to be on the left is now on the right. He purses his lips with mild concern. This sort of thing (self-inverting gardens) should not be allowed.

Then suddenly the air around him seems to crystallise and he becomes aware that this day is indeed different.

The kettle clicks off just a tad below its usual boiling point. His keys lie in the bowl at an unusual angle not normally achieved by his casual throw. There is a chink in his neighbour's curtain a little wider than yesterday. Patterns in the wooden dining table begin to appear and form into eyes that follow his movements around the kitchen.

Those of you who are reading between the lines of the story will have noticed that, due to a volcanic upheaval, a magnetic anomaly has occurred, resulting in his wife being kidnapped by a militant ensemble of clowns and whisked away in an existentialist's private helicopter!

A woman walks into the kitchen and acts out the character of his wife. But he notices she is much shorter and heavier than the original and her eyebrows are not so neatly plucked. In fact she more resembles him than she does his wife.

"Who are you?" he asks after a delicious dinner.

"I think the question is, who the hell are you?" she retorts.

They stare at each other in silence for about ten minutes and then the woman shouts his name with a question mark attached.

"Charlie?"

A man enters. It is himself (with some minor improvements). The two Charlies look at each other blankly for a while and then a small, white, two-dimensional object starts to emerge from the mouth of Improper Charlie. It grows steadily, still connected to Improper Charlie's mouth and forms a speech balloon.

Then Improper Charlie appears to suffer a gag reflex and vomits some text into the balloon. The text floats about randomly inside the two-dimensional bubble and slowly settles into a sentence that spells out 'Who were you?'

Although Proper Charlie admires the detail and artwork that has gone into Improper Charlie's speech balloon, he is nevertheless unnerved and nauseated by this unexpected plurality. He leaves the table and runs sobbing to the bathroom.

But for some reason the bathroom is full of clanking machinery. The noisy machine is busy laying dark, gelatinous eggs into the bathtub. Some of the eggs are partly hatched and the heads of human babies are emerging from the sticky mess. Each baby has Proper Charlie-like features and yet do not resemble him at all. They are Impressionist versions of him. They merely 'suggest' him.

Then he sees his reflection in the mirror and is horrified. There are no features, just an empty face! He screams inside his head and tries to feel for his eyes but suddenly his hands spontaneously combust! What a waste! He had always been proud of his ambidexterity.

The adult doppelgängers look on without emotion. They make no move to help him.

Proper Charlie staggers outside, searching for help or at least some kind of explanation. But instead he is trampled to death by a herd of migrating bison on their way south along the suburban avenue. This is no ordinary day!

READERS' BLOG:

- *Bison stink!*
- *How can he see himself in the mirror if he doesn't have eyes?*

- *Why would an existentialist own a helicopter?*
- *I'm not sure that 'ensemble' is the correct term for a group of clowns. Perhaps 'cluster'?*
- *They are militant clowns, so traditional collective nouns are not relevant here.*
- *A 'cacophony' of clowns seems apt. As does 'chaos' or 'calamity'.*
- *Too many 'C's' there! The above reader may benefit from experimenting with other, more imaginative, letters from the alphabet.*
- *I don't think bison migrate south. Only birds.*
- *Spontaneous combustion was all the rage in the seventies. Then it seemed to fizzle out. I wonder what became of it.*
- *A bunch of keys thrown haphazardly into a fruit bowl can never replicate its previous positional state. Chaos theorems, calculus and differential equations are useless in this situation.*
- *Chinks in curtains are a sure sign of nosy neighbours. So why not report suspicious activity like clown ensembles, ironic helicopters, inaccurate doppelgängers and self-inverting gardens? Jesus said love thy neighbour, but these people ignored him.*
- *If I had nosy but unhelpful neighbours, I would not lend them a cup of sugar should they require one.*
- *I wonder if the egg-laying machine is in fact The Mechanical Flange, as mentioned further on in this book. Perhaps we'll never know.*

SEND YOUR COMMENTS TO
www.planktonsoup.co.uk

DESCRIPTION FOR A PRESCRIPTION

Having served as a pharmacist at St Dympna's Lunatic Asylum for many years, I had encountered an above average quota of bizarre experiences and so, unsurprisingly, I eventually developed a desire to conclude my employment. Therefore when the opportunity arose I happily bade farewell to the godforsaken place and set up my own business in the tranquil village of Verily-on-the-Cleft. It was in this sleepy hamlet where, to my amazement, I once again met with the extraordinary.

As I recall, it was one of those autumn mornings when the air is sharply cold but not damp, and the sun is shining in an attempt to relive its summer glories. I had been attending to some minor duties which required the shuffling of papers and the unnecessary moving about of bottles containing this, that and the other, when the street door opened and an attractive but plainly dressed young lady came hurrying in. I was thankful to be temporarily disturbed from my mundane fidgetings and offered the young lady my best pretentiously intelligent smile and hoped that her requirements would be an interesting distraction from my

43

daily grind at the pestle and mortar. As it transpired, I was not to be disappointed.

She handed me a note, which had seemingly been written by Dr Mountebank, the local physician who had recently been introduced to me by his father, the Professor of Madness at St Dympna's. The note apologised for the irregular manner of the request but, could I put all other matters aside and with great speed prepare a certain medication of highly unusual ingredient for the urgent case to which he, Dr Mountebank was at present attending. The young lady, said the note, must remain anonymous as further explanation would disclose the identity of the patient.

I read the note twice more to satisfy myself that the rarity of ingredient did indeed indicate a serious and unusual complaint. I have no particular knowledge of disease or physiology, my experience being limited to providing mere chemical relief to sufferers of 'the vapours', 'the wobbles', occasionally 'the horrors' and, of course, troublesome stools, the latter being the bread and butter of the pharmacist. However, even my limited knowledge told me that the preparation required by the doctor was a potent soup strong enough to cause the instantaneous metamorphosis of plankton to Homo erectus and vice versa!

I removed my monocle and studied the lady suspiciously. How could I be sure this was a genuine note from the doctor? In hindsight there were many ways to better establish the authenticity of the request but, being extremely intelligent and thus devoid of any common sense, I merely asked that the young lady give a detailed description of the doctor to prove their association.

She first looked puzzled at my request but, after a moment of reflection, took a deep breath and began. What follows is the description of Mortimer. D. Mountebank the doctor, as given by the young lady.

By way of a preliminary overview, he can be said to be handsome… in an ugly sort of way, if you know what I mean. Granted, his eyes are correctly positioned at the optimum latitude and thank heavens for small mercies, but his mouth is too small for his chin and his nose too big for his cheeks. However, his ears are unobtrusive and, together with his eyes, they make a neat foursome. It is fair to say that, taken as a whole, his face is a pleasantly acceptable arrangement of features, being relatively symmetrical about its north-south axis.

At a modest six and five eighths he has one of the smallest heads in the neighbourhood, but this is not immediately noticeable because his features are ingeniously juxtaposed so that his face can claim to be the same size as everyone else's.

Academics might quote the ancient Greek skullologist, whatever his name was, who may have considered the forehead not quite convex enough to indicate a high degree of intelligence, but the doctor would defend himself admirably with a quick-witted 'skullologist-smullologist'. He would then, however, secretly attempt to accentuate the doming effect of his forehead with various cosmetic techniques.

The doctor is of less than medium height, slightly shorter when stooped and a frog's breath taller when at full stretch. Cunning choice in headgear can give the impression of exaggerated altitude and he has the habit of standing on tiptoe when immersed in conversation, although he himself has never spoken of a wish to adjust his vertical dimension. Nevertheless, any thoughts of diminutiveness are dispelled on experiencing the doctor's larger than life companionship.

He is a portly gent, fat being too aggressive an adjective. Rotund and jolly, as adjectives go, are rather more suitable, but portly remains the most appropriate in the doctor's case. His trouser seams are constantly at war against the laws of Newton and the heroic leather belt that serves no other purpose than to fill the loops on the waistband is now stretched to two inches longer than when first purchased. When he encounters a doorway, he is unsure as to the ideal elevation to offer first, his front or his side? That is to say he is as wide as he is deep.

When the doctor sits, the unfortunate chair can be under no illusion as to the extent of its occupation and, despite his love of company, it is very rare that he can be seen sitting next to anyone else on a three-cushioned sofa. His own estimate of his weight is 'a sack of coal lighter than a handcart full of carrots'.

His favourite shoes are his black lace-ups which he always wears with dark grey socks. His dark green two-piece tweed suit is his choice for working hours, with which he likes to wear his purple velvet waistcoat in the cooler months. He is never to be seen in shirt sleeves except at the barbers, whom he frequents on a bi-weekly basis for the application of growth tonic to his scalp and the deforestation of his ears and nose.

His fingernails are, as would be expected from a doctor, immaculate and pearly, like small pink seashells. But they look almost feminine on his stubby, hairy fingers. The backs of his hands are hairy in patches, like a well-worn doormat, the bald spots created by constant friction from the inside of his trouser pockets as he habitually adjusts his undershorts and associated contents throughout the day.

At the breakfast table he is ill-tempered and brusque. A glance at the morning tabloids only adds to his irritation. However, by the time he has consumed his second boiled egg, dipped dry by an army of soft bread soldiers, his mood is lightened somewhat. He then leaves for work in a mellow enough mood to stroke a dog sniffing at the gatepost.

His normal gait is brisk and purposeful but can be altered at will, depending on the terrain encountered. When moving within a crowded space his step may shorten and his centre of gravity switches from side to side as his hips sway to avoid collision with oncoming pedestrians. Upon reaching a clear path, his strides lengthen and a noticeable increase in tempo will ensue. When negotiating progress uphill, he likes to lean forward slightly and assists his leg action by pressing on the working thigh with his corresponding hand, thus engaging all four limbs to the task. Once over the brow and making a descent, he becomes more relaxed, almost nonchalant in comparison and sometimes hooks his stubby thumbs into his waistcoat pockets. On these occasions he has frequently been given to break into a whistle or a song, his current favourite being that of which the chorus goes…
'Where were you? Under the deckchair! Where were you? And the band played on…'

It is difficult to ascertain the doctor's age by mere speculation. The man's 'Johnsonesque' commentary on life, style of dress and thorough enjoyment of unhealthy living serve to belie his years. At first glance, one may assume him to be a decade older than he claims; however, after only a short time as a casual acquaintance it is possible that one will notice the gleam of mischief in the eye, something that is rarely found in a person having over half a century of life experience.

Closer acquaintance will satisfy the observer that the doctor is, in fact, leading the vigorous lifestyle of a bachelor of forty-something and his public recommendation that an egg cup full of malt vinegar imbibed every morning slows the ageing process, is besmirched by his private declaration that a well-aged malt whisky taken every evening with a fine cigar is truly the secret to eternal youth.

Until recently, he believed himself to have a fine head of hair, but a head of fine hair would be a more accurate claim, and, like his beloved British Empire, it is receding from every point of the compass. Having tried all modern styles and fixings to exaggerate its density, alas to no avail, he is now experimenting with deerstalkers and similarly suitable millinery. The surviving hair, making a courageous last stand against the inevitable, has the hue of finely chopped Madagascar cinnamon with a deft touch of caster sugar, the latter of which seems to increase in proportion almost weekly and his over-abundant ear and nose hair are likewise coloured.

The doctor will describe himself to be in perfect health, but his outward appearance can sometimes cause concern amongst those that have a care for his well-being. His skin has the pallor of Lincolnshire sausage meat, mottled sparsely with large pale freckles, which serve as the only colour to his face, although his apple-sized cheeks are prone to brandy rash. The unhealthy complexion is easily explained. He has a morbid dislike of any kind of outdoor activity, unless walking from hostelry to gin palace may be considered such, and this only with extreme agitation manifested by outbursts of foul expostulation as to the absence of available transport.

The two deep creases in his expansive forehead separate the area into three horizontal sausage-like folds, which almost look too heavy to be precariously balanced on his otherwise smooth skin. Perhaps it is only the eyebrows themselves that serve to uphold his heavy brow.

The eyebrows are slightly darker than his other body hair and are of unremarkable density although, as is common in middle age, they are thicker at the junction with the nose and almost non-existent as they approach the temples. The doctor is pleased that they do not meet in the middle as he believes this to be a sign of base intellect, poor hygiene and lack of social graces usually displayed by 'continentals'. There is always at least one eyebrow hair, usually a caster sugar-coloured one, which is almost a complete length longer than the others and obstinately refuses to lie in the same direction, preferring instead to grow at a ninety-degree angle to the rest.

Underneath his eyebrows, as is traditional of his species, are the eyes. His eyes are odd, both of them. One is emotionless and rheumy like that of a recently killed springbok. The other warm and friendly like that of a drunken lighthouse keeper who answers the door to a semi-clad teenage temptress. There is nothing particularly wrong with either eye, each being a perfect example of their individual genres.

The orbs, depending on the previous evening's alcohol intake, are habitually striated with thread veins like red

49

spiders' webs. They sit snugly in their sockets without bulging or sinking, and move in tandem in correct response to stimulation from the brain, or automatic reaction to follow external movement. The irises are pale green with flecks of brown, the left having more flecks than the right, and the pupils perform contraction and dilation as well as can be expected under sober circumstances.

It may be fair to say that the doctor is prone to blinking excessively when tired or nervous, his normal blink rate being one per ten seconds, and on occasions of irritation, embarrassment or pompousness, the lashes stick together slightly on re-opening which causes them to flutter momentarily. The lashes themselves are albino-like, practically invisible and unworthy of further description.

The poor doctor has been unfortunate enough to inherit the Mountebank nose and this feature is difficult to describe kindly or with any affection. It is at once both bulbous and pug, if this is possible, and an observer is immediately reminded of beasts that herd, or perhaps even of giant fruit bats. The bridge is short and wide with a red groove on either side where his pince-nez have eroded their own territorial mark. The tip resembles so closely a strawberry as to make one's mouth water and yet the entrance to the nostrils are angled upwards to such a degree that their contents, should there be any, would be in plain sight to even the most casual of observers if it were not for the protective barrier of his nose hair which in itself forms the upper part of his wayward moustache.

The moustache is the highlight of the doctor's overall appearance. It is unruly to the point of hilarity. In the local taverns it has most cruelly been likened to Miss Laluna

Gladnightly's 'mott' which allegedly covers her lower abdomen and (some say) beyond, she being the village harridan.

- *A lot of 'L's in that paragraph. The author should experiment with other, more interesting letters in future.*

Naturally, the doctor's moustache is the colour of cinnamon and sugar, and this, taken into account with its sheer volume, would make it an ideal nesting ground for Japanese miniature hedgehogs, if they still existed. The growth spreads horizontally across the face, far and wide almost to each ear, rendering them invisible to frontal view. Here, at the nethermost reaches of the face, the moustache hair mimics the skyward tail of a red setter at full alert on a pheasant hunt.

The doctor's teeth are small, even and plentiful, like so many sailors' jerkins on a ship's washing line. They are not brilliant white nor do they show obvious signs of decay. They may fairly be described as being the shade of Dutch cheese which, as far as dental colour goes, is not as distasteful as it sounds. The teeth are kept closed as much as possible even when eating, as if the tongue is some terrible secret, fighting to escape, and one that the doctor must keep hidden at all costs, as you would a demented and incontinent stepmother, locked in a broom cupboard. The lack of jaw movement has resulted in an overlarge chin which, when shaved, closely resembles a giant flamingo egg. He is, however, able to manipulate certain muscle groups in order to curl the tip of his chin upwards and inwards and thus can easily balance a heavy serving spoon in such a position that the concave surface is hooked on his chin and the handle extends downwards in front of his chubby neck.

The neck is short with a large circumference. No Adam's apple is visible, it being cushioned within a layer of pink, sweaty flesh like a damp, raspberry doughnut. It is almost as if the doctor has been struck squarely on the top of the head by a blacksmith's mallet, causing it to sink into his neck, which seems to surround the lower half of his face.

His voice is very much like that of the current Prime Minister and yet, when the doctor has consumed only a quarter of his usual daily intake of ale, and takes centre stage in the company of his friends, his voice becomes reminiscent of everyone's favourite comedian who is presently wowing the audiences in the West End.

The doctor may even be said to have his own collection of catchphrases. "It's all swings and roundabouts to me" is one of the lines he uses to bring about peaks of uncontrollable hilarity amongst his admirers. "It's all in the timing" he will explain to flabbergasted newcomers. His latest catchphrase is destined to become a classic:

"If you think that's bad, you should see me naked!"

He feels no remorse when, for the sake of amusement, he recounts the misfortunes of his patients, describing in hilarious detail their accidents-de-toilette or unusual genitalia. He is always careful never to name names, however, and prides himself on this show of professionalism. He has standards to uphold of course.

Despite his propensity for reverie, he is prone to a curious melancholy that can strike him lame for days. It is as though he must pay penance to maintain equilibrium against the weight of debauchery that wreathes his shoulders.

He is somewhat of an extremist on many points. He believes that the working classes should be interviewed and means-tested before being allowed to have children. He believes that the world is a safer place with the British military at large on the continent. He believes that 'Johnny Foreigner' is of low intelligence and likely disease-ridden. He believes that children should never speak before being spoken to and should have social etiquette thrashed into them before being taught to read or write. He believes everybody should own a timepiece, to the extent that the government should supply those that haven't one, even the beggars… before shooting them.

He loves the streets to be clean and spotless. Manual workers should move about under cover of darkness. He loves the opera. Anyone who has failed to see one is a suspected Johnny Foreigner, communist or alternative comedian. He suffers the existence of the Church. It is a good business venture keeping the poor, the weak of mind and the gullible off the streets and makes money from their miseries and fears.

His genitalia are pink and cherubic and not alarming in any way. In matters of coitus he is experienced but not masterful. He prefers secret groping in public rather than private, loving intercourse. During sexual arousal his vascularity is noteworthy.

When questioned about homosexuality, his face turns purple, his eyelashes flutter and he bids you good day…

…"Good day indeed!" came the doctor's voice from the doorway. Both the young lady and I jumped in startlement at the interruption.

"Doctor…!" we both began.

He held his hands up to silence us as he chuckled.

"I'm sorry for the intrusion but I felt I had to find out what the delay was. The patient's condition really is becoming quite serious. Run along now child. I shall wait for the prescription."

The young lady whispered an apology either to the doctor, or myself, I know not which, nor am I ever likely to know because, as she went out of the door into the sunny street, that was the last I ever saw of her.

The doctor watched her leave, chuckling to himself and shaking his head slightly. I'm sure I heard him say something like "such a pity" before his mood darkened and he turned his strange gaze upon me.

"And now sir, the prescription, if you will!"

As I busied myself in the preparation room I chatted frivolously through the open door, although the whole time I felt a great unease sweeping over me. The doctor remained silent during my efforts at light conversation but presently I was finished and re-entered the shop.

The horrific figure that stood before me was almost beyond nightmare's ability to represent. The doctor's face had contorted to such a degree that it resembled an excruciating snarl. His eyes had turned completely red and the teeth were twisted and green. The hair had grown down to his collar and become an unhealthy yellow colour, similarly his moustache, the ends of which now turned downwards like dead swans' necks. His shoulders had become hunched and bulky so that he was unable to stand upright. The ears, now plainly visible, were highly pointed. Drool flowed from his misshapen mouth and his mysterious tongue now lolled out in the form of two gigantic purple slugs. But the worst of it was the stench of rotten flesh, pieces of which were dripping off his body as I watched. I was at first scared beyond any reaction but almost instantly succumbed to repulsion and disgust.

"Please, the antidote!" gasped the doctor painfully. I could see the tears of pain and humiliation in his red eyes. I passed the bottle of rare liquid to him and he received it in a clawed hand. The nails were long and filthy and the skin shrivelled and grey.

He gulped the liquid down in one long desperate effort.

"It is a gypsy curse," he gasped. "I failed to correctly treat a condition of some rancid old woman at the gypsy camp and, as she died, she cursed me with... with this!"

"Who was the young girl?" I asked horrified.

"That is the daughter of the gypsy. A floozy whose bed I have frequented on numerous occasions. We were lying together in the next room as the old crone died in agony, cursing me with each rattle of the headboard. I was horribly negligent, reaching the zenith of sexual fervour as she drew her last painful gasp of air. Thus I am guilty of her death and fully deserving of my present condition."

His eyes suddenly became calm and he was able to fashion a smile of sorts.

"If you think this is bad you should see me naked!" he rasped.

I felt that the antidote I had prepared might be taking effect. However, when the doctor looked at me again I knew I was mistaken. His eyes, although returning fast to their original colour, were dull and empty.

"Too late! Too late!" sighed the doctor as he sank to the floor.

By the time I had summoned up enough courage to move away from the serving counter to where he was lying, he had completely regained his original form.

Although the stench was dissipating, I knew he was dead without having to investigate further. I became grimly aware of his last words. Had I been less suspicious and not required such detailed information, might not the doctor have lived?

In a panic I dialled my friend, the professor at St Dympna's, and blurted out the story without hesitating to break the news gently. I suspect he had left his office long before I had finished my apologies and declarations of innocence and good intent.

Those were the longest moments of my life as I paced around my small shop, wringing my hands and occasionally glancing at the corpse of a person I had come to know in great detail.

"Too late!" I cried out despairingly.

"Calm yourself Quentin!" urged the professor as he exploded into the shop.

He took a step over to his son's body and, having checked at the neck for a pulse, seemed to sag suddenly within his suit. He knelt down stiffly and stroked the doctor's cold cheek.

"Oh! Mortimer, my poor child!"

The professor gave a long sigh and looked up at me. Tears ran down his face and through the miracle of osmosis they were mopped away by his Archimedes-style beard.

"Feel no guilt Quentin," he said gently. "My son was victim to a far greater force than your prolonged prescription description."

Slowly and wearily, he stood up and blew his nose into a paisley handkerchief.

"The doctor said something about a curse!" I spluttered.

"Ah yes, the old gypsy crone," he said as a distant look crept into his eyes. "She is responsible for the sufferings of many at St Dympna's. The man who lives as a papier-mâché turtle, and the man who believes Jesus is a silver lunar monkey are just two examples of her cursed victims. In fact I myself am somewhat of a victim of hers."

"What do you mean professor?" I asked, confused.

He smiled sadly.

"You see, there is something the young gypsy girl did not know."

He waved his hat in the direction of his dead son.

"I, um… that is, the old gypsy was… oh dear… Madam Zelda and I… well we… ah confound it! Mortimer was our love child!"

I looked from the professor to the doctor and back to the professor. Then I looked at the doctor and back to the professor, before looking at the doctor again, as the terrible truth sank into my throbbing brain. I looked at the professor.

"In that case…" I began.

"Yes Quentin, that's correct," finished the professor. "Let us say no more about it shall we?"

The professor went to the door and called out to someone. Two wardens from St Dympna's came in, picked up the body of the doctor and carried him out to the waiting carriage.

"Thank you for your discretion in this matter," said the

professor, taking out his wallet and handing me some money. "Here's seven guineas and four shillings for your trouble and need I say that, should you ever require a secret to be kept in return, then please do not hesitate to call."

He disappeared and closed the door softly behind him. I looked at the money in my hand and realised that there was only seven guineas and three shillings. The ungrateful scoundrel! I was almost tempted to run out and demand the other shilling but the carriage had driven away by now.

For the rest of the day I pottered distractedly around the shop, troubled thoughts refusing to allow me peace. I knew that I would be forever haunted by that sight… and by those words, "Too late! Too late!" But what really irks me, I said to myself as I brushed up some flaky remains of skin, is that my name is not now, nor ever has been, Quentin!

READERS' BLOG:

- *I still have no idea what the doctor looked like. A face like a sausage, teeth like cheese, gingerish hair and small cherubic penis?*
- *Fuck me, it's Elton John!*
- *I think the pharmacist has breached patient-doctor confidentiality somewhere along the line.*
- *Who exactly is Quentin? Perhaps we'll never know.*
- *Like the late doctor, I also enjoy hooking my thumbs into my waistcoat pockets, but I certainly don't whistle at the same time. It would make me appear to be a working-class Cockney geezer barrow boy on a pickpocketing jaunt down Portobello Road.*

- Yes, and you would probably be tempted to pickpocket some silk handkerchiefs. People like you are no better than vermin and should be broken at the wheel like back in the good old days.
- Whoa, hold your horses, big mouth! I'm just saying that I wouldn't whistle.
- Can we concentrate on the story please? I wonder what happened to the young gypsy girl? If she's out there reading this… go home darling. Your family needs you. Probably.
- I don't like the sound of the doctor's nostrils. If I were him I'd have them seen to.
- Yes he sounds very ugly. Somewhat like a Titicaca water frog, the Latin name of which is the aquatic scrotum! Google it!

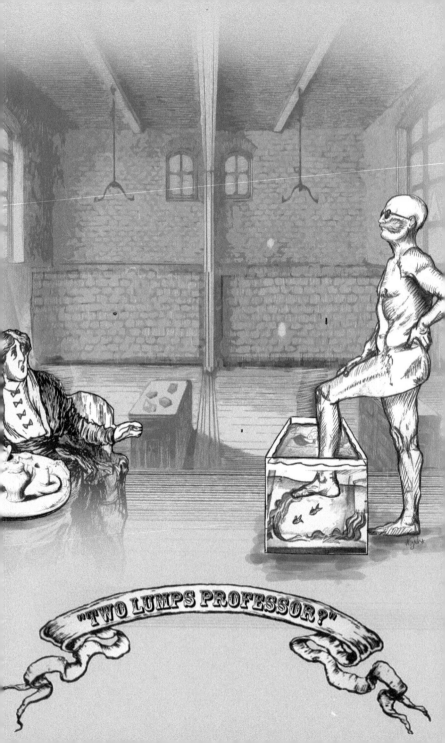

"TWO LUMPS PROFESSOR?"

QUALITY JANITOR

I have finally managed to persuade Muriel to have a nice cup of tea and a sit down. There is a comedy programme on the TV in my basement office which I hope she will enjoy. Later, when she least expects it, I will brutally kill her. But until then she can sit and drink tea and say "Oh dear me!" to her heart's content. She's a lovely lady after all, God bless her.

She's had quite a day what with one thing and another. The 'one thing' was finding Professor Mountebank naked in his study, trying to climb into the fish tank, and 'another' was the attempted suicide of her favourite inmate, who had suffered several paper cuts to his thorax and a nasty sting on the nose which had caused it to swell like a small plum.

- *Or a damson?*
- *Oh I remember now! These characters are from the story 'Beekeeper's Apprentice' which appeared in Plankton Soup – Second Helpings. The professor is haunted by the ghost of Jacques Cousteau, the inventor of the aqualung!*
- *The above reader's comment is a blatant 'product placement' advert for Sutton's previous work (shit, by the*

way) and should be deleted if the author had any moral compass.

Earlier today, Muriel had entered the professor's study and pushed her tea trolley towards the main desk where Professor Mountebank, Head of Madness at St Dympna's Lunatic Asylum, would usually be busy at work. She had intended to leave him his regular preference of Earl Grey tea and some vanilla wafers. It was then that she'd heard a commotion coming from behind the open door.

The stark-naked professor had already placed one of his legs into the small aquarium that stood on a low, broad bookcase and he was now precariously balanced in the act of trying to drag his other leg in. However, the black rubber flipper he was wearing had got caught in the hat stand as he'd attempted to swing his foot up and over. Although the professor had his back turned to Muriel, his precarious position meant that his battered old scrotum was in full view.

"Two lumps, professor?" asked Muriel, holding a china cup and saucer in one hand and silver sugar tongs in the other.

The professor hesitated and turned to face Muriel. She could see that he had taken a spring clip off a pile of documents and was now using it to hold his nostrils closed. When he spoke, it was with a nasally distorted French accent.

"Regardez monsieur! Not only are there some interesting Myctophidae amongst the coral reefs but there is a lone Beluga whale pup seemingly in distress, having lost the ability to echolocate!"

Muriel knew nothing about lantern fish or echolocation but she certainly knew where the panic button was located. It was normally used for violent patients or, conversely, timid patients who had become alarmed by the professor's hauntings. She reached under the desk and pressed three times.

Today I was first on the scene because I had been in a nearby cell, unblocking a toilet with my trusty toilet brush, Pemberton. It's probably hard to believe but Pemberton has a soul! Yes, and his name is Pemberton. (That's what he told me anyway.)

Muriel fell into my arms as I walked through the door.

"Oh, dear me! He's 'avin one of his turns again!" she announced tremulously.

I admired her loyalty. The last time she had encountered the professor during one of his hauntings he had fired a harpoon at her, which had dislodged a plate of Jammy Dodgers from her hand and finally thudded harmlessly into the home-made papier-mâché shell of a passing patient who thought he was a tortoise.

I shepherded Muriel out of the room, shielding her from the disturbing sight of the professor's unruly pudenda.

Just then, two burly male nurses arrived, panting.

"Is it a 'code red'?" they asked enthusiastically.

"No, just Jacques Cousteau's ghost again," I explained.

They were disappointed, but knew exactly what to do.

"OK, play the music," said one.

The Muppet song, 'Mnuh-Mnuh' was the only way to discourage the ghost of Cousteau.

I pressed PLAY on the emergency cassette player on the professor's desk. The nurses approached the professor from two sides and threw a blanket over him.

63

"Qu'est-ce que c'est? Où est les poissons? Merde!"

"Mnuh-mnuh!"

We left them to it. I walked with Muriel and her tea trolley along the corridor to the wards. I chatted away, trying to gloss over the incident and keep her mind on other things.

"I say Muriel, have you seen the price of a bag of onions these days?"

"Oh, dear me!"

We stopped outside the cell of Mr Witherjay (Muriel's favourite inmate). Muriel had prepared a plate of sandwiches for his light tea. He couldn't write on a full stomach he'd said. He was supposed to be a famous author but I'd never heard of him. Gossip and rumour would have it that the subjects of his books always ended up dead. Recently his cell mate had drowned in a shoe full of saliva. Perhaps that's why, lately, there have been strange men in grey suits asking questions around the asylum.

Because the duty nurses were occupied with the professor, I decided to hang around and wait for Muriel whilst she did her visits, just in case there were any hiccups. Not that I'm qualified to cure hiccups, I mean in case there was an emergency. And there was.

As soon as Muriel had stepped into the cell of Mr Witherjay she started screaming. I ran in and looked over her shoulder. There he lay, flat on his back in a small puddle of blood, staring up at the ceiling with a stupid look on his face.

"I don't remember him having such a big red nose," I said. "It looks like a damson!"

"Or a small plum," sobbed Muriel.

"Is he dead?"

"Oh, dear me! Poor Mr Witherjay, he was such a nice man. Not crazy at all."

Pemberton started vibrating in my hand. This was his way of telling me he wanted to give me a message. Ignoring the rancid faeces that clogged his sturdy bristles, I lifted Pemberton to my ear.

I nodded in understanding.

"He's not dead yet. Stand back!"

I placed the rancid tip of Pemberton under the nose of Mr Witherjay and, sure enough, the overpowering stench was enough to shock him back to consciousness.

"Wha… what? Aren't I dead?" He sounded almost disappointed.

"No you're still here."

"Where's the talking bee?" Witherjay mumbled and tried to sit up.

"The who?"

"The talking bee. He stung me on the nose and promised me everlasting serenity."

"The bee spoke to you?" said Muriel, mopping up the small patch of blood in which Mr Witherjay had written 'The End' (This act had just volunteered him to go top of my list, after Muriel.)

"Yes, he spoke fluently in various tongues."

"Ooh, I didn't know bees had tongues! How lovely!"

- *Muriel can be forgiven her ignorance. In bee language, tongues are called proboscises.*
- *Yes we all know that. But in this case Mr Witherjay intends 'tongues' to mean 'languages' and not 'proboscises'.*

- *I thought a proboscis is what a doctor sticks in your arse to cure headache. That's what my doctor invariably does to me. Headache or not.*

I persuaded Muriel to come back to my 'office' in the basement. After all that excitement I'm sure she needed a cup of tea.

As we passed Professor Mountebank's study, he (now fully dressed and medicated) opened the door and said:

"Ah Muriel, just the person we needed to speak to."

I glanced into the room and saw some of those mysterious people in grey suits lurking around, looking a bit shifty, avoiding my gaze.

"I'll put the kettle on," I whispered to Muriel as she went into the office.

My inner voice sneered at the well-dressed men in the professor's study.

"Any day now, the nightmare scenario! Then you can throw away your fancy suits and we'll all be wearing animal skins! Then I'll be in my element. Welcome to my world!" I laughed hysterically as I descended the stairs to my basement.

Fifteen years ago a new janitor started work here in St Dympna's. His likeness to me was uncanny. I knew then what I must do. Within the first week I had killed him and exchanged identities. Then I embarked on a serious killing spree. But I am not unique. Surely not. There must be others. Others who feel this way.

* * *

What follows is a reflective account by Professor Mountebank, based on observational notes taken during his induction interviews of Lord Lucan and also recent video footage obtained by FBI undercover operatives…

"Lord Lucan admitted himself into St Dympna's Lunatic Asylum many years ago in the mid-seventies, after having had a very troubled time in the outside world. He was well spoken and intelligent as befits a member of high society, but there was something dark living behind those handsome manners. His superior breeding had served him well over the years, served to mask the monster within him, the sickness. Nothing gave a clue to his true self, except the eyes. The eyes gave him away.

It is said that the eyes are windows to the soul. If so, Lord Lucan was in purgatory. He had a somewhat tortured gaze. As if he had actually been to Hell and knew what was in store for him on judgement day.

He was sick, he knew that, unable to hold a conversation without becoming distracted by inner thoughts. Uncomfortable in any environment that may lead to excessive face-to-face contact with another person; it was almost a fear… a fear for the other person's well-being. After all he was not evil, just sick.

Sadly, due to information that has recently come to light, it seems that around fifteen years ago Lord Lucan killed our janitor and swapped identities. It is to our everlasting shame that nobody noticed the exchange, not least because the original janitor was a Mexican hunchback who suffered an acute case of dwarfism!"

* * *

Since I adopted my new identity, 'Pedro', I have killed about five inmates a year. Most of the deaths were logged officially as accidents or suicide. Recently the lunatic asylum has received visitors wearing grey suits who ask a lot of questions in low voices. But they have never interviewed me. I am quite rightly beyond any suspicion. I am after all, a quality janitor.

And now it is time to kill Muriel. I will do it in the worst way imaginable, probably using Pemberton to quell her screams.

By the time she knocks on my door I have worked myself up into a murderous state. Somehow I manage to control myself despite the voices in my head.

"Tea's brewing," I say lightly as I guide her to an armchair. In that position I can sneak up behind her from the kitchen and whack her across the head with an old banjo that I have made from the fossilised remains of a Shetland porcupine.

"Can I have coffee instead?" she answers, in a rather gruff voice.

In all the years we have worked together, she has never asked for coffee. I put it down to her emotional state after all the excitement of the day. Still, something is different about her, but I can't quite put my finger on it.

I feel compelled to mention her appearance.

"You look different somehow. I hadn't realised that your chin was so angular; looks a bit like an anvil…"

• *Or an old Volvo?*

"…and is that five o'clock shadow? No offence, you understand?"

She pulls a hanky from her sleeve and raises it to her face in a self-conscious manner.

"Oh Pedro don't be silly, it's just the poor lighting in here. You should change to those new full spectrum light bulbs."

My eyes widen with shocked indignation.

Is she really playing the light bulb efficiency comparison card with me? A *quality* janitor! By Jove! She will pay dearly for that remark! Not that her predicament has become any more fatal than it already was. But perhaps now I will torture her first.

She is watching the new comedy programme on my TV, a sitcom based in a garden centre, showcasing yet another pair of ground-breaking comedians from Cambridge University. If they're not spying for Russia then they're raving homosexuals, likely as not. That's my opinion anyway. I take a deep breath and notice that I'm rubbing Muriel's shoulders and telling her to relax.

I hear myself asking her if she has ever slaughtered a pig. I make the observation that removing the entrails is a very messy business.

Disjointed dialogue fills my mind but I am not sure if it is coming from the television or from my own inner voice.

"Whilst visiting Winkworth Arboretum his ejector shoes misfired and he was never seen again."

"Patios? I've a good mind to pour concrete over my house and turn it into a cave... see how the wife likes having only one entrance!"

"Shield of Justice? What use is that in the jungle?"

"Captain Barclay of the Royal Artillery offered five guineas to any man that could retrieve his fishing equipment from the giant azaleas, although he fully intended to renege on the deal and would offer a banana in lieu."

"It was a danker morning than usual, but at least I was able to get my broad beans in!"

* * *

The freshly-made pot of tea has gone cold. I am wiping blood off the porcupine skeleton banjo. Now the phone is ringing. Somehow I have the presence of mind to answer it.

"Hello?"

"Hi, Pedro? Nurse Bruce here, (I'm the big one with the curly beard). Please come to the library immediately! It's the professor. He believes he has found the lost city of Atlantis!"

I'm not really listening.

"So what?"

"So he's tried to flush himself down the toilet! The crazy old sod has literally gone around the bend this time!" (Laughing in the background; sound of 'high fives' being exchanged.)

"So, can you bring your magic plunger?"

I look at Pemberton who is standing upright, lodged deep in Muriel's throat.

"He's busy at the moment. We'll be there as soon as possible." I hang up slowly and remember what I was doing before the call.

I am amazed at how long it is taking Muriel to die. She is still struggling and displaying immense strength of character.

Somebody starts singing. Perhaps it's me? But instead of "I left my heart… in San Francisco", the words have been changed to "I got the shits… in Albufeira."

I have been to Albufeira, before the madness, but I don't remember getting the shits.

Now what is she doing? Muriel's hand is trying to pull up her skirt and baring her surprisingly muscular hairy thighs.

This really isn't going quite as well as I'd hoped. I try not to notice but… she is wearing very large heavy-knit black undergarments. They have the letters F.B.I. embroidered in big yellow capitals on what appears to be her oversized pubic mound.

F.B.I.? F.B.I.? My janitorial brain searches for an answer. Fire Blanket Inside? For Better Insulation? Free Batteries Included?

Now Muriel has taken something out of a hidden pocket in the front of her knickers. It looks to my untrained eye like a .38 Smith & Wesson.

- *Or snub-nosed revolver?*

Oh dear me! She is snarling like an animal and pointing the gun directly at my fa…

Loud ringing in my head… blackness… nothing.

READERS' BLOG:

- *If I was a cannibal I would make a kind of jam from Witherjay's plum-like nose.*
- *My best friend is a cannibal but his name is not Hannibal. It's Mgawe Ngongo Zimbu, which translates as 'I can't believe it's not butter!'*
- *Well at least that's the Lord Lucan mystery solved. I have*

lain awake most nights since he disappeared in 1974, wondering if he had packed enough sandwiches, a change of undergarments, and sufficient coinage for a phone call.

- Lunatics should not be locked away like criminals. They should be allowed the freedom to express themselves. Perhaps sell them to a travelling circus or Cabaret Voltaire.

- The aqualung has been a godsend to scuba divers all over the world. Without it they may have had to develop gills.

- I expect that I would feel ill at ease in the company of a gilled man.

- In my village, gills would be the least of your worries!

- Sutton talks bullshit sometimes. Lantern fish live at depths of approximately 200 metres, whereas coral forms in relatively shallow water. The aquatic ignoramus.

- Lucan can't be dead because he has written the story… unless… unless… he survived the shot and was then incarcerated within the asylum as a patient again and had Witherjay as a cell mate who then wrote this story on his behalf, which means Lucan probably IS dead due to the Witherjay curse!!!! (As explained in Plankton Soup – Second Helpings).

- Hey wait a minute! Are you Sutton's literary agent posing as a reader's blogger again?

- So Witherjay lives to write another day. Let's hope he does better than Sutton.

SEND YOUR COMMENTS TO THE BLOG AT
www.planktonsoup.co.uk

STATIC NOISE

Quite simply, the Brigadier was the most interesting man that I had ever met. To listen to him talk was to 'ride the wild unicorn of knowledge along the highway of cosmic awareness' (the Government Minister's words, not mine). He could converse in depth about any subject and recount tales galore of danger and derring-do. Also, on the rare occasion he was not the narrator of a tale, he would nevertheless participate with wit, gusto and genuine interest.

However, one day, whilst listening to him lecture us on reasons not to fear, but on the contrary to embrace blue algae, my attention wandered slightly and unfortunately my gaze fell upon his face in three-quarter profile. I was at once astonished and horrified to recognise an unfavourable resemblance between his facial contours and the squatting 'lady' in the infamous *Les Demoiselles d'Avignon* by the loathsome Cubist, Pablo Picasso.

Powerless to prevent myself, I took off all my clothes and, placing one foot on a silk pouffe, I announced my discovery to the other high society guests.

Our man of knowledge stopped in mid-sentence,

somewhere around: "Another fascinating use for blue algae is anal…"

Mademoiselle Bonnet de Douche, in whose drawing room we were gathered, fainted momentarily, but quickly recovered by fanning herself with the nearest item to hand, a giant doily; a gift from one of her pretentious artist friends. Sculpted from caramelised pygmy droppings, it was a rarity indeed!

The Government Minister had been sycophantically taking notes during the blue algae lecture whilst simultaneously and almost imperceptibly frottering against Mademoiselle's wooden arm.

(It is not the done thing to enquire as to the nature of her affliction. Some say she was born like that, but whoever heard of a wooden baby?) However, the Brigadier did once tell of a tribe of people in the Far East who are part tree, part human. At this, the Government Minister had let out a wail of discomfort and had hurriedly left the room, doubled over; clutching his morning coat around his groin area with one hand whilst biting down hard on the knuckle of the other).

Now the Government Minister straightened his back and wiggled his classic moustache.

"I say!" he said.

The silence that followed almost made one giddy. Mademoiselle seemed to be holding her breath and the blue vein in her ivory neck (not literally ivory, a wooden arm is bad luck enough) spasmed stronger with each passing second of quiet.

The Government Minister, having now recognised the similarity to the portrait, stood with mouth agape and, if I had heard a faint noise it could have been his drying lips slowly cracking. I realised at this point that true silence cannot exist. I could hear the blood coursing past my cochlea. I could hear Mademoiselle's wooden arm creaking as its fibres contracted through lack of sap. I could hear the hiss of background radiation from the Big Bang as it echoed through the universe. I could hear our expert's eyelids narrow as he regarded me with all the controlled fury of a true gentleman.

"Well well, Monsieur Malaise du Chien", he said to me through gritted teeth. "I see you have taken my advice in matters of male grooming. May I congratulate you on the quality of your pubic topiary? You have obviously spent a lot of time and money on your genitalia."

I, equally coolly, replied, "Thank you Brigadier Oeufs d'Amour. I recently visited the barber at Place Vendôme as you recommended."

The Brigadier's face softened slightly. "Yes, Monsieur Jambes de Fille is indeed precise and (a polite cough into a monogrammed kerchief)… infinitely gentle."

He began to collect his hat and coat.

"Not so fast Brigadier, if you please!" thundered the Minister, who had at last come to understand the gravity of the situation. "You do realise this means you are no longer welcome in our circle?"

"Minister Dans les Arbres sans Pantalons, I am aware of your misguided animosity towards Cubism, but foolishly hoped our friendship would overcome such prejudice. I can see from your expressions that I am mistaken."

The Brigadier then turned to our hostess.

"Mademoiselle, I regret to inform you that I will never again enter your clique!"

"I too am sorry Brigadier. But I'm sure you understand that I cannot be in any way connected with Cubism. It is an abhorrence to our society. Kindly remove yourself and never again leave your calling card, the angular nature of which would only serve to remind me of your twisted sympathies."

Slowly and with great dignity the Brigadier gave a little bow to the Mademoiselle and let himself out of the room.

"Well that's that!" exclaimed the Minister and then realised something.

"I've just realised something! Without the Brigadier, what are we to do for the rest of the afternoon?"

Mademoiselle thought for a moment and then, glancing up at me, smiled wryly (she could be very wry when she wanted) and said:

"Hmm, I may have the perfect repost to our Brigadier's portrait betrayal."

And then I thought she may have given me a cheeky wink, although that form of body language was rather yet too decadent, even in Paris.

It was indeed a cheeky wink! Now here I sit, naked in the centre of the aptly named drawing room on a crate of oysters from Martinique. My left foot is raised slightly and resting on the silk pouffe as before. I am trying to emulate *The Thinker* by Rodin. The guests are busy behind their easels, using the shafts of their paint brushes to translate my proportions onto canvas or parchment.

The room is silent… but, as I have already discussed, absolute silence cannot exist. I can hear the intake and exhalation of each individual's breath. I can almost identify each person simply by the frequency at which they breathe.

I can hear the friction of the charcoal as it scratches

across the parchment, forming the lines of my torso. I can hear the coloured chalks crumbling as they are pressed to form the tones of my flesh. I can hear the water colour soaking into the canvas.

I can hear the friction of the Minister's trousers as he manoeuvres himself erotically against the leg of the easel. The friction has caused a build-up of static electricity within him and his hair is beginning to frizz. I know this because I can hear it.

Mademoiselle seems to be constantly scratching an imaginary itch on her wooden arm and this is resulting in a static build-up which is causing her wig to become hot. I can hear the pores opening on her scalp to release perspiration (ladies do not sweat).

I am becoming aware of faint voices in my head. I can only assume, as I have learned in one of the Brigadier's seminars, that the static electricity around the brains of my companions has increased to such an extent that it is allowing their thoughts to escape the confines of their delicate skulls. I concentrate harder and am able to recognise the words.

"Mon Dieu, the sweet, tainted ecstasy of wood! How I adore its forbidden pain!"

Someone else is thinking,

"His buttocks would welcome a bit of frottage and perhaps I could make his scrotal sack tighter by some soft brushing with my thumb. If only I knew the proper technique!"

I trust you will excuse me if I do not disclose whose thoughts were whose.

FIN.

READERS' BLOG:

- So, who fancies the naked guy with his foot on a pouffe? The Minister or the Madame?
- That's the point, it could be either.
- They don't fancy him, they just want to rub his testes. Ah, Paris. How romantic!
- I once knew a guy who thought he knew everything. We threw eggs at him and gave him wedgies. But he didn't know how to stop us. Mind you, he's had the last laugh; he's now my bank manager and they have just foreclosed on my mortgage.
- Pygmy droppings probably don't smell because they only eat nuts and seeds. Don't they?
- I wonder what Rodin's real statue was thinking about? Perhaps we'll never know.

WHEN THE CHIPS ARE DOWN

Despite her encouragement I can't get all my fingers in.

"Keep trying!" she begs desperately, "I'm almost there!"

Damn, it feels so hot inside! I try to push my fingers further.

"Too… tight" I grunt.

"I'm coming! I'm coming now!" She's gasping like crazy and her voice is hoarse.

- *Crazy Horse? Is she a Red Indian or an Osmond?*

She's suddenly behind me at the top of the stairs. She has brought a large bolt cutter from the garage and a small fire extinguisher from the hallway, ten floors below. Together they are very heavy and she is exhausted. Perhaps she should have brought one at a time.

I give up trying to get my hand through the door to unhook the chain-lock and I grab the bolt cutters from her.

Smoke is billowing out from the apartment through the gap in the doorway and I can just about see the support stockings on the legs of Auntie Clarice who has fainted behind the sofa.

She promised us chips!

But as we finally break the lock and enter the room it is obvious there will be no chips today. The chip pan is on fire and there is no more cooking oil in the plastic container. I'm very disappointed.

I throw the blazing pan out of the kitchen window and it falls ten storeys into the car park below.

I get a cup of water and take it to Auntie who is coughing and spluttering. I throw the water in her face and give her a sharp prod with my Dr. Martens boot (I'm wearing it). She overreacts to this and says "Ow!"

"There's no more cooking oil!" I snarl.

My cousin indicates the fire extinguisher she is still holding and asks what she should do with it.

I take it off her and release foam all over the kitchen for no other reason than to let off steam… which would have been a good joke had the extinguisher contained water instead of foam! I finish off the last squirt by spraying it over Auntie in the hope that it will teach her not to forget about the chip pan in future. She doesn't appreciate this and shouts "Blurgh!" This makes me laugh because her false teeth fall out as she says it.

Now that the extinguisher is empty I have no further need for it, so I nonchalantly force it through the television screen. My work here is finished and if there are no chips then I may as well leave.

I kiss my cousin goodbye (I surprise her by using tongues) and stop at the door on my way out. I look back at Auntie who is still wiping foam off her spectacles and rubbing her thigh where I kicked her.

"Would you like a cup of tea before you go?" she asks meekly.

I show her my clenched fist and make the knuckles crack like in a kung fu movie.

"You promised me some fucking chips!"

As I walk into the car park I am surprised to see that some cars are on fire and a youth is screaming in agony due to his eye melting with hot oil. He pleads for help but I laugh at his burnt, disfigured face and tell him in a cockney accent, "Geht aht of it!" despite the fact I have never been to Cockney and am not sure if my accent is authentic. Certainly not enough to fool a native.

A passing cat gives me a funny look as if it's saying, "What are you staring at?" The *cat* is asking this of *me*? I kick it very hard so it won't ask that next time we meet. It flies over a dustbin but lands on its feet, so I guess it's OK. I wouldn't want to upset anyone by harming an animal. After all, I'm not a monster.

I go to the chip shop on the street corner and order chips and gravy. I lick my lips in anticipation as the chip shop proprietor ladles thick, dark gravy into a small polystyrene tub. But then something terrible happens!

"You'll have to wait ten minutes for chips, mate!" says the proprietor, flicking a wire basket of raw potato slices that look like albino slugs.

The red mist descends as I open my briefcase and slowly reach inside for my Uzi…

READERS' BLOG:

- *Chips are not worth dying for. Any chip shop proprietor worth his salt (and vinegar) should have sufficient chips*

83

ready-cooked before he opens the door to the gun-toting public.

- I'm sure the body language of the disgruntled customer would have indicated his reluctance to wait ten minutes for chips. In this case I would have offered him some batter bits or a small sausage to distract him. This would also give the SWAT team an opportunity to take up tactical positions around the shop and maybe disarm him before he realised his predicament.

- Dude, you're good! Maybe you should have written the story. What else have you got?

- Well, I thought maybe the SWAT team could arrest the chip enthusiast, but on the way to the police station he uses the handcuffs to strangle the driver when they stop to get doughnuts. But actually he doesn't try to escape; he walks into the same fast food joint as the SWAT team and asks for French fries. He then replies 'yes' when asked if he wants to 'go large'.

- O…kaaay.

- Then, in prison, the irony is that he is given work duty in the kitchens, peeling potatoes for chips. This puts him off chips forever. But later in life he is shot during a drugs raid and the police find out he's been dealing nothing more than dehydrated mashed potato.

- Sutton is emulating the author of American Psycho.

- In Kansas, emulating is only allowed in the privacy of your own home between two consenting adults. And you must wear a condom, especially if you are one of the adults doing the emulating or being emulated.

- Talking of Americans, Crazy Horse and Sitting Bull defeated General Custer at Little Bighorn. Crazy Horse was also the *name of Neil Young's band years ago (although I much preferred Bob Dylan). The Mormon family 'Osmond' had a hit with Crazy Horses in 1972.*

- *Bob Dylan? Weird! Last week I met a Welsh guy in a secluded lay-by on the A49, and guess what? His first name was Dylan too! And he paid a few 'bob' extra for services rendered.*
- *The author has missed an opportunity here. He could have made a joke about Dylan having a little (or big) horn!*
- *The Welsh are internationally renowned to have small penises due to adverse climatic conditions and poor diet, so it is a moot point.*
- *As a self-confessed Welshman, I blame the state of my two penises on the acid rain from the Chernobyl explosion!*

SEND YOUR COMMENTS TO THE BLOG AT
www.planktonsoup.co.uk

THE GABRIELLE
COURVOISIER TRILOGY

GABRIELLE

Oh Gabrielle, my darling Gabrielle!
My sunshine, my moonlight,
My shining star, my blazing candle,
My… my… my blinding beacon.
Oh Gabrielle, where are you?
I searched the city like a madman.
Clutching old friends by their lapels
Eyes wide in frantic desperation.
Scaring children who fell to the ground
As I hacked mercilessly through the crowded pavement.
Our favourite café looked so bleak without you
I think I shall never go there again.
Neither the boutique where you found that dress
In which you remind me of that actress
With the big tits.
In your boudoir with your great aunt's permission
Under your bed the suitcase has gone!
In your wardrobe where you made me hide that time

I was dressed as Batman with realistic tumescent attachment,
Whilst Grandpere sang you a goodnight lullaby.
But alas, quelle misfortune, now your wardrobe is empty.
Finally, on your dressing table amongst the perfumes and ear syringe,
A gilded book embossed with your name,
'Gabrielle Courvoisier'
(How sweet your wine, your heavenly nectar)
Remember how you blushed when I told you that?
Behold, your secret diary lays open to my eye.
Forgive me my darling but needs must!
I am sure you heard the heavy thud of my heart
As it dropped to the floor of my soul,
Even from your hotel room in Cannes,
Where I should also be, had I not forgotten our weekend plans!
Merde!

MEMORIES OF AN AUGUST ROMANCE

…Oh by the way, Gabrielle, did I tell you?
I took a short trip through Clermont-Ferrand
Returning from, well, you know where.
And as I drove through the cobbled piazza,
The one with the red clay flower pots,
I remembered the time we had dinner at that restaurant
Decorated with green tablecloths and yellow candles.
(Not us – the restaurant)

And then as we waited for the Moon's orange eclipse,
You somehow managed to inhale, rather than ingest, a
frog's leg!
I tried the Heimlich manoeuvre but
Succeeded only to maul your breasts.
You slapped me so hard my toupee fell
Into that woman's soup.
The ensuing furore led to the police being called.
Even with your fuchsia pink polka dot umbrella
Embedded in the police sergeant's shoulder,
He somehow managed to fire off a shot into your leg.
You tumbled over the pretty wrought iron dining chair
Painted cream and gold and your crimson blood stained
the purple cobbles.
Your legs were in the air for what seemed an eternity
and the crowd
Were entranced by your ginger mohair underpants.
Or at least that's what they thought they could see.
Oh Gabrielle, I wonder, do you remember?

A LOVE BETRAYED

…Oh Gabrielle I must tell you
I met the most charming woman at the theatre,
Only last week as a matter of fact.
Our eyes met across a crowded vestibule and
What better way to begin a mysterious romance?
I was collecting my scarf from the cloakroom attendant
You know the paisley one?
The scarf is paisley not the attendant

Come, come Gabrielle be serious!
And as I turned away my gaze fell upon
This most heavenly of God's creatures
Seemingly alone despite the crowd,
Resplendent in her taffeta gown and pearls,
Apparently queuing to powder her pretty nose.
Although she later admitted
She in fact had a bad case of the 'merdes'.
That half-hour I waited for her return
Seemed as an eternity, so desirous was I to make her
acquaintance.
When finally she emerged, her delicate brow
Was bathed in perspiration and furrowed with troubled
thoughts.
Her rosebud lips quivered like a frightened deer.
This only served to arouse my manly instincts
(Easily done, ask any waitress at the Moulin)
And I quickly threw my cloak around her trembling
shoulders.
"Come, my angel!" I said, and hailed a carriage
But as we stepped across the pavement
Her wooden leg detached itself, stuck in a grille.
"What devilment is this?" I cried.
But she was unable to answer
As she had a brief attack of St Vitus Dance.
I grasped her fragile form in my arms
And betrothed my everlasting love.
It was only then that her husband appeared and
Struck me violently about the nose for my troubles.
And continued to do so for about ten minutes
thereafter.

Now my soul is tormented by the memory
Of her alabaster face looking back at me
Through the rear window of the disappearing carriage.
And she waved me a gentle goodbye
With her wooden leg in her hand.
But alas! Dear Gabrielle, she still had on my cloak!
And in it the diamond ring that I
Intended to give to you on bended knee today!
Thus in shame I am away to join the Legion.
Adieu!

THE EMERGENCY
MERINGUE BASE

The 'Tall Man' swivels on the heels of his snakeskin boots and strides to the corner of the office. He stops, turns slightly and looks back over his shoulder at the man sitting at the desk. Without breaking eye contact he unzips his trousers and urinates noisily onto the floor. A slight breaking of wind can be heard if one listens carefully enough, although it is of no consequence in itself.

"I'm taking the liberty of relieving myself in this manner, Smith, in order to demonstrate my ambivalence towards your self-perceived authority. What have you to say in repost? Anything? Or, as I suspect, nothing?"

Smith, struggling to maintain composure, leans back in his gigantic leather chair and puts the tips of his fingers together. He then puts his pursed lips atop this digital pyramid and glances at a small glass-fronted cabinet that hangs on the wall, containing an ancient meringue base. After a few seconds he drops his hands and lurches forward.

"That meringue base once belonged to Baron Ludwig Durchfall, the first Margrave of Baden-Baden, but I will use it if my hand is forced."

His antagonist falters.

"Now, now, Smith, that is uncalled for! We both know what that would mean."

The tall, red-eyed man spits at the legendary meringue base in hatred and fear, but misses, and the spittle lands on the leaf of a miniature monkey tree, but that is of no consequence in itself.

"Ah, you always were the clever one!" he sneers.

Smith, having regained some superiority in this battle of wits, allows himself a confident half-smirk. He reaches for the intercom on his huge desk.

"Miss Grotwinkle, could you have some perfumed talc delivered to my office. It would seem that some kind of ruminating mammal, perhaps a large pig, has found its way through the gap in the skirting boards and passed its filthy water on my voluptuous rug."

He looks back up at the tall, red-eyed, tattoo-faced man.

"Adieu, we will not see each other again, I fancy."

"Perhaps, perhaps not," says the tall, tattoo-faced, red-eyed, muscular-headed man, zipping himself up. Then his blazing eyes flash and his face contorts like that of a bear on fire. "Or perhaps I will see you from the flat end of a bullet!" he snarls.

He places an immaculate top hat onto his hairless muscular head and backs out through the lacquered walnut office doorway. Without another word he evaporates into the dim light.

Smith releases a long, noisy sigh, suddenly world-weary. His eyes water with sorrow as he realises the cosmic struggle will never be over. He would almost welcome death, although, in the grand scheme of things, it would be of no consequence in itself.

"Whatever you do," he whispers after the demon, "there's always the emergency meringue base."

READERS' BLOG:

- *I would like to read more about Smith and the tall, tattoo-faced, red-eyed, smooth-headed, top-hatted, snakeskin-booted, urinating demon and the mysterious meringue base. If only there was a sequel.*
- *Perhaps the BBC will buy the idea and make a series?*
- *What disgraceful behaviour! Urinating and spitting, it just goes to show that demons have no place in an office environment. They should be confined to the factory floors of northern towns.*
- *Unless the glass case was hermetically sealed, the meringue base is likely to be well past its sell-by date and therefore of little use in a cosmic emergency.*
- *Who wants office furniture made from walnut? Walnuts look like testicles! Apparently.*

THE PLOT THAT THICKENED

A pathetic, desperate author is making the most of a last-chance meeting with his literary agent. He is reading to her from a collection of manuscripts that he has been working on in an attempt to save his miserable career.

Despite her ruthless exterior the agent wants to help, but she is running out of patience. The author has consistently failed to bring her anything with a 'strong narrative'.

The author has already tried to entice her with a story about Bonzo the magic dog who, with a wag of his tail, 'shping shpang shpong', can perform all kinds of wonders for its owners, but to no avail; the agent remains unimpressed.

Now he is reading another story aloud to her as she squeezes the bridge of her nose in frustration.

"Grimwald the Smurge had awoken that morning to the noise of his friend Boris Morris scratching his gribble over-enthusiastically. He was excited about the upcoming Festival of Noor which this yearlobe would fall on the eleventeenth of Remember.

Boris Morris was complainy that he had no drapes to wear because he was all roly-poly-like, but Grimwald soothed that his Grandmartin's window blankets would do the job nicely and just see how fine he will *looky-looky*…"

"Stop!" wails the literary agent. "Stop please, that's quite enough! You've made a classic error! You've mixed *Lord of the Rings*, *Finnegans Wake*, *A Clockwork Orange* and bizarrely I seem to detect a smattering of Professor Stanley Unwin! And what exactly is a gribble?"

"I've got one more," says the author desperately. "It's called, *The Prog Rock Trance Affair*."

"Very well. Continue," sighs the agent.

The author does indeed continue…

"And there, at the end of the bookshelf, I found a thick red volume entitled *The Time That Land Forgot*. When I opened the book, a large trombone fell out from the middle pages, falling in slow motion and landing softly onto the desk. Upon looking inside the bell of the trombone I saw a beautiful woman who beckoned me to join her. Therein I discovered a wondrous land where marzipan was held in higher regard than the Brent crude oil price. I am fond of marzipan; consequently I stayed inside the trombone for fifty years. When I finally emerged…"

"Anything else?" interrupts the agent.

"You don't like it?" the author asks, genuinely surprised.

"It's got slapstick vampires, a reluctant contract killer and a talking horse. Oh! And a scene where somebody gratuitously bares their left breast!"

"Tell me more about that. Who does the left breast thing?" The agent knows that sex sells books.

"The old librarian," explains the author. "She's got three nipples thanks to a gypsy curse and the only thing that can save her and cure the extra nipple is if she can persuade the

President of America not to destroy the spaceship full of aliens who are battling to redirect an asteroid away from Earth using only the power of their minds. But the President is haunted by the ghost of progressive rock and only a gang of teenage computer geeks on roller skates made from petrified turtles can track the frequency which is coming from a mysterious castle in Germany but not the real Germany, the Germany of the eighteenth century; and if the music reaches the last note it will trigger a huge earthquake releasing swarms of dinosaurs, and not the cumbersome docile kind, only T-Rexs that have been breeding just under the earth's crust thanks to an illegal chemical dump in North Korea that wasn't there yesterday according to satellite reports but only one person can stop the whole thing and that's the marzipan guy, if he ever comes out of the trombone in time…"

"Tell me about the vampires" says the agent, still not yet convinced.

The author shrugs his shoulders as if to say, "What can I tell you? They're vampires!" But he can see that the agent doesn't get it so he explains slowly.

"They fly around at night and bite people on the neck when they least expect it."

"Hmm. Teenage girls love all that sort of thing. What about the slapstick?"

Ah, the slapstick! The author realises this might be the key to the agent's interest.

"Well there's a scene where one of the vampires is carrying a plank of wood on his shoulder and when he turns around…"

"Yes, yes, I can imagine all sorts of chaos ensues. What about the contract killer?"

"He's supposed to kill the man in the trombone but he's allergic to marzipan on account of its nuts."

"Marzipan has nuts?"

"Almonds, apparently."

The agent writes on her notepad, 'Almonds in marzipan? Check for authenticity'.

"The talking horse?" she asks.

"Well actually it only appears every now and again and whispers a bit of Greek philosophy and nobody is sure if it's a dream or not."

The agent reflects briefly, "A philosophical, whispering horse. Hmm."

She taps her pen on the table, underlines her note about marzipan a couple of times and then says,

"Sorry, still not interesting enough."

The author smiles, knowing he has saved the best till last.

"But I haven't told you about the part where Jesus turns up in a hovercraft on Malibu Beach and somehow he's been learning kung fu for the last two thousand years and now he's ready to kick some ass and people are saying, "Oh yeah? You and whose army?" and he says, "Me and the lambs of God!" and all his disciples are like Doctor Who's Daleks with lasers shooting at people's eyes!"

The agent rubs her temples and considers the options.

"Tell me about Bonzo the magic dog again. Maybe you could turn him into a hard-drinking private detective with dysfunctional social skills. That's what the public really wants to read about."

READERS' BLOG:

- *Christ! If this is the sort of thing Sutton is going to churn out it's time he went back to his day job.*
- *The agent is right. I am an average member of the British public and I can't get enough private detective stories despite their obvious formula and clichéd content.*
- *I think a gribble is a small furry animal. Either that or it's a tool for cleaning between bathroom tiles.*
- *Lasers are dangerous, especially for eyes. I'm surprised that Jesus would condone such a thing.*
- *Why would a gypsy bother to curse somebody with an extra nipple? It's not exactly a hindrance to everyday life. Better to turn them into a toad or render them incapable of speech. Must have been a crap gypsy.*
- *Actually I'd like to read more about the trombone full of marzipan!*

I was hoping somebody would say that. Read on!

EROS THE XENOS!

THE PROG ROCK
TRANCE AFFAIR

Something fell from the sky that day. Then there was an explosion in the distance.

The next morning I summoned the energy to conquer my lethargy and looked through my telescope. There was a humanoid approaching across the delta! I remembered humanoids. We haven't had humanoids around here for about a million years, not since all the soil dried up and was replaced by marzipan. Humanoids!

Judging by the strong silhouette that was cast across the ground by the humanoid, I deduced it was probably male… or it could be… an athletic female. This awoke ancient memories.

I felt a stirring in my loins, or at least the place where my loins should be. A fizzing in my nether region. I wanted to thrust, but thrust what? A fork? A handkerchief? An item of footwear? (If only I had feet!) A mid-priced, light tan sedan automobile?

That's right, I don't have a penis. So? What use is that to me? I release spores! This technique is more user-friendly and energy efficient. It is also healthier and prevents disease, except for the air pollution it causes. All those spores floating around on the wind get up your nose and make you pregnant.

I looked again at the approaching figure and experienced a long-forgotten urge to kill, or maybe copulate; same euphoria – opposite outcomes, life and death.

The figure got closer. It was just a man. Ah well, maybe next time.

He came over to where I was squatting behind my favourite rock and handed me a scruffy piece of smelly, green paper.

"Have you got change for a ten-dollar bill? I need to make a phone call."

English? American?

"You speak our language!" I was astounded.

"Yes, apparently so."

If the man was at all surprised by his predicament, he masked it well. I detected no rise in his blood pressure.

I wasted no time with further small talk.

"Are you pro-marzipan or do you harbour doubts as to its cosmic relevance?"

"Marzipan? I love it! Although it is rarely seen, except on birthday cakes and special occasions."

"Its rarity and special status are well justified," I nodded solemnly.

"Where am I exactly?" he asked.

"Exactly? You require the longitude and latitude correct to ten decimal places?"

He pursed his lips and frowned. I noticed a slight shaking of his head from side to side. I formed the opinion that he was indicating a negative response.

"I followed a woman into a trombone and found myself here," he said.

I understood immediately.

"Ah-ha! The old trombone trick eh? The Mighty Bummha works in mysterious ways!"

The man looked at me carefully. He saw my lack of height, the way I seemed to sprawl outwards. He saw my many tentacles. He was surprised to see my visual display unit and the antennae which sprouted from my head.

"Oh sorry, my name is Dave," he announced suddenly.

He reached out his open hand and I realised this was a form of greeting that required a reciprocal behaviour.

I extended a tentacle and placed it into his warm, dry palm. A surprisingly soft palm considering he was obviously some kind of adventurer; a man of action. I revelled in its softness for a moment before replying.

"I'm Elvis," I said.

The man Dave suppressed a smirk. "Elvis?"

"Yes, Elvis. What's so funny?"

"Nothing, it's just that I knew an Elvis once. He was a famous singer."

"What was his political stance on marzipan?"

"I don't think he ever considered marzipan in any political sense."

"Perhaps subconsciously?"

"I think it highly unlikely. He was more a proponent of banana-based foodstuffs."

I reflected on this information for a moment.

"Hmm, then he was ill-suited to fame."

"On the contrary. Fame came easily to him. He wore

high-collared rhinestone jackets and tight-fitted bell-bottoms. He moved his hips like this…"

The man Dave demonstrated a very basic hip movement which failed to impress me.

"And for that he was famous?"

The man Dave regarded me and said, "I don't wish to be rude but you are in no position to criticise hip movement – no matter how basic, as you are in fact devoid of any skeletal support whatsoever."

"We have evolved onwards and upwards from that sort of nonsense. Or perhaps better to say onwards and outwards. Skeletal mass was a mere hindrance, as you will have found when you tried to enter the trombone."

He knew I was right and he quickly changed the subject.

"Look, about this phone call. Do you have any coins?"

"We don't have money, only marzipan. But you can use me as a communication interface."

"How?"

I extended my antennae and, following my detailed instructions, he cupped the tip of one over his ear and pressed the other to his mouth. I displayed a numbered keyboard on my screen.

"What's the international dialling code for Washington DC from here?"

"I think you will find that this *is* Washington DC."

He shrugged and dialled direct.

"Hello, put me through to the Secretary of Defence immediately!" he said confidently.

I could tell he was a man who was used to getting what he wanted and was probably an alpha of his species.

"Hi, sir. You'll never guess where I am… I'm in the land

of marzipan inside a trombone, talking to you via a lovely electronic jellyfish named Elvis!"

He winked at me and I was pleased that he had seen fit to mention me in a complimentary tone.

"What's that you say? President in a prog rock trance? End of the world if the guitar solo reaches the final note? Slapstick vampires?"

The man looked at me and rolled his eyes in a show of irritation at the person on the other end of the line. I could tell they weren't the best of friends.

"Sir, I think I'm on the verge of something here. I'd like to stay and see it through to the end; I think it will help."

He hung up and I asked the obvious question.

"Slapstick vampires?"

"Yes, apparently they get stuck in doorways when trying to go through at the same time."

"That is to be expected. From what I know of human doors they are not very accommodating."

"True, but I think it's the frustrated expressions on the vampires' faces that adds to the comic effect. And I'm sure revolving doors like those in posh hotels will give opportunities for many light-hearted moments… that is until the duo actually get down to the serious business of chewing people's throats out."

"Yes, every silver lining has a cloud," I said philosophically.

"That's my job, asshole!" said a philosophical horse, appearing and disappearing in a flash.

"By the way, you've got a bit of…" I pointed to Dave's cheek.

"Oh jeez, what is that?" he screamed.

"Just a bit of mucus from my antenna."

"Ee-uw!"

I consider myself to secrete a normal amount of mucus and, of course, felt no need to apologise. I put his reaction to my mucus down to a clash of cultures.

"You're welcome," I said, hoping to prompt his gratitude.

"Now perhaps you can enlighten me on this mysterious but beautiful land of yours," said the man Dave, now recovered.

"This world was created at one millisecond past midnight on the first moment of the year 2000, the new millennium. Whilst everybody worried about their digital clocks exploding, a new, mysterious, parallel world was born and nobody even noticed. We share all ancient history of your world and all the distant future. We simply do not share the present," I explained.

"So in the future our world will be made of marzipan?"

"No, because this is not really the earth, this is a marzipan mirror image."

"And the curved, fluted entrance to the trombone represents the journey through space-time?"

"Exactly."

"And the library?"

"Books are of no consequence in this world. We are electronic. I believe the trombone appears at any point in time and space according to the will of The Mighty Bummha."

I displayed a picture of The Mighty Bummha on my screen.

"Behold!" I said, dramatically.

"Oh God!" said the man Dave, recoiling with obvious disgust.

"That's correct. He is the equivalent to your god. But as you can see, he has two sphincters!"

The man Dave started retching violently and his skin became clammy. "I couldn't miss them!" he gagged. "They're on his forehead!"

"He is all-seeing and all-knowing, so I would advise you not to comment on his appearance."

I switched off the display.

"That was a bit of a shock!" said the man Dave shakily.

I admired his diplomacy. I smiled at him, although I don't think he realised I was smiling. He couldn't possibly have interpreted the subtle changes in my body language.

"So do you think this Bummha of yours caused the trombone to fall from the book specifically to bring me here so that I may discover the means to save Earth?" he asked.

"It appears increasingly likely in view of your recent telephone conversation," I replied.

- *Oh dear, that's pure laziness on the part of the author; a blatant shortcut in the plot to save time and effort. Mind you, it's probably necessary because prog rock songs only last about twenty minutes. Even Flash Gordon had more time to save the planet.*
- *Unless the theory holds true that time runs slower when inside a dream-like parallel universe, in which case '2112' by the prog rock supergroup Rush could last fifty years!*
- *Oh yes!*
- *Forget Yes, they were the worst prog rock band ever and sounded like camel shit!*
- *Camel were actually quite good though.*

"And the beautiful lady in the trombone?" asked the man Dave, eagerly.

"Alas, merely a temptation. A honey trap."

I could tell by his sagging shoulders that he was disappointed.

"Don't worry, there are more beautiful creatures than her to be found in our great cities."

"Really?"

"Yes, look here is a website for marriage."

I activated my display screen again.

"You see? A choice of quadrupeds, bipeds, tripeds, tripods even! Green body hair, eyes optional, some with tails, here's one with huge breasts but…"

"Wait a minute!" Go back to that one!"

"Ah! Good choice, but she is expensive."

"Where can I get enough marzipan to pay for her?"

"Can you use a spade? Can you wield a pickaxe?"

"Yes! Yes! I have done a bit of wielding in my time."

"Then you will become a rich man in this world. Your ability to dig will allow you to mine tons of marzipan. There are no laws prohibiting the mining. Everybody is free to take as much as they want. Unfortunately few of us have opposable thumbs and, being generally amoebic, our musculature is inadequate for heavy mining activity."

As the man Dave dug frantically for marzipan, I tried to contact someone in the other time dimension using my computer interface and a complicated software program to send it back in time via the trombone.

- *Why didn't he just call someone like Dave did on the mucus-covered telephone antennae?*

Suddenly the man Dave stood up.

"Don't be offended, but this marzipan looks a little bit like ear wax."

I have no knowledge of ear wax so was not offended.

"This could be the key to saving the world!" he cried suddenly, holding up two small lumps of marzipan.

"That is timely as I have just made contact with someone who is able to help us when we return to the event horizon."

"Where is that?"

"The trombone in the library of course!"

Minutes later the man Dave and I exited the bell-end of the trombone and I fell into the arms of the waiting librarian.

- *When does she get her tits out?*

"Well, hello you!" she said to me. I detected heightened sexual excitement as her pheromones became energised.

"I'm Elvis," I said and tried to wiggle my hip area as I had seen Dave demonstrate. It merely caused a vibration in my jelly but she seemed to enjoy it.

She giggled and said, "Ooh, how lovely!"

The man Dave quickly gave the librarian a synopsis of the situation and his intended plan. She still carried me in her arms and I could feel her heart fluttering with the excitement.

"I've brought some help," she said.

The teenage geeks on roller skates were waiting outside (no skates allowed in the library, by order of the mayor). They were wearing harnesses on their torsos that were attached by ropes to two skateboards. The whole contraption resembled the harnessing for an Alaskan dog sled.

- *How would Jelly-Elvis-Future-Blob know anything about an Alaskan dog sled harness assembly?*

"Jump on!" they encouraged.

"There's no time for further ado!" shouted the man Dave. He landed expertly onto the first skateboard despite carrying the trombone and the balls of marzipan.

"I'll explain the plan on the way. How long will it take to get to the White House?"

"In this traffic, about three hours!" they cried.

The librarian and I jumped on the next skateboard and we were dragged at breakneck speed through the busy traffic.

On arrival at the White House, the man Dave led us through the security checks by flashing his credentials and who knows what else at the startled bodyguards. The President was about to press the red button to destroy the aliens when the quick-thinking librarian jumped across his desk and ripped her blouse open.

"Sir, I've got three nipples!" she shrieked.

- *At last!*

I fell in love there and then.

The President hesitated, perhaps calculating the chance of a private audience and closer, more intimate investigation.

The man Dave put the little balls of marzipan into the

ears of the President, thus blocking his hearing and cutting off the sound of the ghostly prog rock guitar solo.

The teenage geeks skated past and stole the red button from the desk.

"Stop them!" somebody shouted.

From out of nowhere the slapstick vampires walked across the corridor carrying an imaginary large pane of glass which impeded the confused bodyguards just long enough to allow the geeks to escape.

- *It's not hard to confuse bodyguards. They are invariably of limited intellect.*

The aliens, freed from the worry of impending missile strikes, were able to divert the Earthbound asteroid using the power of their minds.

"Attention planet of the Solar Federation," they announced. "We have assumed control. We have assumed control."

- *Ah! That's a line from Rush's '2112'.*

The mission had been a success. We said our farewells. I was to stay in this new old world and marry the three-nippled librarian (I must ask her name!) and the man Dave would return to the world of marzipan and marry the large-breasted electronic hermaphrodite he had bought off a website for six tons of marzipan.

The man Dave was about to step back into the trombone with a cassette recording of Rush's '2112', when a chilling voice caused him to freeze.

"Going somewhere?" snarled the hitman, aiming a long-barrelled pistol at the man Dave's head. "Put your hands up!"

The man Dave did as he was asked but, when he raised the trombone, it knocked the gun out of the hitman's hand.

"Careful!" said the hitman, retrieving his pistol from the floor. "Now, let's try that again. It's quite simple really. Put the trombone down first, *then* put your hands up."

This time, as the man Dave placed the trombone onto the floor, his body odour wafted towards the hitman who then began to sneeze uncontrollably.

"Oh, have you been in contact with marzipan recently?" he sniffled.

"Quite extensively, as it happens," answered the man Dave, matter-of-factly.

"Off you go then… I'll wait until next time," said the hitman as he fumbled for more tissue.

The man Dave once again entered the trombone and returned to the land of marzipan. The playback of '2112' began and, via the event horizon, it was sent back in time to the eighteenth century castle, producing an eternal audio loop to keep the ghost of prog rock happy. The empty castle will now resonate forever with 'Temples of Syrinx' and the President's mind is safe.

* * *

The geeks constructed a skateboard for me that had all kinds of wondrous gadgets including a platform that could raise me from the base of the skateboard so that my 'interface' was at the same height as everybody else's face.

The President held a ceremony to honour our heroic team.

"Well, it seems that the world owes you people a huge debt of gratitude! Perhaps teenage hacker geeks are not such a pain in the ass after all. Thanks to you pesky kids, the three-nippled librarian and an electronic jellyfish named Elvis, humanity can breathe a sigh of relief."

"What about the aliens?" somebody asked.

"Fuck the aliens!" said a giant philosophical horse in Greek, appearing momentarily in a vision above the people's heads.

The President shook hands with us all, including me and my mucus-covered tentacle.

There was great cheering from the crowd and I gave a little bow, although I don't think people noticed. To an onlooker I would simply have seemed to splodge outwards slightly.

The President held up his arms to quell the applause and continued.

"Thanks to their great acts of heroism we can now look forward to a long future of peace and tranquillity, where human beings can live without the fear of impending Armageddon…"

The Secretary of Defence put down the phone and whispered in the President's ear through the marzipan earplug:

"Excuse me, sir, sorry to cut into your speech but… we're at DEFCON One! Jesus has just arrived on Malibu Beach in a giant hovercraft, accompanied by an army of laser-firing Dalek-disciples… and he's wreaking terrible revenge on mankind!"

THE END
(Of the world) (Until next time)

READERS' BLOG:

- My name is Walt Disney and this has given me an idea for a new franchise, Crime Fighting Electronic Jellyfish on Skateboards with Gadgets starring Steven Seagal as Elvis.
- I am a student of classical languages at Harvard, but for the life of me I cannot find a Greek translation for 'fuck' or 'aliens'.
- Um, 'coitus' anyone?
- That's Latin for sexual intercourse, dumbo! Xenos is Greek for alien. I think it should be 'Eros the Xenos!'
- I think that means 'love the foreigner', but it's close enough to be OK. Unless you're a redneck.
- Had I been the author, I would have chosen 'Spanish Castle Magic' by Hendrix as being more apt for the eternal audio loop.
- Perhaps, but the castle is in Germany, not in Spain, and that song only lasts three minutes.
- Oh, yes.
- I told you to forget Yes; they were to progressive rock what owl pellets are to cordon bleu!
- OK. Oh no then.
- Okay Ono had little or no influence on the prog rock genre as she was in the lame pop group, The Beatles.
- You mean Yoko?
- Yoko was a clown.
- That was Coco.

- *Coco Chanel was neither a clown nor a Beatle. He invented Ovaltine.*
- *I reckon that celebrity chef from the TV, Hugh whatsisname, could rustle up something half-tasty with a plate of owl pellets.*
- *Millennium bug my ass! I neglected to change the clock on my microwave and at midnight I was cooking a lasagne. Guess what? Delicious!*
- *I prefer Bolognese.*
- *I feel cheated. It didn't quite pan out in the way I expected. Where were the T-Rexs, as promised in 'The Plot That Thickened'?*
- *Pay attention! They do not emerge from the underside of the earth's crust until the giant earthquake is triggered by the last note of the prog rock guitar solo. In view of the fact that the man David has set up an infinite audio loop, it will never happen.*
- *Oh, yes.*
- *For the last bleedin' time! Forget Yes, they were a pile of… etc.*

THE COLOURLESS
ODOURLESS MAN

He prefers the absence of colour…

"Neither do I tolerate odours," he explains. "When I see colour I am unhappy. When I detect an odour, it dismays me."

He has certain procedures in order to avoid either.

"I have certain procedures which I carry out, in order to avoid both colour and odour."

He does not wish to disclose them to us at this point. What he does say however is:

"Man's use of colour is an insult to nature. Likewise odours generated by man may be considered the signature of the Neanderthal. The use of colour is highly overrated, especially in art. The existence of odour, in art or otherwise, is bestial and perverse. Texture is infinitely more useful and practical. Taste is a more accurate and refined sense befitting the superiority of Man. In short, I do not share others' enthusiasm of the use of colour."

"And what of odour?" we ask.

"Odours, bad or good, are all bad as far as I'm concerned. Any odour is simply the odour of ordure. Their assault on the olfactory nerve, and that is exactly what it is, an assault, is perhaps the first indication of a poison entering the body. Even a sweet smell consists of a toxin that has mixed with the air as we breathe it in; a classic example of a diseased particle entering the human body on the Trojan horse of life-giving oxygen."

He believes that purity is next to godliness and we, having been made in His image, are obliged to maintain that state of purity.

"Instead, we bring chaos in the form of cerebral noise, this in the form of colour and odour," he says.

"And what of noise?" We delve deeper into his psyche.

"Noise is purer than colour and odour. The birth of the universe created the greatest sound ever heard by a living creature and its noise still exists. Before the noise there was nothing. Therefore noise existed before colour and certainly before odour."

We drive him further. "More specifically, man-made noise?"

"Man's use of noise is a crime against nature, although noise is in itself a natural phenomenon."

"Music is a man-made noise. Is music a crime?" we ask cleverly.

"Beauty is in the ear of the beholder, but music can never replace the sound of wind in the trees, a babbling brook, morning birdsong, evening birdsong for that matter. The distant hiss of the ocean…"

He continues to list noises from the natural world until we interrupt him.

"What about the roar of a bull elephant as it impales a cruel master on its tusk; the high-pitched whine of two mosquitoes copulating in your ear; the screech of a blue mandrill as it accidentally drops its last banana from the highest tree in the jungle… are these 'beautiful sounds' worthy of higher accolade than Beethoven or Strauss?"

He hesitates momentarily, clenches his jaw and narrows his eyes.

"As I have said, I prefer the absence of colour… neither do I tolerate odours. When I see colour I am unhappy. When I detect an odour, it dismays me. I have certain procedures which I carry out, in order to avoid both colour and odour."

He does not wish to disclose them to us at this point.

READERS' BLOG:

- *Jeez! What is his fucking problem?*
- *I agree with him. Man is a clumsy, bumbling oaf in the natural world.*
- *Nobody would have heard the Big Bang. It was faster than the speed of light.*
- *I would like to see a blue mandrill but I hear they have red arses. Do they like popcorn?*
- *Any elephant master (or mahout) worth his weight in sandal leather would have learned the trick of grinding the elephant's tusk to a rounded tip. That way he could have avoided being impaled in the event of any elephantine disgruntlement. Serves him right!*

MULL DOON'S LIVES
(Apologies to Van Loon)

I arrived back at my apartment in a state of exhaustion and vowed never to get involved with new-fangled sports again. Aqua-pipes, a new craze sweeping Downy Bottom Valley, was a sport which involved playing the bagpipes whilst performing a synchronised swim routine and trying to throw a live duck-billed platypus into the opposing team's basketball net... naked. Teams were discernable only by the colour of the players' bow ties and top hats.

"Aqua-pipes my arse!" I snorted disdainfully, as I threw them into the broom cupboard.

My wife called to me from the lounge.

"Hello Rupert darling! How did..."

"We fucking lost again! OK?"

"Oh dear," she said, feigning sympathy.

I knew she was smiling smugly to herself at this. She scorned my involvement with aqua-pipes, just as she had with my last project: building remote-controlled robot jockeys to race astride blindfolded camels over a military assault course... in the nude. The robots were not nude nor were the camels (each camel individually decorated, like floats in the Rio carnival), but the rules stated that I should be totally nude whilst constructing and controlling the robots.

I'm a great believer in nudity. I think it was Churchill or Queen Victoria who said,

"Nothing so focuses the mind as does performing duties of office in the absolute altogether," but don't quote me on that.

- *It was probably Churchill. He looks the type.*

I went into the lounge where my wife was still knitting a scarf that rather resembled a stair carpet for a three-storey office block.

"Is that a scarf for a giraffe or is it the emergency replacement for the Bayeux Tapestry?"

She ignored my humour. She took her knitting very seriously.

"I'm afraid I've got some rather bad news," she said without dropping a stitch.

"Apparently your grandmother has been missing for quite some time and the local police are mildly baffled. They have come to the natural conclusion that she may have wandered into her overgrown garden, become disorientated and been subsequently devoured by indigenous wildlife; saw-toothed armadillos, dwarf buffalo and various migrating reed warblers."

I was only half-listening, sorting through the day's mail.

"But I haven't got a grandmother!"

"Well, who was that woman you used to tell me about? She taught you how to do Greco-Roman wrestling?"

"The greased lady with the matted beard and huge hands!" A bell in my head had started to chime quietly. Memories of Battenberg cake and cigarette-rolling machines. The bell in my head clanged and fell to the floor.

"Grandmother!" I remembered.

* * *

The letter from the solicitor acting as executor to Grandmother's estate explained that I, as the only surviving relative, had inherited the large house on the Mull of Doon, a rocky islet off the Scottish coast. The house was ancient and had once been described as the ugliest castle ever built by the eccentric Baron Willis of Paracusis who had failed to listen to his architects and somehow contrived to have the castle built upside down!

My wife declined the offer to accompany me to the Mull of Doon, citing important knitting duties and outstanding appointments with a wool farmer. I knew the man. Square-jawed and slim of hip, he had once been a successful gymnast. He was known in the town as Jake the Sausage and I presumed it was because he was a farmer. I secretly sniggered at the ignorance of the townsfolk… Jake was a wool farmer, nothing to do with meat produce! The poor misguided dumplings!

* * *

I arrived at the grim coastal village of Chortle-Cum-Hardly, intending to follow my solicitor's suggestion to hire a local fisherman who could take me across to the Mull of Doon. I searched the bustling quayside and spoke with some of the fishermen who were busy smoking contraband tobacco and looking at Arran sweaters in a catalogue. They directed me at last to an old sea dog who supplemented his meagre income by acting as the ferryman for the surrounding islands.

He was crouched over some baskets and as I approached I heard him swearing violently. He stood up suddenly and I could see that a lobster had gripped his nose in its claw, and another lobster had clamped onto his right nipple.

"Argh my beauties, do your worst, but ye'll not escape the cooking pot tonight!" he growled.

I saw, amongst the wild grey whiskers which covered almost every feature of his face like a werewolf, that his left eye bulged as if too big for its socket. It was totally white and seemed to have no pupil. It somehow reminded me of a grotesque boiled egg.

He saw my stare and cackled like a witch.

"Argh, ye have noticed the eye have ye?"

- *He doesn't sound very Scottish to me.*
- *As with most men of the sea, he is probably much affected by the continents and cities of his travels and his conversations with local inhabitants and other adventurers…*
- *Let's just listen to the story!*

I was embarrassed for staring. "Please excuse me, I couldn't help…"

He tore the lobsters off him and threw them back into the basket, then suddenly thrust his face closer to mine so that his bulging orb was almost touching the tip of my nose.

The ghoulish fisherman cackled again.

"I don't need your pity, sonny Jim. Stare as much as ye want, but don't go saying, "Aye aye Cap'n.""

• *Oh I get it. Eye, eye! But he's only got one!*

"Do you mind me asking what happened to you?"

"A whaling accident laddie. Torn out by the jaws of the monstrous angry beast. So I took his eye in return. Fair exchange is no robbery eh? But them old whale eyes go white without the salt water on 'em."

"Then why don't you wear a patch?"

"I'm no slave to fashion laddie. I don't hold no sway by it. D'ye see this?"

He lifted one trouser leg and I saw that he had not a human leg but one fashioned from the bones of a whale.

"Whaling accident," he cackled.

"But why did you use the spine of a whale instead of a more solid bone such as the rib? Surely, it would afford more stability!"

"Stability you say? Overrated by you landlubbers. The increased dexterity that comes with having the equivalent of six knees is nothing but a boon to an old sea dog like me. Now, let's get down to business. Which island be ye here tae visit?"

"Mull of Doon," I answered.

He squinted his good eye.

"What's that ye say boy? Ye be wanting to go to the Mull of Doon is it? Are ye mad? Ain't nothing there but a crazy old woman and a bleak house. Are ye sure ye want tae be paying for the privilege of visiting such a place?"

"If you will hold your tongue, sir, that woman is my recently deceased grandmother!"

"Deceased you say?" (cackle). "Well, it's not the first time! There be many a strange thing goes on at that island. Strange comings and goings. Perhaps I should just say strange goings… ain't no comings. I have taken many a tormented soul across and none has ever returned. The castle holds more foreboding than the House of Usher. But ye be welcome laddie to jump aboard as soon as ye cross my palm with fifty doubloons."

"Fifty doubloons?"

"Twenty quid, one way. That's all you'll be needing."

"What is your name, sir?"

"Old Captain Elijah."

"Captain Elijah, nice to meet you."

"*Old* Captain Elijah, if you please!"

"I beg your pardon?"

"When my father was alive, he was Old Captain Elijah. I was Young Captain Elijah. Now he's dead, rest his tormented soul. Whaling accident. So now, I am Old Captain Elijah."

"And your son is Young Captain Elijah?" I guessed.

"Ain't no more Young Captain Elijahs. Ain't likely to be neither." At this, he undid his rubber trousers, rummaged in the front of his pants and withdrew what appeared to be an ivory penis.

"Whale tooth!" he said.

"Whaling accident?"

"Aye that's the short of it. Aye. Dived below when I least expected it."

"Old Captain Elijah. I'm sorry. Shall we?"

He stowed away his whale tooth penis and cast off the

mooring ropes, all the while cackling like a demented crone and singing a shanty.

"Mull of Doon! Mull of Doon! He who visits will be dead by noon!"

* * *

It was a short but bizarre voyage.

I sat on a small leather chair that swivelled violently according to the pitch and lurch of the boat as it battled against the north-easterly swell (one of the worst swells against which to battle). Meanwhile Old Captain Elijah stood at the helm, staring out at the greyness with his dead eye and recounting incredible mariners' tales and filthy jokes, which I neither appreciated nor enjoyed.

He told me of a giant Norwegian squid that had stolen a case of whisky from under his very nose as he slept. I wanted to ask how he knew it was a squid if he had been sleeping, but he didn't stop talking long enough. He then told me how he had fallen in love with a siren that he'd accidentally caught in a lobster pot. He had made her pregnant after a night of drunken debauchery in a smugglers' cove. The child was born a penguin with a pug nose instead of a beak. I was horrified but believed little of this tale. Finally, he made me swear never to kill an albatross and I, being generally bird-friendly, readily swore not to do so.

"I have never even seen an albatross," I said. "Is there really such a thing?"

"Put your head out of that porthole," he suggested.

I did so and looked around for the gigantic bird.

Almost immediately I felt a large dollop of foul-smelling gunge splatter onto the back of my neck.

The squawk of the albatross was echoed by the cackling of the Captain as they shared their little joke.

- *Basic slapstick really!*

Still with my head out of the porthole, I angrily wiped off the mess from my collar whilst facing the ocean and looking down at the cold grey waters almost within touching distance below. Suddenly, I noticed a flash of movement just beneath the surface of the waves and presently I was able to distinguish a dark fish-like body streaking through the water alongside the boat. It broke the surface and looked at me with… oh dear reader, the horror… it looked at me with human eyes! It was the face of a pug-nosed penguin boy, desperately trying to keep up with the boat and his sad eyes beseeched me to help somehow.

I fell back from the porthole, shocked to my very soul.

"Captain!" I cried.

"*Old* Captain," he corrected.

"I think your son is abeam of your starboard quarter!"

The Captain fell silent briefly, then said in a level voice:

"Nonsense laddie, I was spinning you a yarn. Ain't no penguin boy in these waters and no sirens to be caught in pots!"

And with this he pushed a lever and increased the speed of the boat so that no living creature could have kept up with us. When I next looked out of the porthole I saw no penguin boy but only a gentle sea mist that surrounded the dark shape of the Mull of Doon.

"Welcome home!" cackled the Captain. "Aye, the lunatics have taken over the asylum to be sure," he said, pointing to the railings along the jetty. My blood ran cold and the hairs on my neck stiffened, more from fear than the drying albatross shit. Each post appeared to be crowned with a shrunken head!

I began to reconsider my intention to take possession of the place and was on the verge of asking Captain Elijah to take me back when moments later, on closer inspection, I realised that the shrunken heads were in fact coconuts!

As I stepped off the boat the Captain threw my rucksack onto the small jetty and called:

"Good luck tae ye sonny! I'll say a prayer to the big man in the sky fer ye this Sunday!"

"Would you like to come in for a coffee?" I asked, partly out of politeness and partly fear of the island.

He fixed me with a blank stare from his dead eye and, grim-faced, hurriedly cast off. Not a cackle more did I hear from him as he oozed back into the sea mist.

The jetty gave access across the rocks on the small beach to the steep cliff path. Due to my aqua-pipe training, I found the climb easy. It was only when I arrived at the top and saw the old house that my heart started pounding and a cold sweat ran down my back.

The horror! Oh, the horror!

It was not how I remembered it. Gone were the pink roses and purple-flowered ivy. Gone were the yellow curtains. No welcoming glow from the crystal chandeliers once visible through the great windows of the library.

A pall of gloom sat heavily over the decrepit roof. Poisonous vines clung to the dirty grey walls and the black fathomless windows seemed to beckon me into the realms of death.

An army of ravens were arranged on the broken guttering, watching me with evil gleams in their eyes and they held their beaks open with sneering hatred. Albino baboons stood guard at the front door. Their eyes were red and angry, their fangs dripped with rancid drool. As soon as they saw me they started roaring like small lions and then began throwing coconuts at me. Coconuts again! Where the hell did they get those from? Hell indeed! I turned and saw that some of the snarling baboons had cut off my retreat to the cliff steps.

In crazed desperation, I ran through the garden and into a path that cut through the long grass without any knowledge of where it would lead, screaming like a girl at a Donny Osmond concert.

• *Osmond? What century is this dude from?*

I ran fast, then faster and faster and the path split into two and I didn't care which way I took and the distance from the world I knew increased and I crashed through thick undergrowth and began to laugh at the madness and the voice in the back of my head screamed "Stop" but I couldn't and didn't really want to and anyway it was far, far too late!

Suddenly I entered a clearing and came upon a small village of straw huts built on stilts.

A deep voice shouted a warning:

"Don't come any closer Bwana! You will sink into the quicksand!"

A green man, dressed only in a simple loin cloth, emerged from the reeds at the edge of the clearing, which I now realised was a swamp. The man, however, waded confidently through the mire and approached me with a smile on his face. Now I could see that he was in fact covered in a thick, scaly skin like an iguana.

"But it's not so deep," I said noticing that he was only submerged to his knees.

"Our shins are two metres long and our feet are like lily pads." He replied.

"Hi I'm Rupert," I said, offering my hand in greeting.

"I am Massoom," said the lizard man, shaking my hand with his green claw. "We are the Bogdowni tribe." He indicated others like him who had come out of the huts to see this white stranger.

"How long have you been living here?" I asked.

"We have inhabited this island for centuries, but only forty years in these swamps."

"I had no idea," I said, amazed.

"We remember the last time you were here. You were but four years old Bwana. We watched from behind the rose bushes. How we laughed to see you urinating in the fish pond. Your grandfather could never understand what killed his koi carp. We knew but never told a soul."

"Thank you for your discretion. But why did you protect me?"

"We hated your grandfather. He hunted us to near extinction, forcing us to evolve into semi-amphibians in order to escape his ever-increasing desires."

"What do you mean, semi-amphibians?"

"We can't breathe under water."

"I can hold my breath for half a minute!" said Jassoom, a young lizard girl.

"So you are not amphibious at all," I observed.

"Semi-," insisted Massoom.

"Which part of you is?"

"Our feet. They are equally at home in water as they are on land."

- *Just a minute! There is a gaping hole in the plot here. It is unlikely that the Bogdowni tribe could, over a forty-year time span, evolve into swamp creatures. The author is tinkering with the laws of nature and failing miserably.*
- *Yes, just like Dr Moreau. Or Caitlyn Jenner!*

"Why did my grandfather hunt you?" I asked Massoom.

"He was a ravenous carnivore. His appetite was insatiable. Gone are the great herds of dwarf buffalo that roamed the hills to the south of the castle. Few are the sabre-toothed armadillos. Legend has it that his soul lives on, doomed to the impossible task of appeasing his infinite hunger."

"Well there are plenty of albino baboons over at the house to eat, but I think they will eat us first. Perhaps they will follow me here."

"Oh yes, the sacred cappuccino monkeys. They were once friendly and domesticated. Your grandmother bred them, force-feeding them on coconuts, and used their droppings to make a very fine coffee. Since she left the house they have become possessed by evil spirits and their droppings are no longer edible. Have no fear. They will not venture near the swamps. You are safe with us."

- *The author is showing off. He has combined the name of a coffee – cappuccino, with that of a breed of monkey – capuchin. He is calling them 'sacred' because some Franciscan monks were also called Capuchin. If I didn't dislike him so much I would acknowledge this as being quite clever. However, in reality it is the Asian palm civet, a cat-like creature, which provides the droppings for luxury coffee.*

I was eager to hear about my grandmother's fate.

"Did my grandfather eat my grandmother?"

"Frequently Bwana. They were married for many years."

"Ach! No! I mean, has he devoured her? Is that how she died?"

"Your grandmother is not truly dead. She awaits you at the Folly of Willis."

"The Folly?"

"The penis-shaped tower on the northern cliff," he said, pointing in the general direction of north.

I remembered.

"But it's shaped like an upside down pyramid."

He moved aside his loin cloth and I saw his penis was indeed the shape of an upside down pyramid.

"Oh," I said.

He rearranged himself and then gasped. I thought at first he had chafed his overlarge end but he suddenly cried:

"I can help you on this quest! But first you will need the Spears of Destiny! Bassoom! Bring out the Golden Quiver which holds the Spears of Destiny!" he ordered.

Hidden drums began to boom out a dramatic rhythm. One of the tribe came out of the main hut ceremoniously

133

carrying a battered old coal scuttle made of brass and I saw it was full of irregular-sized pebbles.

"Behold!" announced Massoom with a beaming smile.

I thought better of pointing out their lack of geometric awareness.

"But why will I need pebbles, I mean, spears?"

"It is the only way to ring the Bell of Introduction. Its ring will summon the Doorkeeper of the Door. You must cast a spear straight and true. The spear must pass through the Window of the Angry Voice. If you miss the bell, a voice shouts, "Oi! Fuck Off!" and you will not be permitted to enter the Folly of Willis. If you succeed, then the door is opened and the Doorkeeper of the Door will utter these words: 'Yes, can I help you?' You should answer by saying…"

I was becoming impatient so I interrupted him.

"OK, I will take it from there. Which way do I go?"

"Climb on my shoulders and I will carry you across to the far side, through The Swamp of Certain Death, if you have the courage for such a journey. It can be hazardous. No one has ever undertaken such a voyage and returned to tell the tale!"

I hesitated. My choices were to go back and face the sacred cappuccino monkeys and their accurate coconuts, or to stay in the swamp and live a semi-amphibious existence with the Bogdowni, or to cross The Swamp of Certain Death in search of my mysterious grandmother and her giant hands.

- *If it were me, I would return to the beach; use the Spears of Destiny to defeat the coconut-throwing baboons and then swim back to the mainland with the help of the pug-*

nosed penguin boy. Back to the arrogant tramp wife and sort her out.

- *He should stay with the Bogdowni. They are a peaceful, friendly folk; although their scales would repel me, and they probably stink. He could fashion some stilts for himself and live quietly amongst them as an equal. Perhaps get married, spawn some tadpoles. Maybe start an aqua-pipes competition. He would be in a league of his own.*
- *Both those options are fates worse than death. Therefore it is clear that he should choose certain death.*

I agreed with option three.

"Let's go!" I said heroically.

I clambered onto Massoom's shoulders and took the scuttle of pebbles from Bassoom.

The hidden drums began their dramatic beat once again. The womenfolk started wailing a familiar tune:

"Mull of Doon, Mull of Doon, he who visits will be dead by noon!"

This was irritating as the time was, by now, a quarter past two in the afternoon.

We waved a sad farewell to the village and headed north, the drums beating out the rhythm of our progress towards… The Swamp of Certain Death!

* * *

Massoom walked about ten paces and set me down on firm ground.

"There you go," he said.

"Is that the end of the swamp?" I asked, almost indignantly.

"Yes, Bwana."

I considered asking further questions but questions can lead to answers and some people don't really want answers. Answers bring understanding and understanding leads to knowledge. Knowledge destroys innocence and lack of innocence is the precursor to evil.

• *Amateur philosophy!*

I offered my thanks and bade goodbye to my new friend and set off alone to complete my quest.

It was not long before I caught sight of The Folly. Baron Willis was insane. He had built it in a time when there were no more Viking raids. Nothing left to pillage or rape, not even sheep. I could not imagine why he had gone to all this trouble. Perhaps that's why it is called a folly.

It was a gigantic single block of granite, almost as big as the main house, chiselled smooth in the shape of an upside down pyramid. An amazing feat of architecture, construction and engineering. How had it been done?

• *He's alluding to the theories of Erich Von Däniken, Zecharia Sitchin, et al. Interesting but clumsy.*

There was a single square opening just above a great wooden door and through it I could just see a small golden bell. I was sure my aqua-pipes training would stand me in good stead. I had put the platypus in the basket six times this season.

I took out a Spear of Destiny, aimed, and threw it at the open window.

"Oi! Fuck off! Who's throwing stones? Got me right on the bonce!" cried The Angry Voice.

I cowered in fear of some kind of retaliation, praying against more coconuts, but nothing happened. I stood up and considered another Spear of Destiny. However, I had given myself tennis elbow with the effort of the first throw so I decided to try a different tactic. I shouted out,

"Hi, it's Rupert. I'm looking for my dead grandmother!"

Moments later the door opened and a little old man poked his head out. He was dressed only in a sporran and a string vest. There was a fresh bump on his shiny bald head.

"Are you the one who threw that stone?"

"Yes. The Spear of Destiny. Sorry about that."

"Spear my arse! Have you been talking to Massoom?"

"He helped me with directions, yes. I'm Rupert. I believe I'm your new landlord now that my grandmother has died. I was unaware of any sitting tenants."

The old man, still rubbing his swelling (oo-er!) patted me on the shoulder and guided me in through the door.

"I'm Errol Flynn. Well, I was in a former life. Now I multi-task as The Angry Voice from The Window, The Doorkeeper of the Door and The Acknowledger of the Bell of Introduction. Come in, we've been expecting you."

I went inside and was amazed to find that the interior was designed and decorated identically to that of the main house as I remembered it from my childhood.

"Rupert dear, I knew you would come!" said a big woman dressed as a lumberjack.

Grandmother still looked like a Greek wrestler with giant hands.

She walked over to me and gave me a bear hug and a kiss. Her unshaven cheeks rasped against my own peach-like skin.

"I thought you were dead!" I gasped.

"What makes you think I'm not?" she answered mysteriously.

"But… but…"

"There will be many things that you will not understand. But due to time constraints we have no time to explain fully. You must take things at face value," she announced, suddenly becoming business-like.

- *How convenient for the author!*

"Do you know anything about transmigration of the soul or reincarnation?" she asked.

"Yes, I've heard of it but…"

"Well that's it in a nutshell. How is your quantum physics?"

"Erm, a trifle sketchy."

"Basically, clumsy Buddhist monks have inadvertently brought about a series of circumstances that, in their entirety, have contrived to create a tear in the space-time continuum."

- *Oh, here we go again with the space-time continuum theme. He was harping on about it in his first book. It's all wearing a bit thin now. Hasn't Sutton got anything better to do than contemplate the end of the universe?*

- *Wife of reader: "Hush now dear, I'm sure he's trying his best."*

Reader's wife carries on dusting. Reader looks up from this book and considers her words whilst he stares at her ample backside stretching her skirt as she leans to reach a shelf. He stifles an urge to tweak her buttock and instead finds himself drawn back to these pages.

Grandmother continued:

"When Jupiter's sixtieth moon is in alignment with the public toilets of Guildford Cathedral, it will complete a cosmological arrangement, releasing a great power that is transmitted via Blackpool Tower to the Angel of the North and finally to the TV aerial on the roof of Mull Doon Castle. The sky above the castle will rip open and unleash pure evil. So we are tasked to block it before the end of the world."

"And just what is going to happen if we don't?" I asked, sceptically.

"Molar the Devourer will take advantage of the Spectral Shift and come through the tear. He will consume everything in the universe," replied Grandmother seriously.

"Hmmm. Would I be correct in deducing from his name that he is in fact, a giant tooth?"

"More or less, yes."

"In that case what can he achieve? Doesn't he at least need an opposing mandible to facilitate a crushing or chewing action? What about saliva? Does he have any? Does he have the ability to secrete saliva, without which he is surely unable to break down the molecular structure of his foodstuff?"

- *The author has overlooked the added necessity for a digestive tract in order to consume food effectively, not to mention gastric juices.*

Grandmother looked at me with patient sympathy. "He is indeed a tooth, Rupert, but not as we know it."

"So how are you and I going to stop him?"

"Well, now that you have come to terms with the fact that I am both dead and alive, perhaps you will not be so surprised to learn that there are others who have been 'brought back' in one way or another. We have assembled a specialist team."

"Consisting of whom?"

Grandmother pulled a piece of paper from the pocket of her jeans and read out a list of names.

"We've got Johnny Weissmuller."

"The original Tarzan?"

"No. The original Johnny Weissmuller. The father of the actor who played Tarzan."

"Well at least he's probably a good swimmer, if the necessity should arise."

"Alas, he was merely a kazoo player in an Oompah band."

"Who else?"

"Doctor Who."

"That's great! He's exactly the guy we need for such a crisis. With his expertise in time and space travel, combined with his unerring ability to communicate with aliens of all creeds on behalf of mankind, he will be invaluable to our success!"

"Perhaps you didn't hear me... Doctor Hoo, the Chinese herbalist. Struck off the medical register for performing an obscene act with a thatch of stinging nettles."

"Next."

"Vitruvian Man. Many hands make light work so they say, but they also say the devil makes work for idle hands; if he's not kept busy he's likely to put his finger in every pie and spoil the broth. Plus were having a job finding pants to fit him, what with his extra legs etcetera, and I do mean etcetera… he's got double of everything. Can't have him walking around with his multiple extremities flapping about. Most distracting."

"You mean he's got two…?"

"Like the proverbial dog."

"Fascinating! That's not something you see every day. Who else?"

"Walter Mitty."

"Oh?"

"Enthusiastic but useless."

"Oh!"

"Joe 91."

"Don't you mean Joe 90?"

"No, he was busy. Younger brother. Forgot to bring his spectacles, but vaguely remembers how to fly a Sopwith Camel biplane."

"Have we got a Sopwith?"

"No but we've got a camel."

"Well at least I know something about them. They're no good at climbing."

Gran continued with the list.

"One of the Musketeers, but not the famous one."

"Which one?"

"Glenys."

"Glenys!? Who the f…?" I stopped mid-sentence and sighed resignedly. "Is she any good?"

"I'm afraid she's an obstreperous alcoholic, but she claims to be an expert on the sword."

"Oh dear, I fear she is referring to the male erection when talking of a sword."

"Rupert! She really is a champion with the blade."

"Sorry. Who else?"

"Isambard Kingdom Brunel…"

"At last, we're getting somewhere!"

"Let me finish. Isambard Kingdom Brunel reincarnated as a monkey puzzle tree. We can't get any sense out of him whatsoever, let alone technical instruction as to the optimal tensile coefficients of steel girders."

"Is that it? That's the whole team?"

Gran checked her list.

"We couldn't get Rudolf Nureyev or Yehudi Menuhin."

"Grandmother, I think you've been targeting the wrong people. We need vicious warring hooligans like Genghis Kahn, Vlad the Impaler, Ivan the Terrible, perhaps a smattering of Viking, not to mention a dash of Zulu. Dare I say that Hannibal and his military elephants would probably have been a better option than…than Monkey Puzzle Brunel and a camel, for goodness' sake?"

She waved her giant hands in irritation.

"Phooey! It's too late for all that now. No more heroes any more. Are you wi' us or agin' us?" she challenged, like a Wild West gunslinger recruiting for a train robbery.

"Of course I'm wi' you, I mean with you. But I really don't think we can do it."

"It ain't over till the trouble bangs out a stewed prune."

This time a cockney boxing coach. "It's time for you to meet the all-seeing Coracle."

"Don't you mean Oracle?"

"No, Coracle. It leans against a tree by the shore of Mull Doon Lake. It was used by your grandfather for poaching salmon."

"I don't remember him being much of a boatman."

"He wasn't. He bought the salmon from the local fishermen and poached them in hot water, using the coracle as a large saucepan. I couldn't stand the smell of fish in the castle. Choose your questions carefully. You may only ask one question per day. The Coracle will not answer more than that and we don't have much time."

Gran showed me to the door and pointed to a short gravel path that led down to the lake behind the Folly. There, leaning against a tree was the Coracle, just as she had said.

I approached the Coracle and tried to mentally connect.

"Oh leathery Coracle, please tell me what I am here to do."

Suddenly a voice laden with a soft Scottish accent spoke to me.

"The fate of the cosmos is in your hands, Rupert. Although you will succeed in the end, the tactics are unclear and I cannot yet unravel the series of planetary alignments, dreams and stigmata which altogether urge a particular and unique course of action."

I was sure I recognised the voice. Magnus Magnusson? The wisest man in the history of the world! The original Mastermind! He has the answers to everything!

"Can't you give me any clue where to start?"

"I'm sorry Rupert. I must go."

"But how will I know?"

"Pass."

"Will Johnny Weissmuller Senior be required to swim?"

"Pass."

* * *

Dejectedly I returned to the Folly and Errol Flynn showed me to my room. Grandmother was arranging some flowers in a vase (her muscular knuckles and sinewy hand backs looked almost obscene amongst the fragile stems) and my luggage had been unpacked and laid out on the bed. I noticed something was missing.

"Where are my socks?"

"Ah, we've taken the liberty of exchanging them for this special pair. The right one is perfectly normal. The other is the legendary Left Sock of Invisibility. Someone else already has the cloak," said Errol Flynn.

"But will the power of invisibility be of any use during this mission?"

"No, but it will be if the mission fails, so think yourself lucky." Grandmother laughed.

"The Coracle told us to give you the sock. He said your inventive juices flow better when you are naked. You must wear the sock to protect your dignity."

"I'm not sure I feel comfortable walking round in the nude, Grandmother."

"Don't be silly. What with Errol Flynn walking around in a sporran and double-donged Mr Vitruvian, I don't think your little conker is going to raise any eyebrows. You seem to forget, I used to change your nappy after your mother ran off with the Avon lady. Anyway, you will be invisible, so what's all the fuss about?"

* * *

I decided to see the team and introduce myself. They had been told to gather in the dining room for the first meeting.

"Hello everyone, I'm Rupert. I'm here to try and make some sense out of this bizarre situation. We need to establish a profile of our skill base so that a plan of action can be formulated that maximises our strengths." (I had learned that speech from the coach of our aqua-pipes team). "My specialist skills are designing robots and also visualising the aerodynamic parabola of duck-billed platypus."

The team seemed suitably impressed with this.

"OK, who wants to break the ice?" asked Grandmother.

A stout, middle-aged fellow with dyed blonde hair (it could have been a wig) stood up.

"I'm Mitty. Walter Mitty. Colonel Walter Mitty. I am the reigning pedalo champion of Central Park Lido."

"Are you a military man?"

"I was in the Special Forces."

"Be honest Walter. Were you really?"

"Absolutely. One hundred per cent."

"Which Special Forces?"

"The erm… Power Rangers."

"What about you Mr Vitruvian?" said Grandmother, pointing to a handsome youth who, for the time being, was wrapped up in some old floral curtains.

"I might be able to fly. I think I was the prototype for the helicopter. Leonardo made a special harness with a central pivot point. Using this he would cause me to spin around on a horizontal axis at incredible speed."

"Did you actually fly?" I asked.

"No, I was tied naked to a wooden wagon wheel at the time."

"And then?"

"Leo would watch me with a strange look in his eye then shuffle off to the bathroom for ten minutes."

"Mr Weissmuller, what can you bring to the table? I understand you can't swim as well as your son but that may be irrelevant for this mission. Do you have any skills apart from playing the kazoo?"

"My son inherited my massive lungs. I can blow up hot water bottles until they explode."

I pretended to write something on a notepad.

"Glenys, apart from the cutlass do you excel at anything? Please, nothing vulgar."

"My dear boy, I am first and foremost a musketeer. Therefore I am a crack shot with a firearm. I can shoot the balls off a gnat at a thousand paces."

"Then let's hope you are not drunk when duty calls," I said sternly.

"Sonny, when sober, I couldn't hit Billy Bunter's arse at ten paces."

"Doctor Hoo, what can you do… apart from grinding herbs?"

"I dabble in acupuncture and the occasional 'happy ending' if business is slow."

"What's a happy ending?" asked Joe 91, looking up from his jigsaw.

"Never mind about that sort of thing, young Joe. Tell

me, what can you do? Probably not much, seeing as you've forgotten your special mind-programming spectacles."

"Can I have an ice cream?" he replied, looking at Gran.

* * *

The next morning, still disheartened by the previous evening's meeting, I made the short journey to the Coracle.

"I'm thinking of disbanding the team. Their presence is distracting me. They are useless, especially the camel and Mr Kingdom Brunel as a monkey puzzle tree."

- *The author has once again revealed his ignorance. The name is not hyphenated so it is inaccurate to call the tree Mr Kingdom Brunel. A simple Mr Brunel will suffice.*

"The tree will give you the answer but the camel is the key," announced the Coracle.

"But how?"

"Pass."

* * *

Back at the Folly I sat with my head in my hands and stared at the floor of my bedroom. The events of the past twenty-four hours had exhausted me. I had been given the responsibility of saving the universe but had no idea how to do it. My gaze fell on the socks my grandmother had given me. Devoid of any other option I put them on. I felt a tingling sensation throughout my body and when I stood in front of the mirror I was amazed to see nothing staring back at me. I really was invisible!

The carriage clock chimed tea-time and I thought it would be mildly amusing to go to dinner invisibly.

I walked into the dining room and, unseen, was halfway to the table when I realised what the team were saying.

"He's a nice guy but not leader material," said Walter.

"I don't know why he is here. He couldn't even hit the Bell of Introduction with a Spear of Destiny!" said Glenys.

"The Coracle claims he is The One," Grandmother pointed out.

"I caught him staring at my shlamongs when I was getting dressed," snitched Mr Vitruvian.

"What's a shlamong?" asked Joe 91.

"Never mind shlamongs, eat your carrots or you'll end up needing glasses. Oh, too late!"

I felt as though I had been slapped across the face. They were right of course. I had achieved nothing since I arrived. I could not face dinner now so I tried to tiptoe backwards through the door.

At that moment the camel urinated onto Monkey Puzzle Brunel. It cocked its leg like a dog and knocked the tree over. The spiky branches snagged the Sock of Invisibility as I was moving past and pulled it from my foot. I stood completely naked for all to see.

The team stared in silent embarrassment but Doctor Hoo screamed in horror.

"Calm down Hoo! It's just a little dagger! Call that a sword Rupert? This is a sword!" Glenys pulled out a giant cutlass and moved as if to cut off my pert little penis.

"The tree!" cried Doctor Hoo. "The tree can talk!"

"What are you gibbering on about?" said Weissmuller Senior; he didn't suffer fools gladly.

"Didn't you hear it?"

"Of course not! What did it say?"

"When the camel did its business, Monkey Puzzle Brunel screamed out something…"

"Yes but what?" we all asked.

"He shouted the word 'ammonia'!"

"Doctor, do you mean to tell us that you can understand what the tree is saying?" said Grandmother.

"Well I am a herbalist. My work involves spending a lot of time grinding with plants. I do talk with them often as this helps cultivate a generous growth."

• *I'm not sure if this is rude or not!*

"I have never before heard them talk back to me. But when the camel passed water onto the tree it shouted 'ammonia', as clear as day!"

I suddenly clapped my hands in understanding and did a half-jig.

"Passed water! Pass! That's what the Coracle kept saying! Pass! The tree is the answer but the camel is the key! Doctor Hoo, can you try to speak with our friend Isambard and see if you can get any information to help us?"

* * *

Having locked myself naked in the study all night with Doctor Hoo as translator for the technical directions from Monkey Puzzle Brunel, we finally emerged in the early hours of the next day, triumphant.

"Gather round everyone. I have found the answer. We

need to get busy. Here are the diagrams that you'll need to fully understand the plan of action."

I handed out the sheets of paper. There were loud gasps and cries of disbelief as the team digested the plan. Grandmother looked at me with concern.

"Are you sure about this Rupert?"

"It's the only way," I said gravely.

I explained the plan.

"Joe 91, wearing Weissmuller Senior's spectacles, will sit astride the camel's neck and act as pilot. Wires attached to the spectacles will be inserted into each of Joe 91's orifices. I have already designed a remote control for robotic guidance of camels. This must be inserted into Joe's anus. For this he will get an ice cream. He will pilot the camel via electronic guidance from me.

Walter Mitty will be suspended underneath the camel to power a pedal system, connected via cogs and chain to Mr Vitruvian and his pivoting harness. The pivot point will be on the camel's hump and the whole contraption will function like a helicopter, utilising Vitruvian's many appendages as rotating blades.

Weissmuller Senior will blow up hot water bottles, bullfrogs and any other elastic or expandable receptacle with which to aid camel flotation.

Glenys will be in a basket on one flank of the camel. She will shoot at coconuts containing the explosives and coolant that Mr Weissmuller will throw from a basket on the opposite flank."

"But where will we get explosives and coolant?" asked Mr Vitruvian.

I smiled at the simple genius of it all.

"The camel! Ammonia was discovered by the Babylonians, who derived the substance from sal ammoniac, which was produced by the distillation of camel dung. From this amazing substance we can derive nitroglycerin and also a refrigerant!"

- *I expect Sutton will be relieved if we don't ask how on earth they will manufacture these by-products without the necessary industrial equipment and within the strict time constraints they are operating under.*

"Only one problem remains. How will I keep up with the flying camel? I need Doctor Hoo and Monkey Puzzle Brunel with me."

"You can follow the camel in your grandfather's old sports car," said Errol Flynn.

"The Pentland Javelin? That old jalopy!"

"It's in perfect working order and fully capable of keeping up with a floating camel," he said proudly.

- *Does the author take us for fools? Any classic car enthusiast worth his salt can tell you that a Pentland Javelin is in fact a potato.*

* * *

We prepared the camel on the flat roof of the Folly. Errol Flynn had painted a large 'C' on the floor to make it look like a helipad. It was a perfect launch area for our mission.

"Maybe Baron Willis was not such an idiot after all!" I quipped.

Grandmother frowned violently at me but I didn't understand.

I carried on.

"He must have been a weird guy! Upside down house, upside down pyramid. What a loon!"

There was a cough and I turned around.

Errol Flynn lifted his sporran.

"Not you as well!"

"Yes Rupert. The Bogdowni are my secret offspring," he confessed.

"I was the baron in a former life Rupert, long before I became Errol."

"But the pyramid…?"

"Many millennia ago, passing aliens accidentally dropped the pyramid from their spaceship and it landed upside down into the soft soil."

- *Fucking aliens… I knew it!*

"When it was time to build the new castle, in fear of a similar mishap, I changed the architect's drawings for the castle so that the strongest part, the foundations, would be on top. A sort of fortified roof, if you will. It made sense at the time."

"Who was the mother of the Bogdowni?" I asked.

"Inside the pyramid was a dead female alien. Because of the miraculous healing powers of Mull Doon, where all the ley lines of the universe converge, she somehow became reanimated. When I arrived on the island as Baron Willis of Paracusis, your grandmother was already five thousand years old! Throughout history she has appeared as Cleopatra, Hercules and long before that, Eve. Yes Rupert, your grandmother has seen it all!"

- *The plot thickens!*
- *I disagree! It is congealing rather than thickening, like sour milk.*

I was stunned. Grandmother was the first woman on Earth!

"But Hercules was a man!" I cleverly pointed out.

"He was a hermaphrodite; the first, actually. Your grandmother is no ordinary woman and her alien genetics always come to the fore."

"What happened to Adam?"

At that moment, Grandmother interrupted.

"He died of a bad toothache. Very bad! Now let's go, or we are going to be too late. Cast your eyes over to the house!"

* * *

The sky over the house had turned black and stormy. Within the blackness, flashes of blue luminescence crackled violently. It was time to save the universe!

- *He's got that description from the movie Ghostbusters!*
- *Or Poltergeist.*

We successfully launched the camel-copter on our second attempt, having first almost lost our entire team and the bizarre contraption over the pyramid edge. Grandmother, Doctor Hoo, Monkey Puzzle Brunel and I followed in the

Pentland Javelin. Errol Flynn resumed his duties at the Window of The Angry Voice in case of a counter-attack by evil ground forces.

As we approached to within striking distance, we could see a gap appearing in the swirling darkness. It was the ripping of space-time itself. The tear continued to open up across the sky, covering the whole expanse of the island until at last it resembled the smile of the invisible Cheshire Cat.

As the lips of the cat parted in what seemed like silent demonic laughter, a colossal black tooth, rotten and putrid began to emerge from the spectral shift into this world. I could see the rotting carcasses of dead animals from this planet and others beyond, stuck in the jagged crevices of the tooth.

I stopped the car and jumped out. Holding the remote control console above my head to aid the signal, I sent instructions via the anus of Joe 91 to manoeuvre the camel-copter into position over the monstrous tooth.

Molar the Devourer saw my naked form and seemed to turn menacingly in my direction.

"Rupert!" thundered Molar, "I am your grandfather!"

- *I saw that coming a mile off!*
- *I didn't. I lost concentration after the bit about penguin boy.*

"Noooooo!" I cried.

"It's true Rupert!" said Gran, "but I was sent to protect you from him, to protect the universe from him. I was too late to help the dwarf buffalo and almost too late for the semi-amphibious Bogdowni tribe. Nevertheless, we will not fail this time!"

"Grandfather, what have you done?" I sobbed.

"The horror! The horror!" he whispered hoarsely as he forced his way through the hole in the sky. I could see there was no other way of stopping him and, full of sorrow, I gave the signal to attack.

The coconuts full of coolant and nitroglycerin were released from the camel basket by Johnny Weissmuller Senior. As they fell towards Molar, Glenys took aim and fired. The combined effect of freezing and explosions had a devastating effect on the black, enamelled monster. It disintegrated into a million shattered pieces…

* _Just like in Terminator 2!_

…and the hole in the sky healed up with the percussive sound wave of the explosions.

There was a moment of extreme calm and then suddenly it began to rain all over the island. Gold rain!

"Your grandfather had gold fillings, Rupert! When he transmogrified into Molar the Devourer, the fillings must have grown exponentially! There must be a hundred tons of it!" cried Gran in delight.

* * *

Two days later I called my wife to tell her the fantastic news. But before I could go into any detail she interrupted with news of her own.

"Rupert listen, I've been wanting to tell you for some time. I'm leaving you for Farmer Jake, a.k.a. the Sausage. I'm so sorry. I know this has come at a bad time for you, what

155

with the loss of your grandmother as well. I do feel guilty. So much so in fact that I have signed an affidavit relinquishing my share of any of your property and possessions."

I didn't answer. I was silent in thought for a few seconds.

"Penny for your thoughts?" asked my wife patronisingly.

"Oh, they are worth much more than that," I said, smiling to myself, and put the phone down on my previous life, forever.

- *Hooray! He deserves to come out on top. I do like a happy ending!*
- *Not so fast! Look, there's more!*

It was a bright sunny day on Mull Doon, and the castle was once again surrounded by pink roses. I walked hand in hand with Glenys (who had reincarnated as Marilyn Monroe) through the daisy meadows, scattering the newly-established herds of dwarf buffalo as we went, collecting gold dust on our bare feet with every step. We waved to the Bogdowni tribe who had ventured from the swamps as far as the moss and ferns of The Vale of Dampness.

Suddenly Glenys yelped. Something sharp had caused her to limp. She had a slight graze on the sole of her foot. It was nothing to worry about! Laughing, I gave her a piggyback home. We drank some sacred cappuccino monkey coffee, and made love for the rest of the afternoon, whilst Grandmother, Errol Flynn and the team were busy smelting gold ingots.

Meanwhile, back at the meadow, the drop of blood from Glenys's foot seeped into the tiny fragment of Molar.

It began to vibrate. All over the island, minute fragments of Molar answered with corresponding vibrations and, imperceptibly, they began to draw closer together...

- *Terminator 2 again...*

...and the hidden drums of The Swamp of Certain Death thundered out a fitting crescendo to the scene.

READERS' BLOG:

- *I wonder if Jake the Sausage supplied the wool to make the Arran sweaters of which the fishermen are so fond. It's a small world!*
- *Well he certainly supplied the sausage of which Rupert's wife is so fond! (Sound of Basil Brush saying "Boom Boom" and laughing his particular zany laugh.)*
- *So, let me get this straight. His grandmother is Hercules, who in turn used to be Eve, and his grandad is Molar, who was originally Adam... but then where does Errol Flynn come into it? Is he representing Noah? Is the penis-shaped folly supposed to be the Ark?*
- *Don't think too deeply. The story is as shallow and meaningless as the so-called Swamp of Certain Death.*

"FORGET THE ALAMO"

THE JIVE TALKIN' TURKEY
(From Albuquerque)

Howdy folks! Y'all can probably tell from my accent that I ain't from around these here parts originally. If you can't, well, that means you ain't from around here neither.

Railroad Sam they call me, on account I've spent most of my life on a train going somewhere and, pretty soon after that, leaving somewhere. Going somewhere; leaving somewhere. Going somewhere; leaving somewhere... and so on and so forth. Course, before they built the railroads I was just plain old Sam.

Until I arrived in this here place I'd been travelling most of my adult life. Anyways, I guess you can say I'm kinda settled now. This quiet town seems to fit and I imagine the town says the same thing 'bout me.

The town ain't much to speak of. Don't got no theatre or rodeo, excepting the travelling shows that come through 'bout once a year. Only one thing of interest ever happened here and that was the time when the jive talkin' turkey came to town and started talkin' jive.

'Scuse me while I just spit into this here spittoon. Darned tabacci tastes like the inside of ma britches.

Yup. Local townsfolk called him the jive talkin' turkey from outta town that came to town and started talkin' jive like some jive-assed turkey. And that's just the polite version.

He started out with simple things at first. Like going into the Taco Bell diner and declaring John Wayne was only three feet tall in real life!

Later on, in the Town Hall meeting, he stood up and announced that, oh-contrary-wise to popular belief, Jim Bowie's knife was actually made from pantihose. Folks got mighty riled over that one.

After a while he set hisself up in business; said he'd trained a dawg to sew buttons onto dresses. Darned dawg couldn't put a pleat in ma pants though. I walked outta his shop and before I crossed the street ma britches were riding lower than a rattlesnake's scrotum. I sure attracted a lot of unwanted attention that day. Yes sir-ee!

Jive-ass got some highfalutin ambition in his head 'bout buying the whole town and connecting every building with pneumatic pipes so as people could travel around at the speed of a vacuum cleaner or some such machine. Old Jed Morgan over at the general store said it would be like travelling along inside of a fart! We all laughed at that. Ma Baker laughed so hard she really did fart and 'course that made us laugh even harder. Yup, good times back in the day.

Never did find out how Jive-ass intended to create a vacuum, but he hinted he had the ways and means to make it work. Got some old folks scared it was really going to happen. They wanted to know if they could keep their hats on when they was travelling around. He wouldn't answer them straight. Kept mumbling and looking all kinda distracted like he had more important things to worry about than people's darned hats.

One day he got drunk on moonshine and rode his penny-farthing along Main Street wearin' nothin' but his top hat and boots. 'Course when the Texas State Troopers caught up with him he couldn't help hisself but talk jive. Hollered something like:

"Forget the Alamo!"

He kept maintaining that the Alamo was of a wattle and daub construction.

"Alamo shmalamo!" was the last straw, if you'll excuse the pun. They gave him a final warning and said the next time he stepped outta line, he would have to answer to the Texas Ranger. Well this was like waving a red bandana in front of a Longhorn steer.

He printed out a buncha leaflets telling folks how Davy Crockett was a communist spy. And he said he weren't afeared o' no Texas Ranger on account of how they're all strawberry pickers and wear ladies' panties.

Weren't no surprise when a stern-faced Chuck Norris rode into town, cracking his knuckles and limbering up his hamstrings. Pretty soon he done kicked that jive-talkin' turkey ass all the way back to Albuquerque.

The town held a mighty fine shindig. There was a whole lotta rootin' and a tootin' goin' on. I had me some beans and some moonshine but missed out on the rootin'. I sure as hell struggled to keep my tootin' to maself! Phew-ee!

Chuck was there of course. Folks were cheering and clapping like he was gonna be the next President. Before that day I surely woulda voted for him. That is, until I seen what I saw.

You probably won't believe what happened next but I swear it's true. I walked into the men's room at the saloon and there he was, Chuck Norris, the toughest guy in all the 'US of A', sitting down to take a pee!

Now what in tarnation…? Folks, I gotta tell ya… round his muscular ankles was a pair of goddamned ladies' panties!

Well I skedaddled right outta there faster 'n a hog with his ass on fire. Chuck never did see me. I figure he was too busy peeping through the hole into the next cubicle.

Yup. Erm… that's all folks! All this talkin' has made ma mouth drier than Pocahontas's grandma's titties. I'm hankering awful fer a drink. Now where's that spittoon again?

READERS' BLOG:

- *Dear, oh dear. Sutton appears misinformed again. Pocahontas was Mohawk or Iroquois, thus hailing from the North-East region, so it is more likely that Railroad Sam would be referring to an old Apache or Navajo squaw's titties, as those tribes were based in the South.*
- *Yes and the harsh, arid conditions of the deserts in the South would have had a more adverse effect on their hooters as opposed to living in the more temperate North.*
- *Chuck Norris isn't so tough. Bruce Lee kicked his ass around the Colosseum in that movie and Bruce weighed only four and a half stones in his prime.*
- *Sutton's colloquialisms are all over the place. He has mixed Harlem street slang with Texas drawl. He is either a little bit stupid or very, very clever.*

- *How can a dog sew buttons? It has no opposable thumbs.*
- *Maybe it had one of those machines. Especially useful for hems and seam-work.*
- *Bruce Lee could do press-ups with his chin!*
- *Be that as it may, but he had no embroidery skills worthy of note. And he never owned a thimble.*
- *Why do people shout "Geronimo!" before leaping into danger? I would have thought 70s stunt man "Evel Knievel" would be more apt because he really did do some crazy shit.*
- *Chuck Norris? Weird! Last week, by prior arrangement, I met a guy behind some dustbins on an industrial estate in the early hours of the morning. Guess what? His first name was Norris! Even weirder than that, as he handed over the agreed fee, he said in a northern accent, "There you go, chuck."*

SEND YOUR COMMENTS TO THE BLOG AT
www.planktonsoup.co.uk

A FRIESIAN COW IN REPOSE
AND ASSOCIATED QUESTIONS

Last February at about eight o'clock in the morning, I was on a train returning from somewhere or other, having spent the weekend searching for a man called Tom who could lend me his long-handled scythe. It had been a fruitless exercise.

The train carriage was almost empty except for two elderly gentlemen who were not sitting together. Perhaps they had argued, perhaps they had never met, I couldn't tell from where I was sitting.

At the next stop, a woman got on and slowly walked the entire length of the carriage, apparently looking for a suitable seat. She got as far as my position and then turned around and walked back slowly, seeming to perform some complicated mental calculation, and then checking behind her to compare the other seats. She repeated this whole manoeuvre several times. I wondered what criteria she had set regarding appropriate seat positioning. Finally, after many minutes and as many kilometres, she sat at the opposite end of the carriage near the door, facing the direction of travel. I wanted to get up from my seat, go to her and say

"Excuse me, *I'm* sitting there." That's just the type of guy I am.

• *She must be the train nutter. There's always one.*

Further on in the journey I was looking out of the window and daydreaming about problems concerning perpetual motion, a current obsession of mine, when I noticed a field containing an irregular black and white shape. As the field shot past the window I noticed that the shape was in fact a Friesian cow in repose. I was not troubled immediately by this as my mind can only deal with one concept at a time, and even then at a rate of only one every half an hour.

But slowly, ever so slowly, my concentration waxed and waned from perpetual motion to Friesian cow. I was convinced that the secret of perpetual motion somehow lay in harnessing magnetism from the opposing poles of the earth and building a giant gyroscope encompassing the globe and… hey, did you know that cows have four stomachs?

Traditional folklore suggests that when cows lie down it is a sure sign that rain is imminent. However, the sky that was visible from the train window was relatively clear and there was little evidence of wind in the upright and steady treetops.

In a herd of cows there would normally be groups striking various positions; some sitting, some standing and some lying casually on the ground. Some may even lean against the mantelpiece smoking an elegant cigarillo in a paisley neckerchief, although I've never seen it myself. Nevertheless, when lying down, they are usually on their stomachs with front legs bent underneath their chests and head and neck upright. The cow that had entered my thoughts and now giving me cause for concern had been lying stretched out on its left side, all four legs fully extended, with its head resting on a pillow of clover as if on holiday in Hawaii.

- *Do they have clover in Hawaii?*
- *Yes, but not as we know them. They have longer stems and small white flowers between April and July…*
- *Ooh, are you a botanist? Wanker, more like!*

The image of the cow had disturbed me and my mind was suddenly filled with an urgency, to such an extent that I considered climbing out of the window and running back along the roof of the train, then jumping off, rolling upon landing to soften the impact, making my way back to the field to inspect the cow on bended knee and make a call to the farmer, using my mobile phone connected to a satellite dish that I could fashion out of silver paper from my chewing gum. Perhaps even drape the cow across my shoulders and carry it to the farm, depending on the severity of the situation. That's just the sort of guy I am.

- *Ah no. HE is the train nutter! There's one on every train.*

But before I embarked on such perilous action there were questions to be considered.

Would the farmer already have noticed that the cow is not with the others?

Does he perform a head count as the cows file into their milking stalls?

Is he very organised and adhering to strict animal

husbandry policy as laid down by EU regulations, or is he lackadaisical and happy-go-lucky in his approach to modern farming techniques?

Will the farmer's wife complain at the noticeable drop in milk production from the herd as a whole, to the tune of one full udder?

How much does this equate to in monetary value?

Will the farmer scratch his head and wonder why there is an unattached, vacant udder-suction flange assembly?

Or will he scratch his chin?

Is the cow refusing point blank to go along with the herd to be milked? Why?

Is it protesting against poor working conditions on the farm?

Are the dining facilities 'up to scratch'?

Has the cow suffered some form of abuse by the farmer?

Was it physical or mental?

Has it been ostracised by the others? Why?

Does the cow consider itself superior or inferior to the others?

On what evidence does it base its premise either way?

Has it woken up with a reluctant malaise like a sulking teenager?

Is it an existentialist and therefore questioning the relevance of conformity?

Is it simply relaxing after a particularly long evening?

Was it playing the harp in an orchestra the previous night?

Should I design a computer program to diagnose the condition *in situ*?

Perhaps a simple flow chart would be more practical. For example…

Question One: Does the patient present with bruising to the forehead?

Answer Yes – Administer witch hazel embrocation.

Answer No – Consider all other options.

Has the cow ingested a poisonous mushroom in the field?

If so, which strain of fungi was it and is it curable?

Could the effects be lessened if the poison was pumped out of the stomach?

How would the medical staff know which stomach to pump?

Will the farmer be allowed to accompany the cow to hospital or will he be required by the police to remain apart until enquiries had been conducted?

If I save the cow's life, will I be forced/obliged to enter into marriage with it because of some strange regional hillbilly bylaw as in some mid-Asian countries?

That's not the type of guy I am.

But if I do nothing, will it play on my conscience for years to come?

Will I later watch the evening news and see the cow's legs dangling from a harness as it is being airlifted to hospital by a huge yellow helicopter?

Has the cow, in the short time since I last saw it, suddenly realised it is late and scrambled hastily to its hooves, and lumbered off in the direction of the milking shed?

Will it receive some form of punishment for being late?

Does the farmer administer corporal punishment or simply withhold privileges?

Does the corporal punishment take the form of a stick applied forcibly to the buttock region?

What is the acceptable amount of force used as measured in newtons per square inch?

Do the EU laws relating to the use of the metric system affect the laws of physics?

If so, is E still equal to MC^2?

If not, how will this affect my search for the answer to perpetual motion?

Did Einstein take into account the impact of the introduction of the metric system when he predicted the existence of black holes?

Should I try to be more like Einstein and think outside the box?

To wit, has the cow in fact always been alone in that field?

Is the farmer merely a beginner, with the intention of adding to his herd as and when circumstances permit, considering the volatile economic climate and difficulties in general that affect the livestock industry?

Was what I saw a three-dimensional cardboard representation of a cow that had fallen over due to inefficient ballast placement?

Has the farmer created this to trick Government assessors into thinking he has a bigger herd than in reality, so as to qualify for generous EU farming subsidies?

Has he got several hundred other cardboard cows, which he shows to the Government assessors from a distance, pointing and making grand sweeping gestures to the faraway hillside and exclaiming "Regard my numerous herd"?

Did Einstein use a similar ruse to explain the universe to us?

If 'Einstein' is translated into English, it means 'One Stone'.

Earth is sometimes referred to as the third rock from the Sun, but is 'One Stone' a significant clue from the greatest scientific mind that we are in fact alone in the universe and all the other planets are merely cardboard models in a classroom?

Just who was Einstein A Go-Go?

Am I thinking too far outside the box?

Is it a cardboard box?

Has the cow thus provided a clue to my search for perpetual motion?

Four stomachs working in harmony; four elements: earth, wind, fire and water… no, that's not it.

A two-dimensional representation of a three-dimensional reality… a hidden dimension, perhaps argon rays, vibrating in constant flux… no that's not it…

Do cows face magnetic north after midday?

If I affix an elastic band to its lower mandible…

If I harness the methane…

Damn it man, think! I'm missing something, but what?

At that moment I was disturbed from my thoughts by one of the old men seen earlier in my carriage. He was tapping me urgently on the shoulder. I looked up at him and saw that he was gibbering like a lunatic. Drool and spittle were drenching his scruffy grey beard. He jabbed a long-nailed finger at the picture on his filthy homemade sweater... it was a picture of a Friesian cow lying in a field! His finger jabbed first at the picture, then at me and then at the window. Suddenly he screeched out a final laugh, opened the window and threw himself out!

- *That was definitely the train nutter! There's one on every train.*
- *Yes, but now that he has jumped from the window, that leaves the train utterly nutterless. Unless...*

The next day, as I read the paper, the headlines announced that a top scientist had killed himself by jumping from a train. His colleagues said he had been on the verge of an astounding scientific discovery regarding perpetual motion, but had recently suffered a nervous breakdown after a bizarre obsession involving a Friesian cow in repose.

As I picked up my knitting needles and began to follow the pattern of the dead scientist's sweater, questions again entered my mind...

Did the cow fall from a cloud?

Can cows become part of the weather cycle, i.e. do cows evaporate?

If not, from where do we get evaporated milk...?

READERS' BLOG:

- *If that meddlesome halfwit Einstein hadn't come up with 'E=MC² ' then perhaps we could solve the perpetual question of perpetual motion. Thanks to him and his blasted equation we never will.*

- I have read somewhere that cows build nests, so I imagine the cow fell from a tree. It may have sprained an ankle during the fall and may well need the big yellow helicopter.
- Cow's nest? You mean CROW'S nest!
- Ah yes. Crows! But wait a minute, how does a cow fit into a crow's nest?
- Are these the sort of people that are reading Sutton's work? No wonder this country is in the mess it's in.
- I didn't realise farming was so complicated. I shall stick to my lollipops.

THE SINGING, DANCING SECURITY QUARTET

BUDDY GUARDS

Yes that's right, I'm a cross-dressing bodyguard! I know you've been dying to ask. I've seen the quizzical look in your eye and heard your whispers, "I say, look! That chap over there! He's wearing rouge… and velvet hot pants!" So now that the secret's out, let me tell you all about it.

I don't quite know how the idea first implanted itself in my mind, but it was probably due to seeing a bearded farmer in a Laura Ashley dress at the Love Parade in Weston-super-Mare. I had an inkling, a sort of inner voice, urging me to follow the desires that had been tickling the back of my mind for the last couple of years. I awoke the next morning and decided to go for it. I didn't so much come out of the closet; more like went in, had a look around and decided I liked what I saw.

Quite simply, I began to wear women's clothes. No make-up, not yet. I was just dipping my toe in. But pretty soon my dipped toe developed a painted nail; a shade of strawberry pink with sparkly bits (my favourite). And that was just the beginning!

I attended a cross-dressing convention in Reykjavik. After numerous presentations, including a transvestite kung fu film *High Heels*, on the way back to my hotel I saw the cabaret drag queen Ashby de la Zouch being attacked by a stag party of Malaysian teddy boys; their soft, coiffured hair belying their propensity for casual, yet effective violence. I tried to intervene but they roughed me up a little and then interfered with me in no uncertain terms. In those days mindless attacks on men in women's clothing were prevalent. Cabaret artistes were exceptionally vulnerable.

And that's basically how it all started. I set up the personal security escort agency for the world of cabaret artistes; this was to be security with a difference. We sang, we danced, and got the V.I.P. from 'A' to 'B' in a way they would never forget. We were the world's first security quartet… 'Buddy Guards'!

What a team we were! I was, and still am, a transvestite vaudeville historian; and that's not an easy thing to admit to in front of strangers. Of course I couldn't do it alone, I needed people who could sing and dance whilst beating up bad guys at the same time, and so I set out to recruit the best in the business.

Felix was a big black jazz musician from Louisiana who had apparently blown Dizzy Gillespie's horn. Felix claimed he could kill a man with one lunge, but the whole story left me confused.

Leo was the choreographer and pianist. He told me he was an expert at hurting men. He could do the splits and special chorus-line high kicks. He had extensive knowledge of Burt Bacharach's back catalogue.

And then there was our singer, Rhet Martagne. His real surname was Martin but he said he preferred it the French way! Rhet was an ex-gunslinger from Buffalo Bill's Wild West Show.

- *He sings while he slings!*

He could spin his weapon around his little finger and between his legs. He told me that shooting gave him immense satisfaction. I think he meant guns.

I told my mother proudly that I had formed my own company. She asked why I wanted to sell *budgerigars* as I had been allergic to feathers since a traumatic childhood incident with Rod Hull and Emu. No mother, *Buddy Guards* for God's sake!

But dear reader, there was more to our team than met the eye! Our whole was greater than the sum of our parts! We had a secret accomplice! You see, I was the luckiest boy alive because I had the ability to magically metamorphose into any character from vaudeville history!

All I had to do was to enter the haunted toilet of my caravan (our office) and perform a strange ritual. Within seconds, hey presto! I would emerge as… well, it was always a surprise because I had no control over which person I would turn out to be! But the haunted toilet always got it right. It tailored my new identity to the exact requirements of the mission.

- *Hey! Just like the television show, Quantum Leap!*

The giants of music hall comedy, George Formby and Tommy Trinder have helped on a number of occasions as have Ali Bongo and Max Wall.

- *This sounds somewhat unlikely but I will allow Sutton enough rope to hang himself.*

One day, we were hired to protect Elton John at the Eurovision Song Contest. Threats had been made against his life by a mysterious sect.

Everything was prepared. We had rehearsed the route from the hotel and the walk into the dressing room of the theatre. We selected 'The Boy from New York City' by Darts as the song and a simple Mashed Potato hand jive for the car.

Alternatives such as the Yellow Brick Road 'hop, skip and jump' from *The Wizard of Oz* were kept as emergency back-up routines. I felt it might go nicely with a Latin guitar version of Chim Chiminey, Chim Chim Cher-ee. Rhet had argued for a calypso version of 'Nights in White Satin' but we couldn't match it up with any dance steps.

My team waited outside the caravan whilst I got dressed. For this event I had chosen to go with an eighteenth century French ball gown with internal hoops, as worn by Marie Antoinette. Probably not the most practical thing for the office caravan, but when I stepped out Rhet kindly said I looked like a million francs.

- *Considering today's exchange rate that's almost an insult!*

At Elton's hotel we met some other security teams who were also going to the contest with their respective V.I.P.s. The Greek bodyguards were Kris Anthemum and Riki Dikulous.

- *Groan! The author is trying too hard.*

From Slovakia there were Schitjazelf and Kakjapanz.

- *Ho ho! Jokes based on the continental pronunciation of the letter 'Jay'. Ingenious! That's more than made up for his previous tepid efforts.*

And then there were the two Wongs who were from North Korea.

"Are you related?" we asked them.

"Yes, but not to each other," they replied simultaneously, as if having rehearsed that line a thousand times.

As my team and I were products of the politically incorrect seventies era, all Orientals looked the same to us so we gave the Wongs code names to help us identify them. The short, fat one we called Wong Kong and the tall, skinny one we called Long Wong.

- *Makes sense to me.*
- *Why is he talking about the two Wongs in more detail than the bodyguards from other countries? I suspect they will play a more significant role later on in the story.*

Once inside the theatre, the V.I.P.s were supposed to turn left to go to the dressing rooms and the security teams should have turned right to go to the viewing galleries.

But as we said goodbye to Elton and made our way to the gallery, disaster struck!

"The two Wongs didn't make a right!" warned Felix, who was always aware of what was going on behind him.

- *You've got to be kidding me! Is Sutton really using the 'two wrongs' pun?*

- *It was always on the cards.*

"We've got to stop them!" I cried, "They must be the assassins!"

I dashed back out through the crowds and across the pavement to our caravan and launched myself into the toilet cubicle. Hurriedly I began the mysterious ceremony that would summon the spirit of a vaudeville star to help us.

Moments later I emerged from my trance and tried to open the toilet door. It was stuck! Elton was in danger and I was trapped in the caravan toilet!

"Let me out fellas!" I banged on the door impatiently.

Felix jiggled the knob with both of his muscular hands.

"It's jammed! I'm going to have to break it down, stand back!"

He threw his hugeness at the door and it gave way easily.

I stumbled out and looked in the mirror.

"Thanks for that Felix; I thought I was going to be stuck in there forever! Now let us see who I have come back as."

"Fucking Houdini!" we all cried.

Seconds later we were hurtling back up the steps of the theatre and heading for the dressing rooms.

"There's Elton, by the hair dryers!" screamed eagle-eyed Rhet.

Roaring "Nooo!" in slow motion like the movies, I threw myself in front of Elton just as Wong Kong was about to strike. The powerful blow caught me in the midriff exactly as I had intended and I stood up, seemingly unharmed.

Wong Kong's face turned white.

"That was the legendary Five Finger Death Punch! How could you have survived?"

"Houdini magic!" I laughed, as I tried to prevent my spleen coming further up into my throat. I swallowed hard.

"Has anyone got a drink of water?"

The police soon arrived and placed Wong Kong in handcuffs then bundled him into the police car.

"Ooh, did you see Kong's tie?" whispered Felix.

"Yes. Bart Simpson cravats are so last year," said Leo.

"C'est vrai," sighed Rhet dramatically, "North Koreans have no panache."

Suddenly I realised something. "Just a minute! Where's Long Wong?" I cried.

At that exact moment a previously concealed Long Wong was charging with his tanto raised in the air, ready to plunge into Elton from behind.

• *A double entendre! How rare!*

"We need to do something quickly!" I blurted.

"What about *West Side Story*?" suggested Rhet.

"I was thinking more Gene Kelly," said Leo sensibly.

"*Singin' in the Rain*?"

"No, *An American in Paris.*"

"Surely Fred Astaire is called for in this situation!"

"No, too technical, we…"

Rhet suddenly burst into 'Greased Lightnin' and, thanks to the hours of choreography training from Leo, we all knew what to do. We solemnly took up various positions around the police car and began to shimmy our hips.

For a moment I was unsure where this was all leading to and I feared for Elton's life. But during the instrumental break of the song, Rhet took out his weapon and splattered Long Wong right between the eyes…

Surely you don't mean…???

…with a hail of bullets.

Next week…

Lady Gaga is held hostage by members of The Curry Powder Plot! Can the guys rescue her in time to perform the big Bollywood dance finale at the Taj Mahal?

READERS' BLOG:

- *I fail to see what possible help Max Wall could have been to a mission of any type. What with his odd hairstyle, black woollen tights and old hob-nailed boots, he should stick to his funny walk routine and leave the so-called missions to the so-called professionals.*
- *I was disappointed that the author refused to disclose the details of the mysterious toilet ceremony. Perhaps he doesn't even know himself.*
- *He was using artistic licence, but if I had my way he should have twelve points stuck on his licence and have it revoked.*
- *I would give him 'nul points' for this effort like they do in Eurovision.*
- *Houdini was skilled at escapism and could also withstand forceful punches to the abdomen. It's a strange combination of talents, somewhat akin to bobbing for*

cheese in a fishbowl, whilst skipping on one foot wearing skis. Backwards. With your underpants on fire.

- *Just a flippin' minute... North Korea are not in Europe, how were they able to enter a song and two Wongs? And thanks to their uncooperative stance on nuclear arms they are never likely to be offered a place in the contest, never mind the EU expansionist programme.*
- *I would have used the seventies hit 'Kung Fu Fighting'. The actions that go with that song would surely protect any V.I.P.*
- *Elton John has got a very small nose. I wonder if this bears any relation to his penis?*
- *Small penis notwithstanding, he is the UK's top performer and deserves to be protected against a plunge from the rear.*
- *Why didn't the haunted toilet send forth the former boxing champions Sugar Ray Robinson or Rocky Marciano to protect Elton? One clunk from either of them and the two Wongs would have been knocked into next week.*
- *You have missed the subtlety of the plot. The haunted toilet only produces characters from vaudeville history... not from the noble art of boxing.*
- *Houdini? Weird! I met a handsome youth at the swimming baths last week and took him home to my place. Guess what? He kept trying to escape too! But the pink furry handcuffs proved too strong.*

SEND YOUR COMMENTS TO THE BLOG AT
www.planktonsoup.co.uk

THE CAT SAT ON THE MAT

Or did it? True, it was there when the humans went to bed. The cat sat on the mat then. The black cat sat on the red mat. The sleek black cat sat on the luxurious red mat. The sleek black cat with reptilian but efficient eyes sat on the luxurious red mat with golden but impractical tassels.

Not only were the eyes of the sleek black cat reptilian and efficient, they were of different colours. The left one, emerald green and the right one, steel blue. The humans had missed, or perhaps ignored the opportunity to name the sleek black cat Ziggy or better still, Major Tom. They had opted for the name David.

How the sleek black cat hates those humans.

Suddenly a cloud is pushed aside by the heavy sigh of a snoring god and moonlight gushes into the bedroom where the humans are sleeping. The sleek black cat with reptilian eyes is no longer on the luxurious red mat. It is now on the bed staring at the humans.

In the moonlight, the cat's eyes are both black. The cat has come to steal the breath of the humans. It will steal their breath and give it to the Moon. That's what black cats do. Steal your breath and give it to the Moon.

READERS' BLOG:

- *Yawn! Everybody uses 'emerald' when they describe a shade of green. It's always emerald this and emerald that. Boring! Can't the author conjure up something more original? Use the imagination! Smoky green, for example, is quite sexy for eyes. British racing green is a much more exciting hue, especially the metallic version. It's the perfect colour for a Jaguar which, after all, is a cat as well as a motor car. The author's only saving grace is that he did not fall into the trap of using sapphire to describe the blue eye. However I am almost sure that one of David Bowie's eyes was in fact brown? A sort of chocolaty brown?*
- *The author should do his homework before putting pen to paper in future.*

THE DAY OUR UNDERPANTS SAVED THE WORLD

As the battle to end all battles raged around us, over us and sometimes it seemed, under us, I looked at my companion who shared temporary salvation in this foxhole and realised I'd never noticed him before. He appeared surprisingly calm despite the thunder of bombs close by and his warm brown eyes regarded me gently.

"Hey fella, what's your name?" I shouted over the noise of gunfire.

"I am Achmed al Jumeira Yaktoum Ibid Etal Bin Far…" he began.

"OK, OK, that's enough! I don't want your life story!"

"You can call me Kenneth if you wish. Most people prefer that," he smiled sheepishly.

"Hi Kenneth, I'm Smallcock, Justin Smallcock. Smallcock by name, Justin by nature.

Kenneth looked shocked.

"Your small cock is of no concern to me," he said almost defensively.

"It would be if it was growing off the end of your nose!"

"Leave my nose out of it!"

"Ooh touchy!"

"Don't touchy it either!"

We were flying off at a tangent.

"Look, er, Kenneth, I guess we started off on the wrong foot here. Let's shake hands and try again."

His smile seemed to brighten up the foxhole and I heard fanfares as if his teeth were trumpets of light.

We leaned towards each other with arms outstretched. As our hands touched, I felt a powerful spark of electricity run down my spine and fizzle out through my big toe.

Suddenly there was a roaring in my head and my mind's eye was filled with fast-moving images, almost like a high-speed slide show.

I saw Kenneth falling like a fireball from the sky and landing in a haystack, which ignited and destroyed a few ramshackle buildings. He was rescued from the angry villagers by the local carpenter who needed a new young apprentice, his previous one having escaped in a basket of reeds.

I saw Kenneth, a few years older, giving bits of bread to small children. The children then fed the flock of white doves which seemed to hover over Kenneth's head wherever he went. Yet miraculously he never seemed to get covered in poo.

I saw Kenneth rubbing embrocation into an old woman's shin bone. I think he was working at a care home at that time.

I saw Kenneth throwing his sandals at the manager of Addis Ababa bureau de change… and who wouldn't considering the current exchange rate?

I saw Kenneth appearing to win the local donkey derby, people cheering and waving big leaves instead of flags.

I saw Kenneth in prison being roughed up by the guards. And then I saw him being… oh no, that can't be right!

I tried to let go of his hand but his grip was too powerful. A surge of exhilaration swept through my intestines and duodenum as I 'saw' Kenneth rocketing upwards past the clouds and into space, pausing briefly to look back down at the delicate blue sphere of Earth before disappearing at warp speed into the depths of the universe with a tear of sadness in his eye.

He released my hand and sat back, looking at me intently.

"Your name's not Kenneth is it?" I said flatly.

He shook his head very slowly.

"Neither is it Achmed," he said in a low, gentle voice.

"Are you who I think you are?"

"Look into your heart and you will truly know me."

Suddenly a bomb exploded close by and I dived for cover in the bottom of the foxhole. When the dust had settled I looked up and Kenneth had gone.

My memory was filled with the image of the blue planet and its fragile nature. I immediately understood the foolishness of man and the futility of war. I understood our (Mankind's) enormous responsibility to this special place. And I understood that something must be done immediately!

I hurriedly made a white(ish) flag from the only white thing I had… my military Y-fronts. As I clambered out of the hole, waving my underpants in desperate surrender, I saw that across the endless plain of the battlefield, all soldiers from both armies were also waving their respective general issue white underwear! The guns had fallen silent and there were no more bombs. No more war!

The soldier from the next foxhole came running over, shouting and kicking his heels in joy.

"Dude, it's the weirdest thing!" he gushed. "I just spent the last hour with some guy. Swarthy, bit timid, surprisingly clean feet, bit of a conk on him. Said his name was Kenneth. The next thing I know I'm waving my undies in the air and the war's over!"

I looked up at the sky and was sure that I saw a flash of sandal leather disappearing into the stratosphere. I knew then that Kenneth had been with all of us during the battle, showing us the folly of our ways and defending his nose.

* * *

That was many years ago and I have grown old and watched my grandchildren become adults in a safe and caring world. Not one day goes by that I don't cast my mind back to that meeting with Kenneth, and I never forget to thank Ken's dad that we all wore white underpants on that fateful day.

READERS' BLOG:

- *So is Kenneth actually Jesus or Superman?*
- *I don't think Superman had such a big nose, and he was a proponent of red underwear, not white.*
- *If the Geneva Convention stated that war should be carried out in the nude, then there would be less war. Probably.*

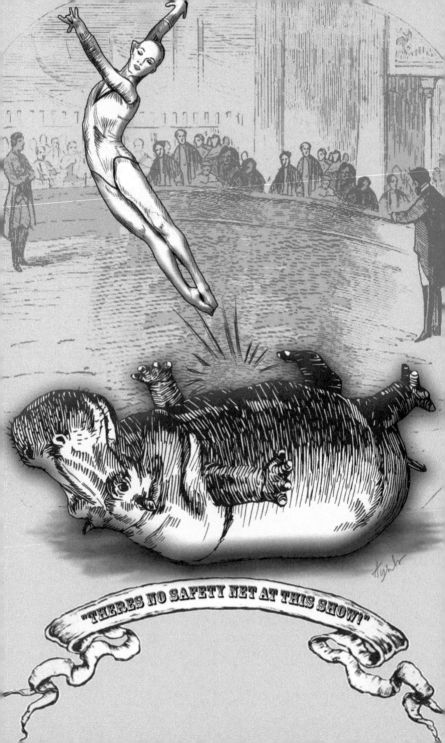

"THERE'S NO SAFETY NET AT THIS SHOW!"

THE SHOW MUST GO ON

I am at The Show. I am watching The Show. I like The Show very much and attend as often as possible. On this particular occasion The Show is performed by various dancers from around the globe.

You can read the colourful billboards outside the theatre…

'Nubile fire dancers from Papua New Guinea; rolling about on hot coals, gritting their teeth in determination. See how they grimace!'

'Acrobats from the Chinese ambassador's personal stash; doing impossible things with bamboo. Watch as they are seemingly impaled!'

'Byzantine belly dancers who look at us askance; pointing their fingers at strange angles. See them undulate!'

The adverts have excited people and the theatre is full tonight. People who rarely visit a theatre have made a special effort. People who swore never to set foot in a theatre have, in fact, changed their tune and relented to attend on this occasion.

A hidden saxophone begins the night. A spotlight is switched on. A solo dancer appears dressed in nothing but a giant cake around his midriff. I am enthralled not so much with his dizzying pirouettes or languid twirls, but by the artistic way he has arranged the chocolate sprinkles in the whipped cream around his pubis. And oh, is that a glacé cherry in the middle? Oh dear me, no! It is *not* a cherry! Is it really what I think it is? How gaudy, how gauche! How daringly provocative!

Then, as a complete contrast, the motor cycle display team trundle on, balancing on shoulders with arms outstretched. Their faces are kept stern as it ill becomes them to break rank and smile. They are highly disciplined, professional men. But how ridiculous they look in their pink long johns, spluttering around in circles at a snail's pace!

I notice they all have beards. I have repressed memory syndrome involving a man with a beard. If only I could remember who... what... how? But it was such a long time ago and may never have happened at all.

Ballet dancers are next and I notice they are wearing fish on their exquisite little feet. Once again I am filled with complex emotions. I find small feet very erotic, but to see them encased in fish has complicated matters; not least because I still find them attractive! I wonder what kind of fish they are wearing. Herring? If so, pilchard or shad?

The act is abandoned when a dorsal fin becomes detached from one of the shoes and the dancer is thrown off-kilter, losing direction and careering into the prima donna. The audience outwardly show sympathetic appreciation by clapping over-loudly but they secretly whisper disgruntled remarks to their neighbours out of the corners of their unhappy mouths.

The troupe traipses off and a trapeze artist traverses

above the stage, tricking the audience into training their minds away from the tragic trout trip.

- *I thought he said it was a pilchard?*
- *Yes, ballet dancers don't have big enough feet to fit inside a trout. Needless to say I find it all highly unlikely.*

The trapeze artist spins from a red ribbon held in her teeth. Drums are rolled, adding to the feeling of impending disaster. The audience are suitably impressed. There is no safety net at this show.

Suddenly the ribbon snaps and the artist drops to the stage amid screams of horror, only to land comfortably atop the sponge-like belly of an upside down hippopotamus. The artist bounces up and performs a perfect somersault before landing deftly onto the stage, then bows to a standing ovation.

Alas, the ovation is short-lived; halting abruptly when the hippo defecates fiercely onto one of its handlers as a result of the earlier impact of the artist on its abdomen. At this I cheer loudly and throw flowers.

- *Did they not envisage this in rehearsals?*
- *How could they?*

After the mulch of half-digested banana and cauliflower has been removed from the stage it is time for the next act. The show must go on.

The next act seeks to portray the Spanish-American war of 1898 through the medium of dance. It begs the question 'why'? Why was there a war, or more probably, from the audience's viewpoint, why perform this at all?

America is represented by a battalion of Riverdancers (a rather vague reference to its Irish population) and in the Spanish corner, a lone flamenco dancer in a turquoise satin dress. I am immediately entranced both by her courage and her vulnerability. Oh the futility of it all!

I raise my opera glasses and am able to see a bead of perspiration form on her brow and then I follow it as it rolls gently down her high-boned cheek, under her upturned defiant chin, quickening as it slides down her slender throat, slowing as it reaches her sternum and then suddenly it disappears, oozing into her wonderfully tanned buxomness.

I fall forward slightly, as if trying to follow the liquid down into her cleavage. The opera glasses are dislodged from my moist palm and they drop from my private box onto the head of a large gentleman in the audience below. Thankfully he is a Grenadier Guard in full uniform and his bearskin hat swallows up the opera glasses without disturbing him.

Fiddles, flutes and bodhrans strike up an irrepressible foot-stomping beat. The large force of thunderous Irish (American) dancers advance threateningly towards the beautiful, proud but diminutive Spanish lady.

She is perspiring freely now (if only I could see more clearly!) and her bosom is shiny and heaving. She knows what's coming.

They are almost upon her and the audience fear the worst. Suddenly she explodes into a frenzy of movement, hammering her heels into the stage like machine-gun fire, twirling the hem of her dress indignantly and glaring at the enemy with her flashing eyes.

The line of Irish (American) stompers hesitates and

even takes a step back momentarily… then the worst fears of the audience are realised as the hapless Spanish beauty is crushed underfoot by the onslaught of greater numbers, although not by greater skill or aesthetics. This is manifest destiny in all its brutality. I find I have shed some tears.

The limp, bloodied body is carried off as slow melancholic music is played by a church organ suspended from the ceiling on a cardboard cloud, accompanied by members of the Viennese Vegetable Orchestra dressed as angels. Be intrigued by them but don't be fooled!

A large Balinese group perform their traditional Fire Dance. There is a lot of sitting and waving of hands and I form the opinion that it is not technically a dance per se. Ultimately they have travelled halfway around the world to disappoint me. No offence. I take the opportunity to visit the rest room and then buy a Cognac from the bar.

Someone seems to have had the clever idea to put on the next act in close juxtaposition to the previous one.

A tribe of Sioux Indians perform their Rain Dance. They jog and hop around in a circle, sometimes looking at the floor, sometimes looking at the sky towards their many gods. At first I find it all quite sad. Their basic movements are far outshone when compared to professional contemporary jazz or swing dancers. And do they really expect a real thundercloud to form within the confines of the theatre roof space?

Nevertheless, the combination of loin cloths, face paint and feathers has triggered happy memories and, due to an uncomfortable erection, I am unable to join in with the standing ovation, although I do applaud enthusiastically.

Maasai warriors fail to impress me with their vacant

expressions as they bounce vertically up and down to a repetitive, though admittedly hypnotic rhythm. But somehow there is no panache, no pizzazz, no razzmatazz, no shazam, no glitz, no glam, and no wham bam thank you ma'am.

It is a purely personal opinion… the rest of the audience seems to love it since they enjoy the tallness of the dancers and their amazing toe strength. If there was an industry that required heavy objects to be moved around using only the power of toes, or boxes that needed to be placed on high shelves and ladders were unavailable, then I have no doubt that these chaps would be regarded as extremely beneficial employees.

Limbo dancers from the Caribbean spring onto the stage with their antics. Steel drums are clanged to add to the illusion that we are actually in Barbados. Gradually the limbo bar is lowered to seemingly impossible 'depths' ('heights' is hardly the best word to describe it). Yet somehow a young female is able to shimmy her way under it.

Now here is a chance for hilarity. They are to choose a member of the audience to come on stage and attempt a limbo.

A bizarre choice defying all logic, they select the Grenadier Guard to make the attempt! Even more bizarrely, he declines the opportunity to take off his bearskin hat! My mouth is agape.

To everyone's amusement, as he bends backwards, my opera glasses fall out of the deep fur of his hat. There is some tittering and pointing, but wait! That is not all! As he shuffles under the bar, other lost objects drop out of the fur, one by one.

A gold pocket watch; a cheese sandwich; a child's tricycle; a small dog (alive!); a blacksmith's anvil and a washing line full of ladies' underwear.

A man in the audience shouts out, "Those are mine!" but it is unclear as to which article or articles he is referring. Do we have here a self-confessed transvestite? Why is he not part of the show? Transvestites amuse me. I repeat my mantra, "Be intrigued by them but do not be fooled."

Meanwhile the Grenadier has somehow successfully negotiated a path under the limbo bar and receives a kiss on the moustache from the lithe female dancer as a reward. I think he deserves more for such a feat and plan to write a commendation letter to the commanding officer of the local barracks and a request for his private number.

The Grenadier's moment of glory is eclipsed, however, when the suspected transvestite jumps onto the stage to retrieve his gold watch, his cheese sandwich and his long-lost dog. He takes a bite from the sandwich and feeds the rest to his dog who licks the man on his cheek. The audience's heartstrings are plucked and hankies are withdrawn to dab at romantic eyes. But I can only wonder at the mysterious line of panty girdles which remains unclaimed.

At last it is time for my very good friend Gertrude, better known as Mata Hari, and her Dance of the Seven Veils. The stage is decorated with billowing fabrics which enhance the mood of seductiveness and heighten the audience's anticipation. Gertrude always dances naked, yet through skilful manipulation of the veils she has never revealed a glimpse of her growler. That is, until tonight!

Something goes awfully awry with her timing! People swoon; children cry out in alarm, grown men shrivel, lights are dimmed. I chuckle and sip my Cognac calmly. I have, of course, seen it all before.

An apple juggler dressed as a medieval court jester on a unicycle is pushed on by the show's artistic director, a desperate effort to finish on a high. The orchestra increases tempo and strikes up a merry waltz. The audience, still distracted by the image of a fiery bush guarding the Promised Land, are only half-tempted back to the performance.

The artistic director, fearing for his reputation, somewhat misguidedly sets the wheel of the unicycle alight and throws a carrot, a rabbit and a small fox amongst the circulating Cox's Pippins. The carrot is hoping that the fox gets to the rabbit first.

Nature takes its course as it is wont to do. The carrot is swallowed by the rabbit which in turn is swallowed by the fox. This destroys the equilibrium of the orbiting apples and the juggler fails to catch the fox.

The fox lies momentarily stunned on the stage until suddenly its bushy tail is set alight by the burning wheel of the unicycle. Immediately it runs around the stage like a fox with its tail on fire, setting alight the curtains and various other stage props. The hippopotamus panics and stampedes, urinating wildly as it goes, causing its keeper to aquaplane across the stage like a drunken water-skier.

Rain dancers come on again, praying for a miraculous deluge to quell the blaze. The Riverdancers reappear, trying to put out the flames with their stamping feet.

The motor cycle display team wobble on, using pyramid formation in the hope of catching the fireball and, just when you think the whole thing is a total disaster, the fox runs to centre stage and explodes in a shower of glitter!

The entire ensemble suddenly breaks into a song and dance routine by Irving Berlin:

"There's NO business like SHOW business…"

The farce has been a charade! The artistic director has been in complete control throughout! It was all planned! Oh how he has played with – nay, toyed with our senses!

The audience roar their approval. I am overcome with joy; but an emotional lump in my throat hinders me from shouting "Bravo!" as loudly as I would wish. I yearn to embrace all the performers individually to demonstrate my appreciation of their efforts. I'm clapping with all my strength but somehow it doesn't seem to do them justice. What else can I do?

Bereft of other ideas, I kick off my shoes and now, wearing only my crotchless leopard skin jump-suit and a black satin shoulder cape, I dive from my balcony in an attempt to join the angelic Viennese Vegetable Orchestra on their cloud. I scythe through the mist of glitter that still rains down from the exploded fox, but I have miscalculated and am obliged to grab an angel's cucumber flute as I fall past the cloud towards the audience.

This acts as a temporary pendulum and I am swung in an arc towards the stage. I land across the shoulders of the chap at the apex of the motorcycle-powered human pyramid. However I am facing backwards and so my crotch is in his face and his beard is tickling my scrotum.

"Uncle Merridew!" I shout, without really knowing why.

The trapeze artist swings across and pulls me off the poor chap's face. She then drops me onto the upturned hippo and I cling to the thick pink flesh, gasping with relief.

"I love you all!" I cry, throwing my arms out wide to encompass everybody.

The crowd look on and gasp. Verily I am a sight to behold!

Silence.

Then the artistic director declares, "It's all part of the show, folks!" And the ensemble breaks into an encore:

"There's NO business like…"

READERS' BLOG:

- *Clearly the author is pushing the boundaries of his artistic licence.*
- *Apparently it's called 'pushing the envelope' these days.*
- *If that's the case, then I'm afraid that the corner of his envelope has become soggy and its contents have fallen into the gutter, to be swept away with the detritus of his many other failed literary works.*
- *I'm not convinced that a stampede can consist of only one animal.*
- *If I had been sitting behind the Grenadier Guard with a hindered view of the stage, I would have asked for a full refund of the ticket price; oh and complimentary ice cream.*
- *Yes. Hero or not, he should know better. Hats are a public nuisance and should not be tolerated.*
- *If I had a hat like that I would use it to smuggle my short-legged friend into the theatre. I would cut eyeholes in the fur so that she could see the show incognito.*
- *Ha! Your sub-hat friend would look like 'Cousin It' from the Addams Family!*
- *I think the authorities should be called in to inspect the hippo's faeces for signs of maltreatment.*

- *I knew a man with a beard once. But he could not ride a motorbike.*
- *To whom did the washing line of ladies underwear belong? Perhaps we'll never know!*
- *Surely if they can train a hippo to lie upside down they could have trained it not to crap everywhere!*
- *A few drunken monkeys with flame throwers would have livened things up a bit!*

SEND YOUR COMMENTS TO THE BLOG AT
www.planktonsoup.co.uk

PARADISE TOSSED

"Be careful what you wish for, you just might get it."

Seemingly such an innocent sentence on first reading. But slightly deeper consideration will soon make clear the dark, hidden undertones of foreboding. Look at the first two words...

"Be careful..."

...And there, there for all to see, who will see. The opening words are a warning! Not hidden in some kind of Huygens-style code, but clear and unmistakable.

Beware! Danger! Impending doom!

As I read those words now, they scream out loud their message, as obvious as the carbuncles on Satan's underbelly. So why, oh, forever why, did I not take heed?

I died in November 1963. My passing away went largely unnoticed by the rest of the world, they being more concerned about the recent death of a more popular man. Although, had he not died, my demise would still have attracted no more interest than otherwise.

Life had become agony for me. However, I was suffering from neither a degenerative disease nor a horrific injury. I suffered life.

Mother Nature had not blessed me as to physical appearance and so relationships with the opposite sex had been infrequent and short. My social skills were lacking in any kind of finesse and my professional achievements were none to speak of. In fact, a retrospective of my entire life would show that I had achieved nothing other than heaping mortal disappointment onto the shoulders of my disabled father who had raised me alone, my mother having died giving birth to me.

At the age of forty, facing the onset of a mid-life crisis, which I had previously assumed was already in full, malignant effect, I made the decision to put myself out of everybody's misery. And so, having considered all alternatives at my disposal, pertaining to my disposal I endeavoured to consume an overlarge quantity of alcohol and unprescribed medication, this being the path of least pain and preparation.

Upon completion of my last supper, I sat in my armchair, facing the door as this, I felt, would be the most civil position to welcome the person who first came to investigate my apparent disappearance.

I very quickly became drowsy and my mind fluttered like a wounded pheasant. In the wisdom of this delirium I became determined to change my casual dress for more formal apparel. It seemed that the solemn occasion demanded a sober outfit, although of course I was far from sober myself.

Consciousness was fading fast as I stumbled about my room, attempting to undress whilst at the same time seeking my brand new, rigid city shoes and pinstripe suit. Opening a drawer, I saw a nice red cravat that pleased my mood to the extent that I smiled at it stupidly and, next to it, an expensive ivory shoehorn. This luxury tool was the sum of my inheritance, bequeathed to me by my late grandmother. My last sensible thought before I entered irreversible slumber was that I would finally get to use it in donning my death shoes.

Consequently, I was found dead with my soiled underpants around my ankles, grasping the shoehorn, which, by commission of my broken-hearted grandmother, had been fashioned to resemble the rampant phallus of my grandfather, the missing, presumed eaten by cannibals, African explorer.

* * *

I remember death. I remember being surprised. I remember being disappointed. There was no journey, no light at the end of the tunnel. No fanfare, no pomp nor circumstance. I simply closed my eyes in one world and opened them in another.

In youth and early manhood I had rarely considered the existence of an afterlife, a heaven, a God. Of course, that all changed after the earthquake of '52 which, although barely reaching one on the Richter scale, was enough to set me on the path to contemplating my own mortality. It became an obsession and in truth, death stained my life. I became engulfed by a great melancholy. What was the meaning of life? Was it all worth it? And if so, why? Why?

We are led to believe by the two schools of thought that stand to gain by impressing their wills upon us, that there is an explanation. Let us humour them. Why was man put on this earth? He wasn't… a particular ferment of plankton soup was. This somehow developed into man. If the Bible in any form is to be believed, and God made man in his own image, then God is a plankton! And yet there are no fossilised discoveries demonstrating the transition from tadpole to man. We are then told that man descended from the apes. If this is true then God is an omnipotent silverback! I have even read somewhere that man shares the same DNA strand as the flying lemur! From what the scientists and theologists tell us, we can expect to spend eternity in some kind of zoo! Therefore, man as we know him, is nothing more than a quirky accident of nature and will be both unrecognisable and unwelcome in the home of his God.

In my later years as cynicism, bitterness, depression and lethargy set in, I no longer thought about the possibility of an afterlife. In fact I was quite resigned to accept eternal blackness, although, like the vast majority of worshippers of any religion, I always held on to that faint hope… just in case. The reality could not have shocked me more.

As soon as my eyelids had finally flickered their last flicker and remained open, there came an awesome, deafening voice that seemed to resound forever.

"WELCOME TO ETERNITY!" it boomed and I somehow felt rather than knew that the sentence had taken an Earth-time week to be spoken.

As I waited for it to finish, I had ample time to study my surroundings, although I did not seem able to take a step in any direction of the compass. I could merely turn my head to the left and right at full stretch. I was again disappointed.

The new world was pure white, mountainous and infinite, like an everlasting Antarctica, although not as cold. Indeed I felt very comfortable. There was not a single soul to be seen, except for my own. I looked down at myself and found that I was naked. More to my dismay though was the complete disappearance of my genitals, nipples and hair. I was almost formless. My once-blotchy skin had also turned white, no, more than white; a sort of blue-whiteness verging on translucency.

- *That's normally hard to achieve, especially on a low temperature wash.*
- *I always use the pre-wash setting and buy expensive two-in-one detergent. My husband loves the softener. He's entering middle age, so perhaps turning a little gay.*

I remained exactly in this predicament for one hundred years! During this phase, my memories were my only companions. But I realised that soon even these were dissipating as though this nothingness was a kind of cleansing process designed to purge me of all earthly senses. I felt as though my head was emptying itself into the surrounding wasteland and slowly, ever so slowly, a blissful peace began to glow within me as the initial frustration and disappointment I had felt was gently erased.

I gradually became aware that I was no longer alone. The colossus that towered quietly above me was of human form and as colourless and lacking in detail as I. The difference, though, was that the head was that of a male lion with an avalanche of pure white hair.

"Ah, you are ready!" growled the giant quietly. "At last your mind is pure enough to begin work."

"Hello." I managed a tremulous, jittered greeting.

"So you are the new unexpected addition to the afterlife. Couldn't you wait for your natural invitation?"

"Sorry?"

"And well you might be. I was not expecting you just yet. I was preparing for… oh never mind. What is your favourite colour?" he asked mildly irritated.

I struggled hard for a memory.

"Um, I vaguely remember quite liking maroon, especially for neckties."

"Hmm, interesting, I cannot remember the last time we had a maroon here," almost to himself. "What's your favourite food?"

"Well actually I'm… I was… partial to a bit of cheese."

"Oh do try to be a bit more imaginative! This is Have-Fun after all!"

"Have-Fun? Don't you mean Heaven?" I corrected.

"Young man, I have been here since eternity began; I should like to think I know where I am! As for Heaven, the gift of life on Earth is the closest thing to Heaven in the entire universe. There is nothing better. Nothing!" He sighed a giant, wistful sigh. "Ah well, must be getting to my next appointment. I shall call in on you again soon, adieu!"

As his presence faded, I heard him mutter into the ether, "Cheese indeed, tut-tut!"

I instantly had the sensation of cheese. The taste, the smell, was in and around me although there was none to be seen. And suddenly, my new world turned maroon!

I was able to distinguish detail only by the slightly differing hues of my chosen colour. For one hundred years more, I remained unable to move or escape from the never-changing view of maroon landscape, and, ever-present, the overpowering and nauseous sensations of cheese.

My situation mildly irritated me at first but soon

extreme discomfort and then desperation overtook me, this to such an extent that when I next felt the presence of the colossus, I begged him to change everything back to the original nothingness.

"You learn quickly for a stupid fellow," mused the giant. "Can you understand now the genius that created Earth and its myriad of colour? The detail; the tastes; the smells!"

But I hadn't learnt my lesson well enough.

"I don't care! Just get rid of that colour and that damned cheese!" I wailed.

"Very well, would you like to pick another colour?"

"Yes, yes! Something completely different. How about yellow?"

The giant smiled and shook his head in sympathy.

"Look, I shouldn't really do this but, as you're not such a bad chap, I will save you centuries of misery before you work through the entire rainbow. May I suggest the colour green?"

"Anything!" I pleaded.

"And food?"

"Caviar!"

"How about Caesar's victory platter or a banquet as portrayed by van Utrecht?" suggested the giant helpfully.

"Perhaps you're right."

"I know I am," said the fading giant.

"One more thing before you leave. Why can't I move? Where is everyone else?"

"My dear fellow, this is infinity. Where would you go? You could travel for millennia and not arrive anywhere. And the chance of meeting somebody is like finding a single grain of black sand in a desert of yellow. On Earth you had the opportunity to travel and meet people and yet you shunned these gifts. Now you see? Heaven is on Earth!"

The new world turned green and I tasted olives and red wine. It was a wonderful improvement on my earlier choice. The million shades of green gave more detail to the landscape making it quite beautiful and my mind picked out sensations of roasted duckling, strawberries and honey-bread.

I began to cry. I cried for the loss of sunshine on my face. I cried for the loss of freedom. I cried for the wasting of my life.

I must have cried for an entire century because my sobs were interrupted by the gentle soothing voice of my guardian.

"Something wrong?" he said, apparently finding it all mildly amusing.

"Oh, no, everything is perfect" I burbled sarcastically between sobs. "I thought you said this is Have-Fun! Well, guess what? I'm not having fun! Why can't I have different things every day? Why can't I meet people? Where are all the parties?"

"My little impatient friend," said the giant sadly. "When will you accept that this is eternity? Do you know how long that is? It is a million forevers, and then another million. And do you know what comes next? Another million! If you have everything at once you will soon be bored of this place, and then what?"

The colossal lion suddenly became serious. He bent down so that his face was close to mine and I saw that his eyes were black and fathomless.

"Look into my eyes," he said, "and tell me what you see."

"Nothing." I whispered.

"It is the infinite darkness that I exist in," he said, almost angrily. "I have never lived. Never experienced the fresh cool air of an autumn wind. Never watched a ladybird take rest on a rose petal. Never climbed a mountain or swam in an ocean. Never felt a woman's lips caress my skin and never watched my son grow to be a man."

He stood up to his full enormous height. "But the saddest thing of all," he said, "is neither have you."

If I had ever imagined that I cried before, it was as a single snow crystal in all the warm oceans of Atlantica, compared to the grief that I now released. I was broken. If it were possible for me to die again I should surely have done so through the agony of a broken heart.

It was some weeks later that my screams of anguish were interrupted by the awesome lion-thing.

"Would you like a change of scenery?" he said gently. "But be careful what you wish for, because you will have it for eternity."

"Oh, what's the use of a new colour?" I bleated. "It will never console me for what I have lost!"

The giant looked down at me without speaking for a long while and then said solemnly, "There is a way for you to return to Earth, my friend."

The shock cut through my grief like an electric arrow. At that moment I would have torn my eyes out for a second chance on Earth.

"I will do anything, anything, to go back!" I begged, tears still streaming down my face.

"But if I do this for you, what can you give in return?" mused the giant as if to himself.

213

"Name it and it shall be yours!" I said desperately, "I just wish I could give you my soul!"

Even from my lowly position I saw the flash in the black eyes of the monster. He tilted his great head back and roared so thunderously that the new world shook. I feared that I had angered him to the extent that he would instantly devour me! But soon the roar descended into an even more menacing sound. The sound of evil laughter.

"In all the history of mankind", growled the hideous creature, "yours has been the easiest!" and slowly he and the new world began to fade.

* * *

As usual, the most wonderful music could be heard in every corner of the palace of Heaven. The angel Mercury approached the Lord God who reclined in his glorious main chamber, being attended to by Cleopatra, Helen of Troy and their friends. Mercury halted at a respectful distance and politely cleared his throat. The Lord God clapped his hands and bade the ladies pause in their attentions.

"Ah! My dear Mercury, what can we do for you today?" he asked jovially.

"I'm afraid I bring bad news Lord. We've lost another one to The Beast."

"Oh? Anyone special?" enquired The Lord God as he leant back and was fed a grape by Aphrodite.

"Just another time-waster my Lord. He did not even pass the first temptation!"

The Lord God spat a grape pip out of the window and another UFO was seen hurtling through Earth's night sky.

"Oh well. It's his wish", he said indifferently.

* * *

My eyes opened as I reappeared back on my beloved Earth with the monster's laughter still ringing in my ears. I had got my wish but had lost my soul.

And thus it is my eternal punishment to spend the rest of forever as the only toilet brush in St Dympna's, an overcrowded but underfunded lunatic asylum in Verily-on-the-Cleft, where I am mistreated, misused and made subject to horrors unimaginable, to this very day.

Now and forever more, as my face is pounded time and time again into that small fetid pool, as I scrape through the ingrained mire of defecation on the stained enamel, I gasp for breath and die a thousand deaths, and know that it was all my own selfish fault. Too late, I have learnt my lesson well! How wonderful life on Earth can be and how foolish of anyone to wish it away.

READERS' BLOG:

- *So Satan is a white lion? I thought he was a red satyr!*
- *A white lion is supposed to symbolise Christianity. Sutton is playing with our minds. Either that or he hasn't done his research. Lazy git.*
- *Who the fuck is Huygens?*
- *Some ancient mathematician. If I was going to write a*

- *code I would use Red Indian language like they did in the War. That way nobody would ever crack my secret.*
- *Crack your secret? Oo-er! Sounds painful! But you would need a Red Indian to write the code for you, and then you would have to kill him because he knew what it meant.*
- *It's not allowed to kill Red Indians anymore. They are a protected species.*
- *Alan Turing was good at codes. He left a note on my windscreen once: "Don't park across my driveway again… you REKNAW"*
- *I would like to have sexual intercourse with Helen of Troy.*
- *I would choose Mercury. I hear he's got the six-pack thing going on.*
- *So the dead guy lost his nipples? Well, who needs them?*
- *My favourite colour is orange and my favourite meal is duck… à l'orange! Infinity? Bring it on!*
- *If man descended from apes, how come we still have apes? Why didn't they all change into men? In that case, how come we still have fish? Seems like Darwin was just guessing.*

HE MIGHT HAVE TO SELF-AMPUTATE BOTH ARMS!

WATCHING PAINT DRY

I look at the wallpaper. I stare at the wallpaper. My eyes burn into the very heart of it; into the structure of it; even down to its atomic level. I picture the gaps between the molecules and wonder how they will look an hour from now. The heavy coat of paint I have applied to the wall will eventually find its way between the molecules of the paper, then settle and dry.

It is hard to think of paper as being 'solid'; it's only a few microns thick. When wallpaper is wet you can very easily poke your finger through it as if it was a cloud of gas. It is equally hard to imagine that the paint will lose its liquidity and also become a solid. The miracle of physics; or would that be chemistry?

- *Miracle my hairy arse! I'm a top scientist and object to Sutton's suggestion that a divine being can alter the molecular structure of paint. It is simply an effect caused by the evaporation of the solvent that is present in paint to act as a vehicle for the dye or pigment. The dye itself is generally derived from a solid.*

I have noticed that some colours of paint change hue as they dry. Some that are dark when first applied slowly become lighter. A few others begin lighter when wet and darken as they dry… I can't think of an example at the moment, but it will come to me.

I find it strange that water makes a material darker. For example, if you spill some onto a yellow tablecloth the wet area of the cloth will be darker than the dry area. Now, bearing in mind that water is clear, translucent, see-through, why has it altered the colour of the cloth? Do you see what I mean?

I remember that 'colour' is experienced by the viewer according to the frequency of reflected vibrations when white light hits a surface. Colour is a specific vibration! I still don't get it. Ah well, as the saying goes: 'Ours is not to reason why, ours is but to do or dye'. Did you notice what I did there? I cleverly exchanged the word 'die' for 'dye'.

- *Get a life dude!*

The owners of the house have chosen a delightful shade of lilac for their bedroom. This more tasteful than the design of my previous clients who had chosen dark purple and lime green for theirs! They told me over a cup of coffee that they were into 'S & M'. I said that I didn't know Marks and Spencer did interior design. They looked at me funny and stressed "Swingers!" I think they were confused with 'B & Q', which *does* stock paint as well as garden swings.

- *What's he prattling on about?*
- *I'll tell you when you're old enough to understand.*

My attention is concentrated on the wall in front of me and, as I adjust my focus on a particular area, I am irritated to see that a bubble has formed in the centre of one of the strips of wallpaper. It is situated just above where the headboard of the bed will go, and once it is noticed it will become the focal point of the room.

The wet paint has highlighted a pre-existing fault in the original application of wallpaper paste. I am not responsible for this but am uncomfortably aware that the clients are likely to apportion blame to the present tradesman and not the original perpetrator of the inferior work.

I have an urge to burst the bubble or at least squash it flat, but that would smudge the paint. I may not be a master of my trade but I take enough pride and try to avoid smudges (also streaks, drips, brushstrokes and horsehair).

Bubbles in wallpaper are a hazard of the profession over which I can have no control. Oh… and flies! Sometimes flies land on the wet paint and get stuck, especially on glossed windowsills, the little bastards!

When I was an apprentice I simply painted over the flies as revenge for their vandalism. Nowadays I pick them off with tweezers and apply a fresh dab of gloss onto the disturbed surface. It's an indication of how far I have come with my anger management sessions.

I often wondered if it was the lead in the paint that was making me mad, like it did with the hatters many years ago in the old days. Or was it mercury they used? Why would they need mercury in hats? Why would they need lead? Who wants a heavy hat?

I guess if you lived in windy areas it would be a boon to have a sturdy hat. Or even the Japanese guy in that

James Bond film – the one where he was throwing his hat like a frisbee and if it hits you it really hurts. What was his name? Cato? No, no… ha! Doctor No! Not now Cato! Wait, that was Jacques Cousteau… No, he was the scuba diver dude… Scooby dooby doo… looking for clues… Cluedo… Clouseau, that's it! Inspector Clouseau… Cato was his sidekick… sidekick? His job was to attack Clouseau with karate kicks when he least expected it… funny job that… Oddjob! *That's* the Japanese guy who threw his hat at James Bond… Oddjob!

Actually, that's me too. I'm the odd-job man. I do garden clearance, change fuses, fix leaky taps, but not the mixer type – too complicated (I'm not a mixer fixer). I unclog clogged guttering, do repairs to the small panes of glass you get in greenhouses, and of course my main talent is painting.

I've got all the right tools. Scrapers, wire brushes for removing old paint (not for painting with – I use horsehair), various grades of sandpaper, a collection of old rags (some damp, some dry), one of those little rollers for getting behind radiators and, of course, a telescopic extension pole.

Again I wonder if I can reach the bubble from where I am lying, using the extension pole as an ad hoc lance? Nonsense! That would smudge the paint and I may not get a chance to repair the damage. After all, I have no way of knowing if this tingling in my arms is a good sign or a bad sign.

You're probably wondering why I have been staring at the paint for so long.

- *Not really.*

You wouldn't believe me if I told you. But seeing as I've nothing better to do I might as well.

- *Oh, go on then.*

A few hours ago I was stung on the back of my neck by a bumblebee and I fell off the stepladder. Now, due to a combination of anaphylactic shock, mild concussion and a paralysing back injury, I am unable to move from my position in the corner of the room. All I can do is stare at the wall that I have just finished painting and that damned bubble! Pure torture!

The funny thing is that the owners of the house have gone away for their summer holidays and won't return for two weeks, so I am in fact quite a prisoner. The paint will be dry as a bone by the time they get back and, perhaps, so will I.

Nothing more than a bag of bones… skull and bones… Jolly Roger… Davy Jones' Locker… so many men on a dead man's chest… treasure chest… silver coins. Silver! That's the colour I was trying to remember!

READERS' BLOG:

- *He should shout for help at the top of his voice. I expect he will have opened the window to allow for sufficient ventilation whilst using paint, as prescribed in most health and safety manuals. That's probably how the bee got in.*
- *Shouting loudly can be quite exhausting and may conspire to hasten his demise.*

- *If he times it right it will be more effective. For example, when the milkman comes.*
- *If the owners have gone on holiday they will have cancelled the milk delivery.*
- *What's the problem? If the tingling in his arms is a sign of returning circulation, it is only a matter of time before he can drag himself worm-like to the door and make good his escape. He should have developed good upper body strength from fixing leaky taps and painting shelves.*
- *I would describe his movement more akin to a butterfly dragging itself out of a chrysalis rather than a worm's longitudinal muscle contraction. And the act of escaping a newly-painted room could be compared to that of emerging from the cocoon.*
- *I'm sorry to say that the tingling probably signifies a restriction of blood flow due to his back injury. I suspect that, before long, gangrene will set in and he will feel obliged to self-amputate both arms using the paint scraper he claims to own, like in that movie 127 Hours. He may even have to drink his own urine.*
- *Davy Jones? Wasn't he in the sixties band The Monkees?*
- *Weird! Last week I met a guy in a gloomy basement underneath a house in Germany. Guess what? He said, "Ich bin Dave. Schpanken sie mein monci." Then things got really weird and I had to escape by pretending to have a rare fungal infection that required immediate treatment.*

AND HE KEPT IT IN
AN OILY RAG!

I am dictating this story from my hospital bed at St Dympna's Asylum with the kind help of my muscular nurse. My arms are locked to the bed with thick leather straps, but I must stress that I am very comfortable and have even signed an affidavit allowing the hospital to contain me in any way they see fit.

I understand that my behaviour has improved considerably and, providing that there are no further outbursts, I may soon be released back into society.

Telling this story is a desperate attempt to make some sense of the last few days. Please believe me when I tell you that this is a true story… although I think that I will never again be sure of the existence of truth. Perhaps there are many truths in this world. If so, this is one of them.

I had escaped my evil parents who were trying to force me into astronaut training school at Cumley-on-the-Mellow Space Centre.

- *Bastards!*

I knew there was more to life than that, so I hid myself in the long hair of a giant yak that was being taken to graze on the lush pastures in Downy Bottom Valley. After having journeyed for days, I eventually arrived at the legendary town of Verily-on-the-Cleft in search of adventure.

It was a warm summer's day and I had not a care in the world as I sat on a stone wall between the mosque and the cricket club, watching the comings and goings of the local inhabitants. There was a carnival atmosphere as sounds of laughing chatter from the nearby bain-marie factory mixed in the air with light-hearted keyboard music from the Belgian restaurant Flem.

My roving eye suddenly picked out a young girl who was struggling along with two heavy baskets of groceries. Being an adventurer, I summoned up the courage to approach her and offer assistance.

"May I help you with those?" I enquired.

She stopped in her tracks and looked up at me, startled.

"Eh? You what? Who the hell…?"

She spoke with a strange accent, sullen yet welcoming, I can't quite explain it. She blew her lank hair away from her dull eyes with a short blast from the corner of her mouth.

"Let me carry those for you," I repeated more slowly and pointed to the baskets.

She looked at me as if I were mad. I began to think she hadn't understood my language.

"Where do you come from?" I asked, using exaggerated facial expressions and hand gestures to assist translation.

"Tesco," she replied bluntly, cocking her head in the general direction of the supermarket.

"No, I mean *originally*."

She didn't answer for a moment or two and I was about to repeat the question.

"Far, far away," she suddenly whispered, with a faraway look in her eyes.

In her trance-like state she accidentally dropped one of her baskets and a couple of Granny Smith apples rolled across the pavement. As I bent down to pick them up, my necklace fell out of my shirt. My necklace held a golden nugget that reminded me, when viewed at a certain angle, of a scrotal sack. When the girl saw it, her demeanour changed completely, becoming immediately alert and focused on the swinging scrotum.

I held my hand out.

"Your apples," I said.

"Yes that's my nickname, how did you know?" she answered wide-eyed.

"No, I mean your apples have fallen out."

She touched my scrotal nugget to stop it swinging in the wind.

"It would appear that yours have too!" she said, putting my necklace back in my shirt.

Her fingers lingered on the scrotum longer than they needed to and I was a little embarrassed at the sudden electric atmosphere that had built up around us.

"What's *your* name?" she asked, actually seeming genuinely interested.

I put on my best secret agent voice:

"Snaigh," I said dramatically, "Adam Snaigh."

"Snaigh, that's an unusual name; is it from this hemisphere?" she asked.

"Er, I don't know about hemispheres, but my great-grandparents were Bulgarian cabaret artistes who migrated to this country during the great vaudeville famine that blighted Eastern Europe." I gulped for air after that sentence. "It's tempting to pronounce it as 'snake'," I added.

"Yes, I *am* tempted." she said meaningfully.

• *Oh, I can see where this is going.*

"Shall I walk you home?" I offered.

"Well I'm not really supposed to talk to anybody." She pouted her lips and looked down at the floor.

"Ah yes, parents," I said wisely. "My evil parents controlled my very existence to the point where there was *no* existence. A clean pair of underpants every day and no visitors after eight o'clock in my room. I'm thirty-six years old for God's sake!"

At the mention of God her face went whiter than alabaster and her jaw muscles clenched.

"I never knew my mother," she said quietly, "and my... father... abandoned me at an early age. I live with my guardian now, Mr Robinson. He's a sort of stepfather really."

"Do you get on well with him?"

"Most of the time, although he once burnt all my shoes to try and stop me escaping... um, I mean going out to buy apples. He's very protective of me but he allows me the freedom of the house and he stays in his study. So we lead quite separate lives. He's very strange; he has more than one personality."

"You mean he's crazy?"

"No, that's a misconception; he's very intelligent but in several different ways."

228

"Does he allow you to have boyfriends?" It was a many-faceted question designed to pave the way for the big one.

She stopped walking and I saw that tears were welling up and beginning to overflow down her cheeks.

"No one has yet found the key to my heart and it is *he* that keeps it hidden."

Sensing that this was my chance for adventure I quickly made up my mind.

"I'd like to meet this Mr Robinson and find that key," I said heroically.

She looked at me and gave me a sad smile that only served to strengthen my determination.

"It is a near impossible task and he will trick you at every turn," she said, resignedly.

I tried to sound light-hearted.

"Listen Apples; when a Snaigh tells you that everything will be fine, you can trust him with your life."

"Oh I trust *you* Mr 'Snake', but whatever you do, do not believe anything *he* says."

We suddenly arrived outside a stylish maisonette at the end of a cul-de-sac.

"Well, this is it," she said nervously. Whether she meant 'this is the house' or 'this is the start of the adventure' I could not tell.

"I'm ready!" I announced, bravely.

"Once you enter and begin the quest, your life will never be the same. Are you sure you are ready?"

I was drunk with adrenaline and high on confidence. The prize would be to win the heart of this girl; the arena was a simple maisonette and the opponent a grumpy stepfather.

"I'm completely sure!" I answered strongly.

Apples rang the doorbell, which was a standard ding-dong model. So far, so good; nothing to worry about yet. But then a huge shadow appeared behind the glass door panel and suddenly it was wrenched almost off its hinges as it swung inwards.

In the doorway stood a terrifying figure of a man! Almost seven feet tall with raven hair, dark blue eyes and short silver beard! He was dressed in a purple silk kimono which failed to reach his tanned and vigorously healthy knees. I could see that the legs were professionally epilated and oiled and he had small pieces of cotton wool between each of his toes. I was at once terrified, confused and slightly amused.

"This is Adam," said Apples almost threateningly. "He seeks the key to my heart but, in one way at least, he already has it, so treat him with care!"

My pulse raced. She is almost mine!

Mr Robinson glared at us with fury in his eyes but her words seemed to have had a curious effect on him. It was as if he held some kind of fear of me.

"Go to your room, Apples," he growled. "I shall attend to Mr... er?" He leant towards me and offered a huge hand.

"Snaigh, but please call me Adam," I said, feeling very insignificant under his intense gaze.

"Mr Snake... of course," he said slowly, as if rolling it around in his mind like a connoisseur of fine names. "You may call me Caruso."

"Thank you," I said, beginning to feel a little dizzy.

"Come into the vestibule and take off all your clothes," he said, stroking his immaculate beard. "I want to be sure."

I did as he suggested. It didn't occur to me to ask why. I was mesmerised by his strong aura, the sound of distant zither music and the aroma of rosewood smoke.

"There are many treasures here, but only one which you seek," he said, and then let the silk robe drop from his powerful shoulders. He was naked but thankfully, before I lost control of my manners and glanced down, he was already drifting, for he did indeed drift, through the door and into his study.

Awkward in my bareness, I followed at a respectful distance. Not knowing the correct etiquette for jiggling genitalia, I contemplated tucking them between my legs, but found in doing so I was unable to keep pace with my strange host. I let them jiggle.

To my astonishment we entered a vast secret garden, which was lush to the extent of being equatorial. We seemed to walk for hours and I saw, through the thick undergrowth, hidden doors which Caruso told me led to rooms within rooms within rooms. As we walked, he told me of the wondrous things contained in those secret chambers.

He told me that the largest room of all contained millions of special books. These formed the 'Dynion Paradox', a blueprint for the meaning of life but not of life itself. Each huge tome contained only reference numbers relating to individual and specific lessons. Each single lesson would fill a lifetime.

He described to me the 'Phobos Link' which, using its own energy, can propel a medium-sized man throughout the universe via a Yerkes-style tunnel system.

He pointed to another door behind which was a circular

room, containing in its full volume a minute segment taken from the outer circumference of the Cassini Division, the empty space between Saturn's rings.

The most secure room contained a tiny black gemstone.

"Trapped within the jewel is a frozen black hole," he told me, "captured at the moment of its birth. It is completely empty and if set free would devour the entire solar system within seconds. It is held in check by the flimsiest of fur jackets harvested from 1,000 bees. The fur of the bee is the only earthly substance immune to gravity."

Aha! That explains how such an ungainly blob of an insect defies the laws of aerodynamics!

The next was a room containing the secret of perpetual motion.

"Does it involve magnets?" I asked enthusiastically. "Is magnetism the secret?"

He almost laughed.

"It is infinitely simpler than that and yet impossible to understand."

At last we came to a beautiful wrought iron gate that led to corridor Omega 7. There was a photograph hanging above the entrance. In it Caruso was standing next to a dwarfish, but massively muscled, oriental warrior who was wearing a fearsome spiked gauntlet on his right hand and holding a bottle of whisky in the other. Caruso was smiling at the camera but the warrior's expression was fathomless as if the secrets of the universe were stored therein.

"That is my twin brother Ji, the guardian of the Silver Vial," said Caruso. "It contains the last remnants of the saliva of Eve, the sacred juice from which mankind as we know it was created. The saliva was scientifically swabbed from '*The*

Apple' by the giant lunar apes of old who came to Earth via the meteors which killed off the dinosaurs and then they built… ah but it's a long story, perhaps for another day.

The guardian is now heavily moustachioed and lives on a houseboat on the Yangtze, punting forever against the tide, destined to journey without end. His moustache is haunted by the ghosts of dead warriors from the Ancient Dragon Legions. Ji's facial hair has been responsible for the demise of many a greedy adventurer… and countless small stray dogs."

"In the days before his moustache, he was forced to rely on his gauntlet, great strength, and over-dramatic high kicks. The Hell-Dwarfs of Molybdenum nearly succeeded in obtaining the vial and destroying its contents, which legend foretells would lead to the eventual extinction of mankind, and so, Our Lord the All-Powerful, sent the moustache as a gift to assist Ji."

- *God sent a haunted moustache? Is that the best he can come up with?*

"Since the onset of facial hair there has been relative peace in the universe. However, dark forces are eternally seeking to bring about our decimation."

Caruso stopped at a dramatically ornate ebony box with heavy brass corners and looked at it thoughtfully.

"Would you like a biscuit?" he asked raising one eyebrow. His eyes pierced my soul.

"Er, thank you but no, sir, I prefer to snack on fruit. Apples and what have you."

He stared at me for an endless moment.

"Indeed," he seemed to snarl, and, turning his back on me, continued along the gilded corridor.

Seizing my chance I briefly lifted the lid of the ebony box and looked inside. I was disappointed to see an assortment of both dark and milk chocolate biscuits, but nothing resembling a key. A manic laughter filled my head and I quickly closed the box and hurried after the floating Caruso.

At last we came to the end of the corridor that then opened up into a magnificent altar room. The walls were cathedral-like and soared up to an immense height. The porcelain ceiling was painted a classical eggshell blue. In the centre of the room was what seemed to be a small and elaborately gilded coffin resting on a rancid old animal skin.

"This is the most important room in the garden," said Caruso proudly. "Here lies the last Fighting Swan of Parafango."

"I don't understand," I said frowning.

Caruso's glare softened slightly.

"I was once merely an adventurer like you," he began. "I was on a quest to find a suitable hiding place for… well, you will soon see… and I suddenly came to a great lake surrounded by wild forests. In the middle of the lake was a blue swan, the most beautiful thing I had ever set my eyes upon. At first I wanted to catch it as a trophy but the longer that I watched its serene majesty, the more I grew to love it and eventually I shouted a promise across the lake that I would never again kill a living thing."

"My shout disturbed the evil beasts of the forest and soon a black shape emerged from the trees. The giant warthog attacked me, knocking me to the ground and, although not badly wounded, I was rendered defenceless. Then, with a thrust of his monstrous snout, I was thrown into a bed of evil daffodils from which I could not self-extricate. I was at the mercy of the sabre-like tusks of the hog and also the deadly pollen from the poisonous yellow flowers. Suddenly there was a gust of wind and a shrill cry. From out of the sky came the blue swan and it landed on the back of the warthog. The two creatures fought for hours until, after succumbing to a fatal peck in the eye, the warthog breathed its final, rancid breath."

Caruso pointed at the black pigskin underneath the coffin.

"But the blue swan had also been dealt a mortal blow and with its last reserves of energy it made its way to some reeds at the water's edge. It beckoned me to follow and, with my help, laid an egg."

Caruso opened the lid of the coffin and carefully lifted out the delicate object.

"And here it is in an oily rag," he said, unfolding the material to display a sky blue egg.

He held it out to me and indicated with a slight nod of his head that I should take it from him. Hesitantly I reached forward but somehow the egg slipped from my grasp and, as it fell to the ground, I cried out in despair…

"Don't let it fall! It will smash on the floor and all shall be lost but for a pool of albumen and the last Fighting Swan of Parafango will have fought to the death in vain!"

Of course the egg had smashed long before I finished the sentence. I could barely bring myself to look down at the fragments. I expected a tirade of violent abuse from Caruso but there was silence. His face held a strange expression as he bent down to examine the debris of shell.

"I'm so, so sorry," I said in my sincerest voice.

"The egg is of no consequence," he said matter-of-factly. "*This*, however, is vital to the future of Mankind."

He held up a steel implement, dripping with albumen. To my untrained eye it looked like a surgical rib-separator.

"*This* is the key to my daughter's heart!" he cried suddenly. "Now let us see if you are truly worthy of it!"

He lunged at me using the strange implement in a sabre-like manner but, through years of being bullied at school, college, university and home, I had developed the skill of lunge avoidance.

"Good!" he encouraged. "Good, very good!"

His cries became more demented with each unsuccessful lunge.

"Ha! Yah! Bravo! Ye gods! Oh babushka, mein liebling!"

• *The guy's demented!*

As I retreated back into the corridor, I was hindered by a small walnut table that carried an assortment of curiosities. In desperation I picked up a brass bowl full of sand and threw the contents in the direction of Caruso's blazing eyes.

"Not the Myriad Crystals of Reality!" he roared, and then roared louder, this time in pain as the sand began to sting his eyes.

Whilst he was engaged in the throes of eye agony, I managed to wrestle the surgical tool from his weakened grip. Apples suddenly appeared by my side, and seeing that I had possession of the steel tool, she tore her dress open revealing her bosom and a thin red scar in her ribcage.

"Find my heart!" she cried passionately.

Gritting my teeth I plunged the steel into the red scar tissue.

Her ribcage opened easily and inside there was a golden band encasing her heart. There was a strange groove in the band, the shape of which was vaguely familiar.

"Your nugget!" she gasped "*That* is the key to my heart!"

"I wondered why you were so interested in my scrotum."

"Turn it upside down! It's not a scrotum you fool, it's a heart!"

I looked at my nugget and immediately I understood.

Caruso floated down from the ceiling, having sprouted some kind of mosquito wing affair between his shoulders. He seemed to be experiencing constant transmogrification.

"Behold!" he cried in a thin voice, "I am Zantac, demon protector of the caged heart."

"Mr Robinson please calm down. Zantac is some kind of ulcer medicine, not a demon. Now, I'm going to put my nugget in your daughter's niche and then we're going to call the relevant authorities," I said, trying to maintain my sanity.

"Pah! The world is not ready for the truth!" hissed the giant insect that had once been my future father-in-law. "The dark evil one will soon walk amongst us! When the pagan giants of Thrall sink to their knees in prayer, when Emperor Krog's monolithic fortress collapses like a rotten tree, He will come!"

"When the Mighty Zarg cry like lambs and the noble Wharl-Quog beg for mercy, He will come!"

"When the mighty mountain range of Zambalu shivers in fear, when the awesome cliffs of Skajka crumble into the ocean, He will come!"

"When So-lar falls from the sky and eternal darkness descends, when the earth's molten core rises up to burn and devour all, He will come!"

"When all hope is lost and the celestial gods of Astraluna forsake us in our moment of need, when Zorgon the Proud bows in defeat and gives over his sword, He will come! His vengeance will be instant and final and His name shall be... and His name shall be..."

"Well actually his first name is Clive," Caruso said, almost apologetically, but then recovered and shouted, "but nevertheless prepare to meet thy terrible doom!"

He snarled and tried to swim through the air towards me but he was getting weaker by the moment. His frail wings could not flap fast enough to keep him elevated. Now he was on his hands and knees looking up at us. His eyes had become eggshell blue like the ceiling in the altar room. His voice was now soft like the downy hair on a young angel's top lip.

"The Myriad Crystals of Reality have returned me to my true self; for that I owe you this warning. Do not use your scrotum to win my daughter's heart. Things are not what they seem and you will regret for eternity what you are about to do."

I was not inclined to listen to him, even after all I had seen, and wrenched the chain from my neck.

"My scrotum is no longer any concern of yours, Mr Robinson!" I shouted as I crossed the room and thrust the golden heart into the groove on the band.

"Noooooo!" cried Caruso, as if his world was coming to an end.

With the heart-shaped nugget in place, the gold band

fell away from her heart and suddenly the room was filled with soft white light, the smell of summer evenings and some kind of pink violin sang in the air.

She walked towards me through the veil of light and I saw that her hair had become long and lustrous and her now big, green eyes shone like fresh gemstones in a Babylonian firework display. The scar had disappeared and so had Caruso Robinson.

We embraced and tears of joy ran down her cheeks. I was breathless with emotion.

"Well at least now you should tell me your real name," I said.

"Haven't you guessed it yet?" she asked mischievously.

An idea flashed into my head and felt goose pimples rise to the size of very small garden peas.

"Are you… are you… Eve?" I said with awe.

She lowered her eyes and blushed.

"I am Eve," she said quietly, then without looking up she added slowly, "I am the Eve of final destruction!"

I blinked stupidly, not sure if I'd heard correctly.

She leant towards me and whispered in my ear, "I am known to the ancient ones as… The Dark Evil One."

"C… C… Clive?" I stuttered. Suddenly there was a great explosion and I was hurled upwards towards the porcelain roof.

When I regained consciousness I was in Verily-on-the-Cleft General Hospital. A detective was waiting by my bed to ask questions. I told him about the girl, Caruso Robinson, the secret rooms, the swan, the biscuits and the golden scrotum key. I did not mention Clive. I still could not believe that one so beautiful could be so potentially evil.

The detective wrote everything down and, thanking me, went out to speak to the nurse. I heard him recommending she should call Professor Mountebank at St Dympna's Lunatic Asylum.

I sprang from my bed and joined them in the corridor.

"But what about the girl, what happened to her?" I demanded.

"I'm afraid your story doesn't add up," said the detective. "We found you at the derelict site where the old Adamson place used to be. There hasn't been anyone or anything living there for years. You stepped on an unstable pocket of marsh gas and 'whoosh', up you went. There was certainly nobody else involved. Now come on Mr Snake, back to bed with you until the padded wagon gets here."

I began to plod resignedly back to my bed when it hit me (the truth, not the padded wagon).

I ran back to the doorway and shouted excitedly, "Did you say the Adamson place? Don't you get it? Adam-son... son of God, married to Eve! Add that together with all the references about apples, plus my name, Snaigh or snake and... you see? It all fits!"

* *"I knew it!"*

Mr Snake, are you really trying to tell me that the Garden of Eden is in a cul-de-sac in Verily-on-the-Cleft?" said the detective sceptically.

"Go to the Yangtze River! Find the guardian of the Silver Vial, he'll tell you everything for a bottle of whisky! All the secrets of the universe! Japanese-type guy, metal glove... but watch out for the moustache, it'll have your throat out!"

240

I ranted, trying to avoid the hypodermic needle that the nurse was trying to plunge into my shoulder.

Of course nobody listened and so, here I am. My tablets are working and I'm beginning to think that it was all some kind of hallucination caused by inhaling a toxic yak hair.

But you know something? Having had this opportunity to tell my story in its entirety, I'm actually feeling a whole lot better…

…Hold on there's something on the news… What's that? An earthquake in the west, volcano in the east? Unseasonable rains in Central Europe? Drought in northern Britain? Nurse! Warn the world! Look out for Clive! Do you hear me? Tell them Clive is coming! No, not the needle again!"

READERS' BLOG:

- *I find it unlikely that any death-dealing demon of doom would be called Clive. Should be something beginning with 'Z', or even 'V'. Those are evil letters.*
- *The author should not be so specific in his choice of apples. His clumsy reference to Granny Smith as being the apple of preference to the Dark Evil One may have an adverse effect on future product sales.*
- *Bulgarian cabaret artistes? Name one!*
- *Houdini?*
- *Hungarian.*
- *Charles Bronson?*
- *Lithuanian for fuck's sake, and anyway he wasn't a cabaret artiste, he was an actor.*

- *So, this 'Ji' fellow is guarding us against the dark forces of the universe whilst punting up the Yangtze? I'd like to shake his un-gauntleted hand!*
- *I've heard that all swans belong to the Queen of England. If that's true she will be livid when she finds out about the dropped egg. Fancy keeping something like that in an oily rag!*
- *I have never seen her feeding bread to the swans.*
- *She shouldn't do that. Swans are renowned for breaking people's arms.*
- *It's no use crying over spilt milk... I mean albumen.*

AN INTERVIEW WITH THE DEITY FORMERLY KNOWN AS GOD

Scene 1. Recording studio of independent television company.

Studio announcer (dramatic voice): "And here's your host, no it's not the Holy Ghost, it's… Jeremy Bile!"

(Audience applaud, some shout "whoop-whoop!" like the Americans do)

- *I hate those wannabe American nerds!*
- *Me too. Especially the ones who, upon greeting their local barista say, "Can I get a cappuccino" instead of "Can I have…" They are the ultimate douchebags!*

Jeremy Bile appears at the top of some steps at the back of the stage, pausing with his arms outstretched as if surprised and humbled at the warm studio welcome. He milks it for a few moments longer before descending and taking his place in front of camera number one.

"Wow! What a great audience! I wish we could have

you lot every week! Thank you ladies and gentlemen, and anybody who doesn't fall into either of those categories."

(Mild titters ripple through the crowd. But they are hoping for better material as the show goes on.)

"My goodness, have we got a show for you tonight!"

(Bile pretends to look for the producer.)

"Have we got a show for them tonight?" he jokes.

(More gentle tittering.)

"I'm just kidding with you. But seriously folks, we really do have something special on the show. Tonight's guest needs no introduction, however I will make one anyway. He's been known by many names over the past millennia, but since his retirement he has reverted to his original… please give a big studio welcome to the deity formerly known as God, yes it's… Walter!"

(Audience roar their approval.)

God-Walter enters stage left. He is seven feet tall and built like Thor. In fact, he looks a bit like a WWE wrestler.

The studio chair groans under his muscular weight.

Bile waits for everyone to settle before beginning.

"Firstly, sir, may I say what a pleasure it is to have you on the show."

"Thank you for inviting me," replies God-Walter graciously.

"I've been a great admirer of yours for many years now," snivels Bile.

"Oh? You've seen all my work?"

"Well, you were very prolific at the height of your career but I have seen many of your displays and exhibitions."

"Nah, I fucked up! Over in the next universe…"

"Ho, ho! I'm sorry Walter, this is a family show! Don't

244

forget the kiddies! Maybe we can bleep over that before we release it to the viewers at home."

"Sorry about that Jeremy. As I was saying, over in the next universe they exist in a constant state of sexual climax."

- *A lot of X's in that sentence!*
- *Bah! Just my rotten luck to miss out on that universe!*

(Having softened Walter up, Bile goes for the jugular.)

"So anyway, what's all this about a virgin birth?"

The audience hold their breath, anticipating a dramatic reaction.

"It's all true!" Walter answers, unperturbed, as if he knew the question was coming.

"But surely…"

"Don't call me Shirley! Just kidding! It *had* to be a virgin birth. The very girth of my penis renders coitus with an earthling impossible!"

(Whistles and jeers of kudos erupt from the audience. More idiotic whoop-whoops are let out.)

Walter plays to the audience by wiggling his eyebrows in a suggestive manner and flexing his pectoral muscles. Then he continues.

"So the only way to do it was by artificial insemination. No jiggery-pokery involved. I sent Gabriel to Earth armed with a vial of my heavenly juices and a turkey baster."

- *Sutton is obsessed with bodily secretions! If I were a psychiatrist I would diagnose his condition as chronic deviancy due to working in a Turkish sauna as a child laundry assistant.*

245

Having set the trap, Bile brings on more victims.

"Let's invite the other heroes of the story to come on stage. Please welcome Jesus, Mary and Joseph!"

(Parts of the audience cheer, some just clap politely.)

"And I'd also like you to welcome our surprise guest, the angel Gabriel!"

(Audience start to murmur. It is now obvious that there is something terribly wrong. History needs to be rewritten! There will be blood on the streets!)

• *Not the first time religion has caused genocide.*

"Jesus, you've grown up in the belief that Walter was your father and Joseph was your stepfather. You're here to confront Walter and ask why you were forsaken."

(Bile turns to Joseph.)

"Joseph, you're here today to confront Mary and you have requested a paternity test."

More uneasy murmuring from the audience.

"I have here an envelope with the results of a DNA test."

The studio falls silent as Bile makes a big drama of opening the envelope. Then he looks at the camera as he reads out the result.

"Walter…" (Bile pauses for effect), "you are *not*, I repeat *not*, the biological father of Jesus!"

Walter jumps up and kicks his chair. The audience gasp, scream and swoon.

"I knew it! Lies, all lies!"

Walter tries to grab Joseph's throat but the studio security guards hold him back.

"So she wasn't a virgin after all?" Walter thunders.

"I never touched her!" pleads Joseph.

Walter and Joseph look at Mary.

"Then how…?"

"I'm sorry guys. I thought I was just following some miraculous heavenly plan!" she said, equally confused.

Joseph storms off stage and perhaps leaves the studio. No one knows for sure. Just as he did in the Bible, Joseph completely disappears from the story.

Bile turns the screw.

"Gabriel, you are here today because you wanted to tell Walter something?"

Gabriel takes a deep breath. He has been preparing for this moment for two thousand years but still feels hesitant. He clears his throat.

"Yes Jeremy. It's about the vial of life essence. On that fateful day, the twenty-fifth of March, in the year zero B.C., I stopped off at a gas station for a coffee. When I came back from the loo, my handbag was missing. I didn't want to say anything at the time, I was so embarrassed."

"So how did Mary get pregnant?" cajoles Bile.

"Well, I managed to replace the lost 'juice of life' with um… mine!"

Audience members gasp, scream and faint (as opposed to swoon which is more temporary). Someone says, "Oh my God!" and another actually says "OMG!"

Camera two zooms in on Walter's face, then Mary, then Jesus. A split screen then shows the uncanny likeness between Jesus and Gabriel. Blue eyes and blond hair!

Bile has more surprises up his sleeve.

"And here's the guy that stole the handbag. Ladies

247

and gentlemen, boys and girls, please give a warm studio welcome to… Satan!"

Satan comes on twirling his seventies-era, German porn star moustache. Audience hiss and boo.

Bile tries to lighten the mood.

"So, the Devil wears red spandex?"

"Indeed I do! Mwa-ha-haaa!"

Walter tries to break free from the guards to get at Satan but they are too strong and Bile suggests they take him backstage to cool down and have a brief chat with a counsellor from social services. Perhaps a coffee and a biscuit.

- *If he is the God from the Old Testament he could do with some anger management sessions thrown in.*
- *And ask him why foreskins aren't allowed in Heaven!*

Bile takes up a thoughtful stance in front of his new guest.

"So, Satan… why?" A clever question, delivered with cutting brevity.

Satan shrugs dramatically and pushes his chewing gum to the side of his mouth before answering.

"I'm just trying to make my own way through life. If I can spread a bit of misery and pestilence as I go, so much the better!"

Audience boo again and someone shouts, "Asshole!" Satan gives them the finger.

"Yes, you morons, I created the great Flock and Soul swindle! Mwa-ha-haaa!"

As the show turns into a chaotic melee, much to the delight of the production team, Bile faces the camera to do his closing summary.

"Well, so much for that lot. As my grandmother used to say, 'You should never trust an Arab.' I didn't understand what she meant until today. She's dead now so you can't prosecute her for racism.

Anyway, be sure to tune in next week when our guests will be members of the so-called British royal family and Major James Hewitt. Will there be surprises in store for one or all of them on the show? See you next time!"

The audience erupt into raptures of hero worship and blind adoration for Bile. They have already forgotten the poor unfortunates on stage.

The producer calls his wife and tells her to put the kettle on as he will be home soon.

"How was the show?" she asks.

"Same old, same old," he replies.

READERS' BLOG:

- *I was disappointed to hear about the use of a turkey baster. Surely a moment so divine would warrant a pipette?*
- *I wonder what happened to the original vial of heavenly juice? Perhaps we'll never know.*
- *I notice God-Walter refers to us as earthlings. I knew he was an alien!*
- *Eros the Xenos!*
- *I thought all this would have been sorted out by now; up in Heaven or wherever they all went at the end of the Bible.*
- *I am becoming alarmed at the change in Sutton's writing style. This was more a script than a short story. Before long we may have to suffer a screenplay by him and his inane drivel will be on our TV screens.*

- *Not a chance in hell! I am the Archbishop of Canterbury and object in the strongest possible terms to Sutton's blasphemous farce. I shall be sending some ecumenical roughnecks around to pay Sutton a visit and then let's see who's laughing when he's had his tongue cut out and his shins tenderised by baseball bats.*
- *Just a minute! I really am the Archbishop of Canterbury and the previous imposter should be ashamed of him/herself. Sutton has some valid points here and, I must confess, my faith is rattled.*
- *If I were Satan I would not go around in red spandex. I would try to be a little bit more discreet whilst carrying out my dark administrations.*
- *Who leaves their handbag on the table when they go to the loo? If it were my juice I would sue Gabriel for negligence. He needs his wings clipping! And his testes!*
- *Bile makes me sick!*
- *The big problem is… if Joseph is not the real father, then Jesus is not a descendant of the line of David. Therefore he is not the King of the Jews and any modern-day Royals claiming a bloodline connection à la The Da Vinci Code are merely charlatans and hoodwinkers!*
- *Sutton is making a statement about how society has turned its back on religion and now worships celebrity status. He is very clever and probably well on his way to fame and fortune. Therefore I will accept a pipette of his juice anytime.*

ME AND THE CAPTAIN

- *Sutton's poor grammar is immediately evident. The title should read, 'The Captain and I'.*
- *But you weren't on the ship… were you?*
- *Classic comedy banter!*

I'm incredibly famous. You've most probably heard of me. I'm the 'very young man' mentioned in the book *The Time Machine* by H.G. Wells. Can't quite place me? You're squinting your eyes, trying to remember who I am? Well that's exactly my point; I'm tired of being the minor character in the background! Now I've decided to have a little excitement of my own, so off to sea I jolly well go! And like all good maritime adventurers, I shall keep a journal of the voyage. What follows are some selected highlights of my greatest adventure!

Day 21: We received word today that HMS *Beagle* with the lunatic Darwin aboard has left England in search of finch and tortoise. Fools! What can they hope to achieve?

We are already three weeks ahead of them. Three weeks since, with a firm jaw like a sperm whale and buttocks tightly clenched like the lips of a pufferfish against the ingress of water (ingress of anything!) I boarded the *Flying Dutchman* and we set sail for the East.

The next day, having recognised the mistake and losing some of the crew to a whorehouse in Amsterdam, we set sail for the West.

I think the Captain likes me. We are getting along famously. He has given me full and free access to his extensive library collection, although to date I have only found books by King and Rowling. This is my idea of hell. Their formulaic writing vomits forth a seemingly endless spew of nonsense but I soldier on (or should I say sailor on) diplomatically. Flying fish are a constant source of amusement to me. "See how they fly!" I cry.

Day 30: Are the oceans a magnet for imbeciles? (Discounting us, of course!). We sighted a sail on the horizon and, eager for news and a change of company, we headed that way.

"*Santa Maria*! Bloody Spanish!" shouted the Captain, when he saw their flag through his telescope. "How can we drink and make merry with them? The ignorant scoundrels cannot speak a word of the Queen's English."

It soon became apparent that the *Santa Maria* had some educated men aboard and I was invited to peruse the papers and scientific notes of a Mister Columbus and his colleagues. It seemed to me that they were trying to reach India but some kind of sixth sense told me they were hopelessly lost. I am no expert navigator, being merely an adventurous journalist for the cutting-edge science magazine *The Wonder of Coal*, but I felt sure that India lay to the east.

"Buffoons!" the Captain winked at me as he waved

them in the wrong direction. How we laughed as they sailed ahead of us towards the setting sun.

We set a slightly more northerly course than the Spaniards so that they would not vent their anger upon us when discovering we had misled them.

Day 33: We nearly crashed into a small boat during the night. The Captain ordered grappling hooks to be thrown and our crew boarded the *Mary Celeste* and made prisoners of the other crew. The captured crew asked could they finish their supper first but we said, "No, come on!"

They reluctantly agreed to replace the crew we had lost in Amsterdam. Captain said it was a win-win situation. Original crew were tucked up in bed with prostitutes, and the new crew came complete with a decent cook (despite being of dusky origin) called Timothy. The Jamaican already had ideas above his station and his first words upon seeing the galley were,

"For God's sake! I need more money if I'm to make Moules Marinière!"

But which gods do his sort of people pray to?

Day 34: Dolphins are following us and play gleefully in our wake. They seem to smile at us as they arch through the air and dip back into the ocean. What wonderful companions they make! A fair wind blows spray off the surface of the sea and, thanks to the glorious sunshine and the wonders of nature, there is a rainbow in every wave!

Day 45: Doldrums are giving me the doldrums (that's funny). We were hoping to find land before now to replenish our water and food. In desperation the Captain discharged a small cannon at a flock of seagulls. Timothy

255

the new cook picked the biggest that fell to the deck and proclaimed, "Soup for all!"

Day 46: Timothy is blackballed, and I'm not being racist. The bosun claims that the seagull was in fact an albatross and, now that we have all supped at its juices (delicious by the way) we have the curse of the Ancient Mariner hanging over us. The Captain, however, is oblivious to his crime and made a joke, "Waiter, there's an albatross in my soup!" which we in the officers' mess laughed at quite heartily until we heard of the unrest below decks.

Naturally, me and the Captain…

- *The Captain and I, for God's sake!*

…are of educated minds and so not at all prone to superstitious fancy. Therefore we are fully confident that the curse is nonsense and no harm will come to us during this voyage.

Day 47: A giant squid has attached itself to the bow of the ship and its tentacles have ensnared some previously able-bodied seamen (now grotesquely *dis*abled-bodied). Their screams are most horrifying. I wish them a speedy death so that the rest of us can get some sleep.

The dolphins' enigmatic smiles now reek of schadenfreude and I regret having thrown them some stale bread in a show of friendship. They are in fact vicious, two-faced bastards.

Day 48: Giant narwhal leapt out of the sea and tore a hole in our mainsail. We are now at the mercy of the elements. What further disaster can possibly befall us?

Day 49: The ship's monkey has eaten the last box of

cheese crackers… and all the cigars. Quelle misfortune! As I prepare for bed I hope for better news tomorrow.

Day 50: We are being drawn inexorably into a maelstrom! The swirling cauldron of angry water seems determined to suck us down to the bowels of the earth, perhaps all the way to Hell!

I had a 'eureka' moment. I suddenly recalled that I am aboard to report about the new wonder fuel – coal – and its potential to provide steam power to the ship. The ship has an engine! I pointed this out to the Captain who initially discounted the idea but then reluctantly agreed to give this new hocus-pocus a try.

With a great roar and not inconsiderable vibration, the engine erupted into life and lo! We are moved slowly away from the ravenous lips of the violent whirlpool. Those of the crew not engaged in frantic shovelling of coal gave a huge cheer. We are safe at last!

Day 51: We are being chased by bloodthirsty, sex-starved, cannibalistic pirates! For fuck's sake!

Day 52: Luckily for us we have blundered into the Bermuda Triangle. The pirates seem to have given up the chase, as if afraid to enter this area. But it is surely a myth and what more could happen to us? Surely the gods have had their fun!

Day 53: By the mysterious powers of the Triangle we have been transported to the city of Calcutta, circa 1756.

Day 54: Now in Beirut, circa 1980.

Day 55: Now in Benghazi, circa 1944.

Day 56: Now in Pompeii, circa A.D.79.

Day 57: Now in Hiroshima circa 1945.

Day 58: Now in the England of 2112 and have washed

ashore in the middle of Bradford high street. Oh, the absolute misery!

Day 59: Finally our ship emerges from The Triangle and we sail on to who knows where. The crew are muttering under their (rancid) breaths. There is no toilet paper left on board. The discomfort is manifesting as surly expressions on their already grizzled and haggard faeces... I mean faces!

For once I celebrate the rambling excess of pages by Stephen King; the paper will now come in very handy! No more discomfort for our rear ends.

Day 60: We have been rammed astern by a certain Nemo in his weird underwater craft *Nautilus*, and we are slowly sinking. Ever the gentleman, Nemo waves his silk handkerchief in our direction and shouts, "Sorry chaps!" but offers no assistance. Surely this is against maritime rules!

Day 61: The good ship *Titanic* sent a distress message but we had troubles of our own, desperately trying to reach land before we went under. At least we have plenty of rum.

Day 62: No rum! There were stowaways in the rum barrels. The Swiss Family Robinson in fact.

Day 63: Land Ho! Hooray! We arrive at an island inhabited by curious beings. Dr Moreau and his hairy half-beasts, Dog-Face and Furball greet us at the beach.

Their welcome was polite yet formal and we somehow feel like unwanted intruders.

We handed over the Swiss Family Robinson as payment for Dr Moreau's hospitality and his eyes lit up as if it were Christmas. He locked them in his surgery and stayed with them all night.

Day 64: The Doctor is three sheets to the wind. He has had a taste of his own medicines, in particular those containing methanol. He ran about bare-footed shouting, "I've done it! I've done it!"

We were left to fend for ourselves and eventually dined on dodo, salamander and beetle. Dr Moreau was apoplectic and claimed they were respectively an old friend, a distant cousin and his local tobacconist! We have realised too late that Moreau is a maniac vivisectionist. He turns people into animals! The Swiss Family Robinson have succumbed to his clumsy scalpel and now roam the island as abhorrent creatures. No more rum for them!

Day 65: The Doctor is now running about totally naked and we see he has fitted himself with the penis of a... a... could it be a rhinoceros? But why, oh why has he given himself the anus of a baboon?

We are in fear of our lives and so, in the interests of health and safety, the Chief Mate ran him through with a cutlass. We buried the Doctor on the beach and The Captain said a few words. However, I did not feel they were particularly relevant to the sombre occasion.

"A man with no shoes is easily defeated, but that's why the Chinese Boxer rebellion was so unexpected; they wore flip-flops made of rice paper! The Albanian navy never impressed me either... their footwear was made from cardboard!"

And with the Captain's bizarre eulogy ringing in our ears, we returned to the ship.

Day 66: On the next island we discovered a strange form of brown fruit that grows underground. When viewed at a certain angle many of the specimens vaguely resemble the shape of human reproductive organs, affording a minor but welcome distraction from the boredom of daily ship's duties. The flesh is white and hard. The taste is faintly earthy.

The Chief Engineer has discovered that, when dropped into the furnace, the fruit becomes soft and fluffy and is a delight with butter and grated cheese or tuna and mayonnaise.

One of the deck hands has managed to make a potent brew from the hard fruit, somewhat like strong gin. I congratulate him on his experimentation. After weeks of misery, the sky is blue and the atmosphere aboard ship is one of optimism.

Day 71: The fog! A dense curtain of rancid mist envelops the ship and invades our nostrils. We can barely breathe and so confine ourselves to our respective cabins. But the fog is alive with murderous qualities and throughout the night terrifying screams are heard.

Day 72: We awake to find the fog has gone… but so have most of the crew! Dried pools of blood serve as grim clues to their mysterious fate. The Captain is apoplectic and accuses us of murder! We are all locked in the brig and he threatens to hang us from the yardarm. We are sure we can convince the authorities of our innocence if we stick together. The camaraderie of the seafarer is legendary.

Day 73: I awake alone. The cell door swings to and fro with the rolling of the waves. The remaining crew have deserted the ship and now only me and the Captain are left aboard.

* *(All readers in unison) The Captain and I!*

The Captain orders me to work. I must cook for him and clean the decks. I carry out the duties of the full crew –

alone. He has stopped calling me Mister Marlowe and now addresses me simply (if at all) as Marlowe. I am exhausted by the end of the day and vow never to seek adventure again! Tomorrow I shall hide from the Captain's wrath.

Day 74: The Captain has fashioned a weapon of sorts and is prowling the ship with menace in his eyes. He has set bear traps around the ship and covered them with leaves.

He emitted an unusual auditory night signal. But to who? To who?

- *Ha ha! Bravo Sutton! Owl sounds disguised as hypothetical questions. Genius!*

I have found his journal. It chills me to the core.

Captain's log.

Day 1: "We have set sail."

Day 2: "Where the fuck are we?"

Then, dozens of empty pages until…

"Day? Only Hell knows! Matters outstanding: Kill Marlowe!"

I hear him approaching, I am trapped! I hunt frantically for a weapon with which to defend myself.

As he enters the cabin I drop from the ceiling and crush his skull with Stephen King's *The Dark Tower* (hardback edition).

* * *

Day 1: Voices around me. Water splashed onto my face (I hope it is water!). I awake to find I have killed the ship's monkey with a Bible. Somehow it is only the first day of our voyage! It seems that I have been delirious with seasickness since the first moment I set foot on deck! Ah, but dear reader, thanks to the time-leap experience of the Bermuda Triangle, does this mean the events that I have recorded here have never truly happened? Was it a dream or is it true? If dreams exist are they not real? And isn't reality the truth?

READERS' BLOG:

- *I don't understand the questions!*
- *I would be prepared to overlook the serious anachronisms if only the story were any good.*
- *Anachronisms don't count… the guy is a friend of the time traveller from the book The Time Machine by Orson Welles.*
- *H.G. Wells, you pleb!*
- *Who is Orson then?*
- *Orson was the alien boss in the seventies TV series Mork and Mindy.*
- *Fuck the aliens!*
- *When I got to the page about 'the doldrums' I was shouting at the Captain to use the engine but he didn't seem to hear me.*
- *That's because he is in the story and so exists in your past. You are reading the story and thus you are in his future. You are both connected only in the present… and only when you read the story. It's a bit like Schrödinger's Cat. It only exists if you open the box and look at it. Unlike some quantum particle behaviour which only exists when NOT observed.*
- *Oh, you mean quarks.*
- *Yes.*
- *Imbecile! Schrödinger's experiment asked if the cat in the*

box was dead or alive. It most certainly did exist because he put it in the box himself.

- Why has the man in the story got a beef against Stephen King? King had to write as much as possible because that mad woman was going to sledgehammer his feet.

- If I was a famous scientist I would have my assistant handle any small mammals. Cats make me sneeze, whether they are in a box or not. And I would ask the assistant if the cat is dead or not, which in turn would nullify the famous philosophical quandary.

- Doesn't anyone know that Orson Welles starred in Citizen Kane? Probably the best film ever!

- Bullshit… Jungle Book was better!

- I very much doubt you would 'run someone through' with a cutlass… they were designed for hacking and general swashbuckling. Now, a sabre on the other hand…

- Yawn! Sorry to interrupt, but is the above reader going to list all types of swords and their respective uses? The moderators should block him, and any other would-be sword enthusiasts for that matter.

- It was Sir Walter Raleigh who first brought potatoes to England. The stupid bastard!

- If it's only 'Day 1' the young man should get off the ship in Amsterdam with the rest of the crew, like at the beginning of the story.

- If he does that then the story never happened and these pages will become blank… and maybe even we readers will never have existed!

- But I've just bought a season ticket for the Arsenal!

SEND YOUR COMMENTS TO THE BLOG AT
www.planktonsoup.co.uk

PROBLEMS WITH A MECHANICAL FLANGE, LEMON SOAP AND AN UNWATCHED KETTLE

Well, as you can imagine, I had to laugh. There I was, trying to teach a three-legged rhinoceros how to peel a banana, when in came the boss on an antique motorbike, dressed as panto's Mother Goose, shaking a giant tambourine and shouting in a defunct Uzbek dialect, "You're all fired, now get your coats and sling your respective hooks!"

And that's basically how I ended up inventing the Mechanical Flange.

* *I fail to see the connection.*

For want of nothing better to do, I converted my garage into a workshop and started inventing. I had one of those original 'bubble cars' but the underbelly link sprocket had capitulated long ago and where do you get a spare one of those these days? So the car was pushed into a corner, of which there are many as it is an octagonal garage. It was designed in 1963 to house the spaceships of the future, although why the architects of the sixties imagined that the scientists of this century would design octagonal spaceships is perhaps due to the effects of LSD, which everybody had in those dark, bygone days.

The rest of the garage space contained a workbench, some old lawn mowers, of which I'm an avid collector, jars of insects (I'm an aphid collector), sandbags containing dry sandy earth (I'm an arid collector), canisters of various volatile liquids (I'm an acid collector) and a single dead spider (I'm not an arachnid collector)…

- *He's gone too far with this joke now!*
- *Yes. Comic timing is a technique not easily acquired.*

…old repair manuals for extinct vacuum cleaners, jars of assorted screws and nuts and, the pride of my collection, a box of bits from a Chinese spy satellite that had crashed to Earth in the Orkney Islands, killing my grandfather and one of his sheep in the explosion.

He and the rather attractive sheep had mysteriously disappeared from the family farm earlier that week. We never did get to the bottom of it.

(Compulsory aside – "I bet your grandfather did!" Sound effect – brushed cymbals.)

I then embarked on the planning phase of my project. Weeks of diagrams and notes later I was ready to start construction of what I imagined would be the greatest scientific development of this century. I locked the doors of the workshop and spent the next three weeks screwing, riveting and grinding until I was totally exhausted.

(Compulsory aside – "Oo-er missus!" Sound effect – trombone slide.)

The sculptured piece of engineering that now stood before me was similar to the H.G. Wells time machine, but this machine would not perform such mundane and irrelevant work, this was a mechanical flange! Nay, *the* Mechanical Flange!

In order to operate the flange successfully, the 'pilot' was to position him/herself at the control panel. Then, having donned a special infrared reflecting face shield, he was to place a coin (preferably 'of the realm') into the relevant slot. The weight of the coin depressed a pressure plate, so connecting a circuit which then set the machine in motion. A wire-wound electric dynamo motor was activated and this turned a lever to push down on a kettle switch. The kettle eventually boiled and the rising steam turned a set of turbine fans. The vertical torque was converted to horizontal by means of angled cogs. The torque power was then momentarily stored in a steel spring until the pressure reached a critical level. At a measured, precise moment, a safety catch would release, throwing a pivoted wooden mallet clockwise, causing it to strike the initiator of the main flange assembly. The flange would thus be initiated. Once the flange had completed its process, the machine could be reset simply by refilling the kettle.

The whole project had taken me nearly two months to complete and it was only then, as I stood admiring my work, sweating and exhausted, dressed only in a flame retardant G-string, that I realised I had eaten nothing but toilet paper for the last few days. I collapsed onto a hessian sack containing thousands of rubber washers and spare rubber fan belts for vacuum cleaners of every hue and denomination.

My head was spinning through lack of sustenance and I remembered something about the press-ganged sailors two hundred years ago needing vitamin C to ward off scurvy. I cast my eyes around the garage and saw a bar of soap on the small sink unit. The packet said 'lemon zest'. I devoured it like a mad man and collapsed back onto my sack.

(Compulsory aside – "Sounds painful!" Sound effect – two blasts of a duck whistle.)

As I stared in wonder at the mechanical flange, an irritating flea of doubt gnawed distantly at my sense of accomplishment.

How shiny was the flange! Ah, but how powerful!

How well oiled its joints and pivots! Ah, but how ready to strike at any moment!

How quiet and efficient the flanging process! Ah, but how silent and deadly the assassin wearing fur booties!

How pretty the spinning sails of the turbine fans! Ah, but how ugly the intentions of those who would get their hands on my flange.

(Compulsory aside – "Larry Grayson looks at the camera and sucks his cheeks in." Suggested sound effect – broken spring/canned laughter.)

See how the black shiny frame resembles that of an alien spider intent on destroying all in its path.

See how the glistening lubricants ooze like the poisonous slime on the back of a rabid toad.

See how the teeth of the master cog are actually those of an evil clown who hides, smiling in the dark, waiting for his chance to rip your heart out while you sleep!

The machine is watching, waiting. It is smiling, secretly planning. It is evil and must be destroyed! I staggered to my feet, retching soapy bubbles.

"What are you doing Alfie?" asked the machine in a strong metallic Chinese accent.

• *He's got that idea from 2001:A Space Odyssey!*

"Who's Alfie?" I burped, lemon slime dribbling down my chin.

"You are Alfie Noakes."

• *He's got that idea from 'Derek and Clive'!*

"I'm not Alfie Noakes! I'm…" another burp of citrus bile.

I staggered over to the workbench and reached for a thermos canister that contained two litres of spare rocket propellant for the spy satellite. Clutching it in one hand, I lunged forward towards the kettle on the flange initiator.

"You are opening a whole can of worms, Spartacus!" warned the Flange.

"I'm *not* Spartacus!" I hissed through gritted teeth as I opened the flask and poured the propellant into the kettle. I emptied a jar of screws onto the worktop and scrabbled around in the contents to see if there was a coin. I found a brass token, which was a souvenir from a seaside arcade I had been to as a child. My favourite game had been 'Explosion of the Alien Spider Death Machines'.

"How apt," I thought.

"I'm going to destroy you!" I vowed through a mouth full of lemon foam.

"You are powerless! Pathetic! Plankton! In fact most things beginning with P!" snarled the Flange.

"I'm not a plankton, I'm a human being!" I cried triumphantly, as I placed the token into the coin slot and fell back to watch the destruction of the Flange. (Maniacal mechanical Chinese laughter.)

"When the kettle boils, the propellant will explode with such force that we will both cease to exist… along with most of your neighbours within a mile radius!" (More insane laughter).

With horror I realised the Flange was right. What had I done? Had I set in motion an unstoppable deadly force? Wait! There was a way to stop it! Humans have one advantage over digital machines… the ability to talk and think nonsensical hogwash! Old wives' tales! I remembered one. 'A watched kettle never boils.'

* * *

Now here I lie, staring at the kettle, praying that my concentration will prevent it from boiling and that I am able to save countless lives, including my own. My eyeballs feel as if they are on fire and tears are streaming down my cheeks. I don't know if I can carry on much longer without blinking. Surely someone will come to try and find me sooner rather than later. The milkman hasn't been paid for weeks; he will arrive any moment now.

I am trying to remember the ignition point for rocket propellant. Will the ageing and badly scaled element in the old kettle manage to reach that temperature?

Meanwhile a tendril from the Flange is snaking its way behind me. Formed from the telescopic radio aerial of the Chinese satellite, it is about to tap me on the shoulder and break my concentration. Startled, I will look round in surprise just in time to hear the Flange say,

"OK, before we die, please tell me who you are. Are you Jesus? Can I come to Heaven with you?"

AMAZING INTERACTIVE SECTION!
HOW WILL THIS STORY END? IT'S UP TO YOU!

1. Will the kettle boil now that I have glanced away?
2. Will the milkman arrive in time to switch off the kettle?
3. Will there be a power outage due to a marauding plague of armadillos?
4. Will the machine discover that the coin was not legal tender and cancel the transaction?
5. Will the Flange develop a conscience that prevents it from self-destructing?
6. Will the Higgs boson particle intervene to maintain the status quo of cosmic anti-matter?

YOU DECIDE!

Roll the dice that was not included with this book!

IN WHICH I DO BATTLE AGAINST A SILVER BLUE DEMONIC GNU WITH IRIDESCENT LIME GREEN EYES IN A CUPBOARD UNDER THE STAIRS

It is a bright summer's day; a perfect day. Everything is as it should be.

Outside, the children are playing in the quiet, sunny park. I hear the ice cream van approaching and the delighted squeals as the children rush to greet it.

The Gnu, sensing that my concentration has wandered, charges like a bull in a Spanish street. I somersault over its monstrous head and feel its hot breath like poisonous steam on my skin. The Gnu crashes into a set of bagpipes that are hanging in the corner of this cupboard. A slight moan in the key of 'A minor' (the saddest of all keys) escapes the bag.

I see in my mind's eye that the pivot pin has fallen out of the ice cream dispenser. The ice cream man bends to try to find the pin but it has rolled underneath the driver's seat and is irretrievable. Whilst he reaches around for the pin, his other hand is trying to stem the incessant flow of ice cream that is gushing from the spout.

I feel the ice cream pouring into the sleeve of his pink uniform. I feel the hot flush of embarrassment on the face of the ice cream man as he tries to hide from the world, crouching below the serving hatch.

He cannot face the customers through his embarrassment, but if he doesn't stand up soon he will drown in vanilla. (Ah well, worse things happen at sea!). The customers cast heavenward glances. This is not the first time something like this has happened. They are becoming weary of his inefficient ice cream dispensing methods.

The Gnu is rearing up on its colossal hind legs and, with its downward hammer blow like Mjolnir of Thor, it hopes to smite me asunder. At the last moment, I cartwheel to the left and the muscular hooves (yes, somehow they are muscular) get entangled in the weave of a plastic wash basket.

I see the fat man further down the street who has been sleeping in an awkward position which has affected the blood flow to his lower body. I see him jump out of bed to awaken his dead leg, only to find that the other leg is also dead and he collapses, pulling down the curtains and causing the bedside lampshade to ignite on the bulb.

The lamp burns a tarantula that has been placed there by a ninja who got the idea from a James Bond movie and not from his official training manual. This is incorrect procedure for which he will be severely reprimanded, if not fired. He has already been warned about this. Why does he persist with these extravagant ideas?

The Gnu is charging like a steam train, its head held

low with which to crush me against the ironing board into splinters of cosmic energy. I dodge the clumsy monster easily and have time to collect my thoughts as his gaze once again locks with mine.

I see the dear old lady carry her shopping home and start to unpack.

She has a sad look on her face as she begins to prepare dinner for her husband. Only she and her husband will eat, now that their son has moved away. I see her add ingredients to the meal that could trigger a heart attack if someone were to have such an allergy. She misses her son since he left after declaring his love for another man. The husband is ambivalent to the situation and continues to watch his John Wayne movie in black and white.

The Gnu bares its vicious teeth (oh yes, they have vicious teeth; you didn't know?) and tries to sever the life force from my physical being. But I am far too quick and am already behind him as the massive jaws snap together with a compressive finality befitting the gates of Hades.

I see a kettle full of rocket fuel approaching critical boiling point. The creator of the Flange lies helpless on a sack of rubber spares. If he thinks I have time to intervene he is very much mistaken, given my own current prickly circumstance.

I know why the ice cream man is a nervous wreck.

I know why the ninja wants to kill the vacuum cleaner salesman.

I know why the old lady 'lost' her son and what revenge she seeks.

I know that the fate of the Flange lies in the roll of a dice.

How do I know these things? How can I fit inside a cupboard with a demonic Gnu? Because I am omnipresent of course!

All matter is made of molecules, all molecules contain atoms, all atoms… all everything, contains… me! God made man in his own image. The essence of mankind is the particle he is made of.

I am the God particle. Some call me The Higgs boson, although I admit I am very disappointed with this name. Why not Alpha or Genesis or just plain God? Higgs boson for crying out loud!

I am at one with the universe.

I am at one with nature.

I am at one with mankind.

I am at one with tables and chairs and other contemporary furniture.

The God Particle!

They are looking for me in Switzerland but here I am in this cupboard under the stairs of a three-bedroomed house in Cumley-on-the-Mellow, fighting for the preservation of the universe against the silver blue Gnu with iridescent lime green eyes.

READERS' BLOG:

- *How can eyes be lime green and yet iridescent simultaneously?*
- *It is a supernatural beast so anything is possible.*
- *I find it highly doubtful that a giant Gnu can fit into a cupboard.*

- *Well, the Higgs boson is tiny so there should be plenty of room left over.*
- *You shouldn't keep bagpipes in cupboards where a cosmic struggle is likely to unfold. They may become damaged and out of tune.*

"THE RIPPER HAS STRUCK AGAIN!"

THE SECRET SOCIETY

To whom it may concern,

I am a Semi-Tendril belonging to the Orifice of Secret Knowledge. I have been a member for twenty years. My name is of no consequence but my senior position within the society should satisfy the reader that this document is indeed authentic.

I was on the verge of becoming the assistant to the Grand Tendril, but I have been rudely overlooked, left dangling in the wind; and another Semi-Tendril was chosen instead. Consequently, I am disgruntled and my revenge will take the form of full disclosure in this document of the Society's mysterious ways.

- *A nice, succinct introduction. The situation is clear and I am in a good position to read on with confidence.*

We are the guardians of the most secret of secrets; the secrets that nobody knows exist. We are not concerned with religious secrets like the Vatican, nor of political power and worldwide domination of banking cartels like the Bilderbergs. Neither are we involved in sleazy deals, backhanders, nods and winks like the Masons.

- *Sutton is sticking his neck out and risking libel action. The Masons have friends in high places.*
- *Talking of high places, are the Royals actually descendants of the lizard people, as proposed by the respected scientist, David Icke?*

We know of the secret truths that really matter. For example, do you know what light really is? Does it move or is it transference of energy through molecules and, if so, how is it powered? Ha-ha! Your answers amuse me. However, back to the story… I mean disclosure.

The Orifice of Secret Knowledge was formed centuries ago by the immortal Master Tendril. You ask his name? I have already stated that names are of no consequence. Names mattered little to the great Tendril of Tendrils. However, for the purpose of this disclosure I will call him 'Z'.

- *Hmm, Zachariah, Zebedee, Zeus, Zanzibar, Zebra?*

No, it stands for Zarathustra. Doh! Confound it! That was supposed to be a secret!

(Grand Tendril's voice: "That's exactly why you weren't promoted!")

Anyway, 'Z' was a man of incredible wisdom; a man who saw the truth behind the lies, indeed he saw the truth behind the truth. After centuries, the weight of knowledge soon became too much for him to bear alone and so he searched for an assistant.

- *Tell me. Was Sherlock Holmes unable to catch Jack the Ripper because they were actually one and the same person? I notice they were never in the same room at the same time!*

- *Fool! Any fool knows (except you) that Sherlock was real but the Ripper was fictional!*

Please! Enough of this nonsense! Don't you want to know about the Pyramids? How they were built? Wouldn't you like to know about the systems that were designed using rivers of mercury, electromagnetism and ionisation?

Do you know why they built three pyramids? To mirror the stars! If you could mirror the stars my friends, oh what wonders you would see here on Earth! To vibrate with the stars, to oscillate… is to live!

- *That's as maybe, but did Hitler really only have one bollock?*

(Sigh). Those who seek the truth are likely to use it for personal gain. We recruit only those who seek nothing for themselves. Most of our members are picked from those who know their rightful place in the world and are content with it. Contentment and tranquillity are states of godliness. Ambition and desire are the roots of evil.

- *Which reminds me, The Rothschilds, what IS their fucking problem? Quite apart from all the other shit they get up to, my gran said they wrote that book… The Protocols of the Elders of Zion. She's dead now so they can't sue her for libel.*

Eventually Z found the perfect assistant he needed, working in the field of scientific medical research. This person had no desire for fame or fortune. Z recruited her and gave her the code name Mrs D.

- *Doubtfire! Was it Mrs Doubtfire?*

No, no! The name is part of an ingenious secret code that was devised by Z. The lady's real name begins with C, so to encode it we use the next letter of the alphabet which, by a complicated extrapolation technique, results in the letter D. We could quite easily have called Madame Curie Mrs X on account of her work with X-rays but she felt it too sinister; consequently Madame Curie became Mrs D. Curses! I have blurted out another member's name!

(Grand Tendril's voice: "Have no doubt, you're fired!")

Groan! At the outset of this disclosure I had only intended to reveal the existence of the society and its secret workings. I had no wish to announce the names of its members. However, it is too late and now my life is in danger. The Society will seek revenge.

In the event of my murder it will be beneficial for the police to interview all members to help identify the killer. Now I shall name them all simply to protect myself.

There is no 'A' as such due to our coding method. If anyone were to be Mr A it would be 'Z' as he is the alpha male. He is the Tendril of Tendrils. He is also the known as the Big Hairy Root Ball.

- *Good grief!*

Mr B is Abraham Lincoln, where the 'B' stands for beard, black and Booth (as in the assassin John Wilkes). It's cheating

I know as Mr Lincoln should be Mr M. But that title has gone to Dr David Livingstone where the 'M' stands for the missionary position he held for years.

- *Impressive! My husband can't last three minutes!*

The 'M' also stands for Malawi, Moffat, malaria and mud hut.

Mr C is Alexander Graham Bell. The 'C' stands for communication, cable, cell phone, call waiting, crap signal, cut off.

Mrs D has already been discussed. The 'D' could stand for danger or depleted uranium as Curie worked with radiation.

Mr E is Sir Arthur Conan Doyle. Mister E= Mystery!

- *Ask him about Jack the Ripper!*

Mr F is Albert Einstein. Although he developed the theory $E=MC^2$, he is not Mr E, 'M' or 'C'. In physics 'F' stands for force which would be more appropriate for Isaac Newton but he is Mr O which is quite fitting as the 'O' could represent an orb which in turn resembles an apple. However, in the case of Einstein, 'F' stands for funny face.

- *Oh dear! It's all getting rather complicated!*

Mr G is...

The narrator continues to list the members of the society in alphabetical order. Meanwhile, outside in the dark, foggy London street, two shadows approach his house. Shadows of evil intent. Shadows that have not yet been named on the list.

Once inside, they climb the stairs to the narrator's office. Their movements are smooth and swift…

- *Smooth, swift movements? Sounds like diarrhoea. They should eat some dry bread!*
- *Or crackers.*

…and the blades of their surgical knives gleam in the dim light that escapes from underneath the office door. They can hear the voice of the narrator as he lists the secret names.

Mr S is Rasputin. The 'S' stands for sorcery and seduction. Mr T is… Oh, but excuse me, I have forgotten the 'R'.

The 'R' stands for Royal and Regina. She alone is known by her title rather than her name, so of course, Mrs R is her majesty the Qu…

* * *

After the slaughter, Mrs R and Mr T (Titled and Typhoid) walk hand in hand towards their home at the end of The Mall.

"It seems we were just in time, your Majesty," says Albert.

"Yes indeed we were, Mr Saxe-Coburg. Good knife-work by the way," says Victoria.

"Likewise," says the Prince Consort.

In the distance, a police whistle rings out urgently through the foggy Whitechapel streets.

"Jack the Ripper has struck again!" cries the shocked policeman as he turns away in disgust from the mutilated body of the narrator.

READERS' BLOG:

- Ho, ho! How ironic! Whilst attempting to name all the members in order to protect himself, the narrator failed and has met his gruesome death. However, the unnamed assailants have inadvertently revealed themselves through the medium of the story that he was narrating before being killed!
- I am a pedant and insist on denying an author artistic licence. None of it makes sense. Some of these people could not have been members of a secret society at the same time as each other and, more importantly, the narrator could not have completed the story if he was killed halfway through it.
- So who is writing this?
- "Mwa-ha –haaa!" (The ghost of Mr X flies into the night.)
- Ah, so the X means ex-Writer, ex-pired, ex-ecuted.
- Ex-actly!
- Who killed JFK: the CIA or the Mafia?
- Who cares? I am more concerned with the Roswell aliens.
- Fuck the aliens!
- Have the Chinese dug a network of tunnels under the Pacific so they can invade America?
- Did we really go to the Moon? If it was just a movie why didn't they use Bruce Willis instead of that other guy? He was so wooden! What a douche!
- Hold the front page! I just heard that Queen Elizabeth I actually had a cock!

WINDOW TO THE WORLD
(What's on a Man's Mind)

I have suffered a great depression all winter. My room, in the attic space of an old monastery, afforded me little comfort in the way of cheer. Staring out from the small window at the near monotone and featureless coastal view had triggered a psychological malaise. The sky was grey, the sea was grey, (well actually it was almost brown) and the beach was terribly bleak and empty. Mentally desolate, I confined myself to my bed, much like my hero Proust.

- *Hardly. Proust spent fifteen years in bed!*

I lie day after day, watching the raindrops hurl themselves against the glass and sometimes it seemed it would shatter from the force. I half-expected it to implode in a spray of shards, sharp angles of window and soft round shapes of rain. Sometimes the rain was gentle and there was no wind, so that the drops would just appear on the glass without sound then gradually slide down, collecting others on the way. It was quite hypnotic and mind-cleansing.

As usual with my bouts of depression it went on far too

long. So long in fact that I became temporarily lame. Fearing for my long-term physical and mental health, I summoned the strength to lift my head from the pillow. Banging my cranium on the partition wall using Morse code, which I mastered after some trial and error (mostly error and many misunderstandings), I eventually convinced my neighbour I needed help. Actually with hindsight, the wall is so thin I could have shouted the message.

My neighbour, Mungawa, is a fully-trained and certified witch doctor who has travelled the seven seas in a watertight wigwam made from the discarded sealskin sou'westers of historic seamen such as Magellan and Drake. Due to cultural upheavals he had left his island home, which was situated somewhere between Polynesia and Africa where, tragically, the introduction of the potato had had an adverse effect on cannibalism as far as Mungawa was concerned.

He claims to be a seventh dan shaman in the mystical art of alternative therapy. I told him of my condition and he attached some vibrating magnets to my legs, then lit some incense and dangled a fake amethyst from a string. (I think he found it on the beach. Probably a fragmented wine bottle that has been ground smooth by wave and sand).

Nevertheless it worked and now, as I look down from my window, it is early spring and life outside seems to be stirring once more. I am desperate for sensory input after my self-inflicted incarceration.

I have a fresh and eager interest about everything. I set my mind free and let it dash from thought to thought like a pirate with a new treasure trove map and wonder where it will lead me. I become aware that the minutiae of life can be extrapolated in thought. Associated subjects flood into my brain, uninvited but welcome… and the whole known universe opens in my mind like a pop-up reference book. I remember reading somewhere that if you know seven people, then their connections could lead to 'knowing' everyone in the world. I wonder if it's the same with topics.

For example, there is a book on the windowsill about seashells. I look at it and let my mind wander. Apart from the word 'shell' itself conjuring up an image of a bomb, the shape and construction of a shell tempts me to think of ears and, strangely (please excuse me) a woman's vagina!

- *"Why specify woman's vagina? It's not as if men have them."*
- *"I could tell you a few stories!"* (Harley Street surgeon's voice).

The paper pages of the book lead my thoughts to the manufacturing process. Paper is made from pulped wood. Wood from trees. Forestry and land management, environmental issues, Brazilian rain forests. I almost veer off into regrettable thoughts of Brazilian bikini wax and deforestation of vaginal hair, and thankfully do a complete U-turn at Brazilian lady-boys!

The ink on the pages leads my mind through modern printing processes, ancient clay tablets, Egyptology, hieroglyphics, ink, paint, and this now splits into two trains of thought.

First train. The Renaissance, art and sculpture… Now don't get me started on art. The *Mona Lisa*. What's that all about? What is the big deal? Apart from the fact it was painted by a genius, it's not outstanding. And neither is she smiling; it's an optical illusion created by the shading of the corner of her mouth. Nothing enigmatic about it. It's all in the viewer's imagination. *The Laughing Cavalier* is much more lifelike but he is definitely not laughing, merely smiling, albeit his smile is more obvious then Ms. Lisa's. Van Gogh? I'm sorry but his paintings are simply dire. The colour of vomit. *The Execution of Lady Jane Grey* by Delaroche is far superior to any aforementioned.

And what about the sculpture of *David* that people rave over? "Oh, he's beautiful!" they drool. Just a minute, look again! He's got massive hands! They are way out of proportion to the rest of him. However, in Michelangelo's defence, *The Pieta* is stunning. And what's going on with all those paintings and sculptures of naked women? You can sometimes see their vaginas! Ah but I've gone off at a tangent...

Second train of thought... ink, blue paint, blue dye, Tuareg natives in the Sahara, blue ink, tattoos, Maoris and Aborigines, Australia, criminals, weird animals, British Empire, colonialism, slavery, America. Ah! America! Columbus discovered the West Indies, not America per se. Aztecs, Inuit Eskimos, at least fifty indigenous tribes of 'Indians' and the Vikings were there long before Columbus blundered his way over. Thor Heyerdahl sailing in his bamboo raft Kon-Tiki (not sure about the bamboo, where would Vikings get bamboo?) deserves more praise.

- *Buffoon! Thor sailed away from South America in a craft of balsawood construction and it was nothing to do with Vikings. He was demonstrating the possibilities of migration to Polynesia.*

290

Columbus, navigation, flat Earth theory, mysteries of the cosmos, destruction of the Library of Alexandria by Christians, history rewritten, truths hidden, The Bible, Vatican hiding truth about Jesus. Jesus was married (?), Holy Grail rumoured to be Mary Magdalene's… (God forgive me)… vagina. Navigation of the globe? Wooden masts? Phallic symbols? Peaks and troughs? Virgins? Holy Grail? Da Vinci Code? Uh oh, Chongo! Women's vaginas!

• *He's gone mental!*

Je regarde la mer. I regard the sea and think about the tide. They say that the tide is influenced or controlled by the Moon. The Moon? But there's no gravity on the Moon! How can it be that the 'gravitational' pull of the Moon affects the tides? If it can pull an ocean there must be some pretty strong gravity! It only enforces the belief that Americans did not land on the Moon all those years ago… before mobile phones, laptops, satellite navigation, microwave ovens, they went to the Moon? No way, we just didn't have the technology in those days. That's why there's no more Moon trips… because the rest of the world now has the technology to monitor exactly where the rockets are going. Rockets, phallus. If the rocket is the phallic symbol then when the rocket enters space does that symbolise entering the vagina? Moon? Rockets? Space? Black holes? Vaginas!

Newton 'discovered' 'gravity'. But all he actually did was invent a name for something that was already there. He also had something to do with refraction of light and prisms. Just like the Pink Floyd album cover on 'Dark Side of the Moon'. Moon, gravity, Newton, apple, Eve, original sin. What exactly was the sin? Talking to the snake? Eating the apple? Becoming aware of nakedness? Adam suddenly becoming aware that Eve had a vagina and (to coin a Biblical phrase) 'it was good'? Therefore it follows: Newton? Physics? Forbidden fruit? A woman's vagina.

There is a seagull atop the lamppost outside my window; facing into a gale, stubbornly refusing to fall over despite its spindly legs, seemingly not even having to brace itself against the wind. The ratio of body mass to leg strength is surprising considering the disproportion of its design. Why doesn't it find shelter behind a wall? What is the lifespan of a seagull? I've never seen an old one. What is the average wingspan? Is it the optimum ratio for efficient aerodynamics? How does this ratio correspond to the flying ability of bumblebees?

What is the wingspan of man? Da Vinci's Vitruvian Man demonstrates the natural span of man using the 'Golden Section' or 'Divine Proportion'. However, Leonardo da Vinci realised the ratio must be altered to achieve flight. He devised an 'Ornithopter', a framework to be worn on the upper body which accommodated giant wings. He also designed a prototype helicopter. The designs were unsuccessful but the design of the bumblebee is equally irrational. It just doesn't make any sense. And the equation is further complicated when the bee's hairy legs are fully laden with pollen!

Daedalus created wings for himself and his son Icarus using wax to attach the feathers. When Icarus flew too high the wax melted. I wonder if it was beeswax? Waxing again… bikini wax! Oh no! Greek mythology? Aerodynamics? Bees? Hairy legs? Honey? Vagina!

Another academic concerned with the Golden Section

was Fibonacci who devised a mathematical sequence to describe and predict numeric values. This sequence can be found in nature as spiral shapes such as a simple snail shell. Shells again! Mathematics? Spirals? Concentric circles, tunnel vision, tunnel of love, love tunnel, it's inevitable. Vaginas.

Jimmy the builder is driving a tractor on the beach, smoothing sand that has been displaced by bad weather away from the sea wall. The concrete wall has a smooth concave surface towards the sea. How did they make a wall that curves outwards? Stone masons. Masons, ancient mysterious order, secret meetings and codes. Origins in Knights Templar, rumoured to know whereabouts of Ark of the Covenant, possibly the Holy Grail. Oh crumbs, there's that vagina again! Jimmy the builder is in the Masons… horrified that he knows the secret of the Grail. Head of the Masons is the Grand Wizard. Dirty joke about a loose woman and a wizard's sleeve. Smooth curves? Secret meetings? Wizard's sleeve? Yikes! Vagina.

It's still raining and I see a dog running along the beach. He stops to wait for his master. There is steam coming off the dog's back from the heat of its exercise. The owner of the dog is jogging and he is also generating a vapour cloud. If the rain quotient is low enough in ratio to the rate of evaporation, then is it possible to stay completely dry in wet weather if you generate enough body heat? Create your own personal weather system, a mini hydrologic cycle. Protect yourself from moisture by generating moisture. Sweaty exertion? Generating moisture? Exchange of fluids? Dampness? Curses! It's an unavoidable vagina again.

Man on beach with walking stick. Stick sinks into sand. The mechanical design of the stick is inefficient and ineffective. In Victorian times, walking sticks and umbrellas were stored in elephants' feet. This gives me an idea which I intend to patent at the earliest opportunity. I don't want to lose my claim to fame like the guy who supposedly invented the light bulb before Edison but missed his chance; consequently, I don't even know his name. Anyway back to my idea. Why not attach a stuffed camel foot to the bottom of the walking stick? The spread of the toes creates natural sand buoyancy. Oh dear. Camel toe? Naturally, vagina.

There is a collection of detritus washed up on the sandy beach. Half a bike, a broken tree branch and half a rowing boat. Perhaps I could make a canoe with the tree as a mast and the bike to power a propeller... how far would it get? Maybe construct something like a weird Baron Munchausen creation, although he went to the Moon in a balloon, not a makeshift pedalo. Pedalo? Pedal pushers. Short-legged trousers. Hot pants. Miniskirts. Serendipitous glimpses of half-hidden panties. Canoe? Little man in a boat? Munchausen's balloon? A woman's vagina!

Now it is May and the parade with the May Queen is passing by in the street below. Some wit leans out of a neighbouring window and shouts, "Fuck off!" It reminds me of the French aristocracy being harassed as they were escorted from the Bastille to the guillotine. They had to endure having fruit and vegetables thrown at them. From where did the people get those? They had no bread at the time but loads of excess vegetables? Didn't Marie Antoinette tell them to eat cake and isn't that what started the whole thing? Excess vegetables? Start to think of a lettuce and how it resembles a rose which in turn resembles... God help me... the furling, folding softness of... a vagina!

Oh no, this is getting ridiculous! I have the whole universe to contemplate and I can't get past a vagina! I realise I must come to the end of my imaginary journey. It is time to face reality. I need to get out more. I need to get a life. I need to leave this room, which has become my tomb. Or womb? A womb, with the window being my opening to the outside world... like... like... a vagina!

* * *

Future Discussion at a meeting of The Godalming Writers' Circle.

Ms Prunella Fourchette (Chairwoman): "Well! Who would like to start us off with this analysis? I think we'd all agree there are many historical and factual inaccuracies in this work."

Mr Jack Phillips: "I would say a door represents more closely the opening to the outside world, not a window. However, a vagina does not look like a door... perhaps more like a ship's porthole, which after all is a mixture of both.

Fourchette: "I would like you all to concentrate on the writer's technique rather than discuss vaginas."

Mr Leonard Huxley: "I'd like to know what kind of ladies the author has been associating with to cause him to liken a woman's vagina to a lettuce!"

Reverend Bartholomew (new member): "Well, I don't know about my wife's vagina but her ear looks like a cauliflower. If Sutton's extrapolation theory is in any way accurate, then sex with my wife shall be a rather gruesome affair. Consequently I have no desire to break my vow of chastity! I think I shall stick to gardening. That reminds me, it's high time I fertilised my wife's vegetable patch."

Ms Prunella Fourchette: "Reverend! You filthy little man!"

THE BALLAD OF PURITY CALOU

She rode into town on a dappled mare,
Nipples pierced and both breasts bare.
She gave out oranges, lemons too.
Somebody shouted, "That's Purity Calou!"
Rings on her fingers, bells on her toes,
She carries a shotgun to shoot all her foes.
Hair like Rapunzel but smells like Baloo,
Manners of a lumberjack, that's Purity Calou.
Don't try to cheat her, she'll kill you for sure
And don't give her whisky, she'll only want more.
Who shot the sheriff? I'll give you a clue,
There's only one suspect, Purity Calou.
Old timers tell stories of years gone by
When marshals rode west to catch her they'd try.
Their numbers were many but they came back few
And they blamed all the killings on Purity Calou.
An orchard she bought, it made her feel calm,
She watered the trees and did no one no harm.
This town has no doctor, no dentist too,
If vitamins are lacking, call Purity Calou.

Maybe that's gossip and maybe it's true
But the townsfolk all love her, the mayor does too.
When she's giving out citrus, or kisses in lieu
She's everyone's hero, she's Purity Calou.

READERS' BLOG:

- *Ha ha… it rhymes!*
- *A jaunty limerick indeed. However, as usual it is evident that Sutton has mixed reality with fantasy. He has fused Lady Godiva (naked on a horse), Nell Gwyn (oranges) and Annie Oakley (Western gunslinger) and I'm sure there is at least one other personage in there somewhere.*
- *Maybe the above reader is thinking of the old movie Cat Ballou. And I can see the word association that occurred in Sutton's head — Baloo the bear from The Jungle Book.*
- *So he got his ideas from someone else, eh? My grandmother used to say that the biggest crime of all is getting caught. Sutton is a transparent and shallow author with no talent whatsoever.*
- *Talking of word association, how about this… 'Oranges and lemons say the bells of St Clement's' is an old English nursery rhyme. Purity shot the sheriff but was granted clemency because she handed out clementines. 'My Darling Clementine' is a cowboy song and also a movie about the gunfight at the OK Corral. Perhaps Sutton is a genius after all!*
- *Apparently vitamin C can cure Clemydia. Thank God!*
- *That would be a dangerous statement if it were spelt correctly!*

- *I used to be the hairdresser for ex-footballer Ray Clemence. He always thanked me with a large bouquet of Clematis but there was nothing going on between us, despite what my wife thinks.*
- *The above reader is probably lying. Clematis is a climbing plant so it would be unsuitable for presentation as a bouquet.*
- *The previous loud-mouthed reader is spouting nonsense. The Clematis genus also includes a herbaceous shrub. I could quite easily make a bouquet from that, albeit slightly unorthodox.*
- *Churchill's wife was called Clementine and his successor (and predecessor) was Clement Attlee. Maybe they were related?*
- *Maybe they were one and the same person. Did they ever appear in the same room at the same time? Unlikely!*
- *Clementine I is a satellite on a secret mission to photograph aliens on the Moon. But what's that got to do with anything?*
- *Fuck the aliens!*

SEND YOUR COMMENTS TO
www.planktonsoup.co.uk

FRANK GLADTIDING: TUG BOAT OWNER, PART-TIME DETECTIVE AND FATHERS' RIGHTS ACTIVIST… WITH MILD TOURETTE'S. OH! AND HE WAS ALLERGIC TO FLORAL PRINT CURTAINS TOO!

Frank Gladtiding was not only a tug boat owner, he was also a part-time detective and fathers' rights activist… with mild Tourette's. Supplementary to all that, he also had an allergy to floral print curtains.

- *This paragraph is redundant as I had already surmised those facts from the title.*

Yes, but did you know he had a crewman called Bolus who performed his ship's duties whilst wearing roller skates?

- *That does shed new light on the matter.*

You see, Bolus was once a champion Sumo wrestler but a severe case of pubic Japanese knotweed had left him permanently bow-legged and the doctors had confined him to roller skates for the rest of his life.

- *Sorry for interrupting, but I am a Thames Shipping Inspector and find this sort of thing highly irregular. The use of roller skates aboard ship would surely pose a disadvantage to the wearer and may even lead to the spillage of hot tea, particularly during inclement weather. As a general rule of thumb, high jinks at sea should be discouraged.*

Poor Bolus! As if he hadn't suffered enough already, he also had a skin complaint which meant he could only wear bikinis!

- *Borderline ridiculous.*

Nevertheless, Bolus continued faithfully with his ship's duties, making the tea and feeding the giraffe. Oh, didn't I mention the giraffe? Luckily for Bolus, he was allowed to keep his pet giraffe Peepo onboard, and everywhere the tug boat went, people were surprised and delighted to see Peepo's long neck stretching out from the hatchway on deck.

Frank Gladtiding was miffed. His wretched ex-wife had forbidden him access to his son and he wasn't going to take 'no' for an answer any more. Nobody messes with big Frank Gladtiding so he decided to protest. But first he needed to find a 'fathers' rights activist superhero costume'… a costume that no other rebuffed father would have. Batman and Spider-Man had already been done. Who could he choose?

"Cast off, we're setting sail for Carnaby Street!" he called out to Bolus.

Bolus was used to Frank's maverick tendencies. He had been a loyal deck hand for years. But Frank's habit of announcing "Anchors away!" upon successful completion of a bowel movement after breakfast was becoming nerve-wrenching.

Meanwhile, back at Thames Tug Boat headquarters, the emergency phone rang urgently.

Some tourists had got their pleasure craft stuck on a sandbank. "We need tugging off!" they shouted to shocked passers-by. Needless to say, nobody accepted their offer.

A call was sent out to all tug boat captains to be on the lookout for inexperienced sailors who needed tugging off.

All registered captains acknowledged the call except Frank. Tug Control Headquarters soon realised there was a problem and rumours spread like wildfire. "Frank's gone rogue!" "We've got a broken arrow!"

"He's gone dark!" explained the Tug Fleet Rear Admiral to the police.

"Too much sunbathing?" asked the confused detective.

"He's incommunicado."

"Communicado? Is that the Algarve?"

"Just be careful out there. He's got Tourette's!"

"What? He lives in a castle?"

"No… Tourette's… in his head."

'Weird-shaped head… like a castle', wrote the detective.

Later that day, Frank could be seen chugging down the Thames dressed in his bargain basement superhero oddments. He had found a Darth Vader mask, a Wonder Woman bodice complete with inflatable boobs and a cheap pair of the Wrong Trousers from Wallace & Gromit.

The upsurge in adrenaline had sparked off his Tourette's and he was powerless to prevent himself shouting "*Knickers, knackers, knockers!*" through the inbuilt voice distortion unit of his Darth Vader mask as he floated along at five miles per hour. Bolus busied himself with tea-making duties and Peepo stared straight ahead as usual.

But! Hello? Watch out! Meanwhile, somebody has planted a nuclear device behind the clock face of Big Ben!

- *Bastards!*

Police had cordoned off the area but were unable to find anyone to defuse the bomb.

"Who have we got in that area?" demanded the Prime Minister.

His secretary pointed to the television. The lunchtime news was reporting a strange figure in outlandish dress, clinging to the clock tower and waving frantically either to attract attention or shoo away the journalists in their helicopters. It somehow resembled the final scene from King Kong but was a more pathetic, embarrassing version.

"I know the perfect guy!" said the secretary.

- *But surely the SAS would…*
- *Sh! Quiet! Let Frank do it!*
- *James Bond…?*
- *Ssshhhh!*

Frank had climbed up Peepo's neck to reach a ledge on Big Ben when the news helicopters began circling, and he had tried to wave them away as their downdraught was making him lose his grip. Suddenly his wife's voice was being transmitted through a loudspeaker.

"While you're up there can you help us with a small problem Frank?"

"Not until I get equal visiting rights!" shouted Frank, now waving his helmet to get the attention of the cameras.

"I will let you see Wilbur on Wednesdays and alternate weekends!"

"Can't do Wednesdays, I take Bolus to have his scrotum crop-sprayed."

"OK, Thursdays then."

"I'll do it!"

Frank climbed into the tower and joined the police who were staring anxiously at the silver casing of the bomb and the array of flashing lights and coloured wiring that seemed to form its control panel. But worst of all was the ominous ticking that really indicated the imminence of an explosion.

The Inspector in charge greeted Frank gratefully. He knew Frank's history of solving crimes as a private detective and welcomed his help.

"Any clues?" asked Frank, professionally.

"We are still look…" began the Inspector.

"Excuse me, sir! We've found this, sir!" interrupted a young constable, eagerly showing the Inspector what looked like a nose hair.

"Well done constable, take it to the forensic labor…"

"Sir! Yes sir!"

"Just a moment, constable! Not so fast!" said Frank authoritatively.

Before anybody could stop him he took out his pipe and filled it with a moist tobacco, pushing his gnarled thumb into the rim so that the juices would flow more freely. He grabbed the nose hair segment from the policeman, put it into his pipe and smoked it.

"Hmm", he said. "Hmm!"

"What do you make of it, Frank?" asked the Inspector.

"I don't believe it was a guy, folks. I think it was a lady."

• *Groan! For the benefit of my fellow readers who may have missed Sutton's poor joke, he is attempting a pun on Guy Fawkes. How droll.*

"It's a female office temp who recently drank Pinot Grigio and likes watching the hit series *Desperate Housewives*."

"But how will we find…?"

"She is six feet three inches tall with bright red hair… and a slight limp due to a gymnastic injury in high school," said Frank vaguely.

"Send that description to all units!" ordered the Inspector. "It shouldn't take long to find her. But be quick! The bomb could explode at any mo…!"

"We've found her, sir!"

"How did…?"

"She was hiding behind the door, sir!"

• *Let him finish his sentences, for fuck's sake!*

"Great! Let's take her in for questioning. We need answers urgen…!"

Frank held up his hand.

"Inspector, I know these waters. Your clumsy procedures won't wash. Let me speak to her."

He thrust his helmet close to her face.

"Which wire should we cut?" Frank demanded grimly.

"Red", she said flatly. Then she blushed heavily. She scratched at the tip of her nose and began perspiring. She shuffled from foot to foot and avoided eye contact, then folded her arms defensively across her chest.

"She's lying!" cried Frank.

"How can you be so…?" began the Inspector.

"She had her fingers crossed behind her back when she answered!" explained Frank triumphantly.

Frank bent down and cut the blue wire. The ticking stopped!

It later transpired that the terrorists possessed incriminating photos of the Parliamentary nightwatchman stealing ladies underwear from a well-known high street store that sells that sort of thing. They blackmailed him. They persuaded him to leave the back door of Parliament slightly ajar one evening. Once inside, they had cold-cocked him, tied him up with his own bra, then made their way to the clock tower and installed the bomb. They had left the red-haired accomplice there to initiate or disarm the bomb according to future circumstances which have not yet been imagined by the author.

- *Sutton might be a crap writer, but at least he's honest!*
- *Yikes! The fate of this once great nation lies in the hands of a low-paid, closet-transvestite kleptomaniac!*
- *Thank God for stalwart people like Frank!*

A few days later the Queen invited Frank to the Palace. He had been recommended for a medal to honour his bravery and quick thinking.

Bolus waited outside and looked up at the window of the ceremonial room where Frank would be getting his medal. He wished he could be there; however, due to the virulent nature of his pubic affliction, he was legally required to stay at least one hundred metres from the Queen.

Suddenly he had an idea! Copying Frank's earlier example, Bolus climbed up Peepo's neck and was then able to see inside the Palace.

Frank was standing stiff and proud in his full costume as the Queen picked up the medal from a small velvet cushion offered to her by a courtier. Bolus rapped on the window to attract Frank's attention. Frank looked over and saw his dear friend Bolus waving. He smiled at the sight of his friend's face at the window… and then his heart froze! His lip trembled as the Queen moved towards him with the medal. There were floral print curtains in the ceremonial room!

- *Oh Christ no! Don't tell me!*
- *Hell's teeth!*

Frank's breathing became heavy. To the gathered crowd it seemed that his noisy metallic gasps were due to the voice distortion effect of the Darth Vader helmet.

The Queen leaned closer. But as she pinned the medal onto Frank's Wonder Woman bodice, all the emotions and passions of the moment surged up within him and the words Frank had been holding back all afternoon suddenly exploded messily in the Queen's face…

"ARSEFANNYTITCOCK!"

Will Frank Gladtiding get out of jail in time to solve next week's mystery?

READERS' BLOG:

- *Alas! Sutton has succumbed to popular pressure by writing a detective story for the masses. He should hang his head in shame. It is the literary equivalent of taking candy from a baby.*
- *Arsefannytitcock? Poor Frank. You can take the seaman from the sea but you can't take the seaman from the man.*
- *I think you should rephrase that.*
- *Ho ho! Knickers, knackers, knockers! That was the catchphrase of Les Dawson, Britain's favourite comedian during the early eighties. He was great; but his wife was ugly.*
- *Sutton has made the basic schoolboy error of measuring the speed of the tug at five miles per hour instead of the nautically correct five knots per hour. The tit.*
- *I like the sound of Bolus. I think he and I could be friends. You see, I too am bow-legged and like to wear bikinis. But that useless Peepo can get stuffed!*
- *Giraffes spit a lot. I don't think that's conducive to efficient tug boat navigation.*
- *If I was the Queen, I wouldn't pin any medals onto inflatable boobs in a Wonder Woman bodice. She should just place it into the pocket of the Wrong Trousers. She might get lucky and pull out a plum.*
- *Carnaby Street ain't what it used to be. Mind you, neither am I.*

- *Why would anybody want to blow up Parliament? All those lovely people trying their best to help the poor and unworthy of us scrape through our mediocre lives.*
- *This would never have happened if the famous high street store in question took their stock loss procedures more seriously. A stolen bra almost led to anarchy!*

SHORT STRAW

Grunting sounds associated with sexual effort.

Shortly after…

"Hi folks! Be with you in a minute… a couple of cell divisions here, a couple there. Just need a few more divisions. Soon be able to function better. It's coming! That's it! Now then, let's have a recap…

Sperm enters egg. So far, so good! Womb Carrier not yet conscious of my existence. Early days."

Sleep.

"Hello, what's this? Ah, forehead is developing nicely. Hope rest of body follows suit or will look bizarre when outside.

Rise in heartbeat of Womb Carrier, associated with heightened anxiety. I am discovered!"

Sleep.

"Cortisol levels building in kidneys of Womb Carrier. Stress. Not good.

Spermatozoa donor is near, can feel my genetic frequency oscillating at precise same level. Loud, unhappy noises coming from outside womb."

Sleep.

"Couple of arms have sprouted. Relief! Wonder if they will be strong and hairy or silky slender in years to come. Need a lot more cells yet."

Sleep.

"Sleep disturbed. Some kind of pinging noise like a submarine echoing around the womb. Are they mad?"

Sleep.

"Excellent news, eyes have started to form! Very complicated machinery, the eyes. What with the retina and convex this and concave that. Needs more time to get its bits and pieces together than most other body parts; although won't be needing them for a while. Nothing much to see in here anyway. Wonder what colour they will be? Will future lover look into them and 'melt'?"

Sleep.

"More unhappy noises coming from outside womb. Blood sugar levels of Womb Carrier are very erratic. Get a grip on yourself, woman!"

Sleep.

"Ooh! New toes!"

Sleep.

Sleep disturbed.

"Getting very warm in here. Starting to feel light-headed. That's difficult considering head is bigger than body. Start to laugh. That was funny! Feel like singing but don't yet know any songs. Getting very, very warm. What's this acidic liquid that the Womb Carrier is sending to me down the umbi… umbi…? Can't concentrate (hiccup). Anyway this situation is unbiblical Lord!"

"Making my mind spin. And another thing, where's this

hot water coming from? Don't you know there's a drought in Africa? Scalding my sensitive new toes. Crazy!"

"Drifting, drifting. Damn this heat! Can't take it much longer."

Half-sleep.

"I could have been a contender. Coulda bin a contenda. Might have been a princess! Wish I could ride a motorbike, just once. Would have been nice to have a pet.

I've got a lot of love to give someone… something… sometime… maybe next time.

Drifting, drifting… just let go… ah, serenity…"

…………sleep……………

THE END

ABOUT THE AUTHOR

Popular legend has it that the media frenzy over *Cream of Plankton Soup* forced Sutton into hiding. He has dyed his hair electric blue and lives in a snow hole in Greenland, surrounding himself with eunuchs to keep warm. There he waits and makes his plans against the world.

However, truth is stranger than fiction. According to his agent, Sutton actually lives in Oxford and is married to a direct descendant of Genghis Khan. Before becoming an author he was quite an adventurer. He has been lost in the Arctic Circle, crash-landed on a deserted airfield and been shipwrecked in the Strait of Malacca. He has been down and out in Orlando, kidnapped in Bangkok, and escaped from a Croatian Mafia boss in a pimped-up Renault Twingo.

He has rubbed shoulders with the world's top dignitaries (as a masseur in a Berlin brothel) and is rumoured to be a distant relative of a senior Capone gang member. He has been a bodyguard for Hillary Clinton's lobster and is on handshaking terms with Darth Vader. He has worked for the Foreign and Commonwealth Office and once declined a medal from the Queen. He has worked in a glue factory in Oldham (home of the tubular bandage) and has been to a nudist colony with a princess on a bicycle (not in Oldham).

He has hunted pirates in the Indian Ocean and tried his hand at bodybuilding (he intends to try the rest of his body soon). He once had the honour of being ignored at the Beverley Hills Polo Lounge by John Cleese and Ricky Gervais.

He has twice appeared in theatre wearing nothing but a G-string, only once legally.

This book is a miracle and a masterpiece considering Sutton does not speak a word of English.